Midas World

Midas World

A NOVEL

Frederik Pohl

To Joe —
With all good wishes —
F Pohl

ST. MARTIN'S PRESS
New York

Library of Congress Cataloging in Publication Data

Pohl, Frederik.
    Midas world.

    I. Title.
PS3566.036M5   1983   813'.54   83-2896
ISBN 0-312-53182-6

First Edition
10 9 8 7 6 5 4 3 2 1

To Horace L. Gold
who made me do it
and
to Robert Theobald
who showed me what it meant

Contents

Midas World

1

THE FIRE-
BRINGER

It isn't love that makes the world go round, it's energy. Everything else can either be produced or substituted for, if the energy is available. Garbage is simply a valuable commodity in the wrong place; an ore is only a valuable metal not yet squeezed free of its impurities; all either one needs to become useful is energy. Therefore, when Amalfi Amadeus learned the trick of trapping plasma in a cup of monopoles and thus produced nuclear fusion power for all, he gave mankind the Keys to the Kingdom of Heaven.

He neglected to keep a set of the keys for himself. He thought he had one, but in order to get things going he went to the businessmen and the banks and they did what they were supposed to do. They backed him. First, of course, they called in their consultants, specialists moonlighting from IPRI and the faculty of MIT. The scientists checked his calculations and replicated his tests—and then did it all over again, because they could not believe what they found. Finally, amazed, they agreed that the thing would work. Fusion power was suddenly real! The endless deuterium fuel of the oceans could be brought to the service of the human race at last.

So the bankers and businessmen called in the lawyers. The contracts were drawn. No Texas wildcatter ever hornswoggled an oil lease more effectively than the bankers benefacted Amadeus. They made him rich, on paper. They gave him stock participation, on paper. But paper has two sides, and on the flip side was the fine print.

The test fusors worked. The demonstration plant was a success. The first full-scale installation was commissioned. As the generators began to spin, thirty megawatts poised to flood into the power grid, there was a ceremony. The President of the United States was there. So was the IPRI engineer; so was the MIT professor. Amadeus watched it on television from his home. He hadn't been invited. The President said, "With this great step forward we liberate our land forever from that worst of deprivations, energy starvation." Everyone applauded. The MIT professor, who had joined the utility conglomerate as a senior executive vice-president, whispered, "The publicity people ought to use that quote." The engineer from the Independent Power Research Institute, who had come aboard as publicity chief, made a note. The President cut the ribbon and depressed the switch and Amadeus turned off his television set, feeling left out.

Well, he was left out. He had done his part. He was permitted to do no more, while gleaming white hemispheres sprouted around every city. Their cooling towers reshaped every skyline. Their reject heat, as wastewater, tempered the cool of every lake and bay. Power became plentiful, then cheap, then taken for granted. Electrical power at a trivial cost rebuilt the cities, sieved impurities out of the streams, cooked plastics out of urban trash and I-beams out of scrapped cars.

The factories boomed.

The living standard boomed too, in a world of plenty. Maybe no one had quite "enough," because perhaps there isn't any such thing as enough, but everyone had more than ever before. And gradually, gradually, surfeit set in. Deserts blossomed. Crops multiplied. Automatic machines became smart machines, became robots. And as universal prosperity became plenitude, Amalfi Amadeus realized that, although he was very rich, so was everybody else.

It seemed to the Savior of the World that he was entitled to more than that. A vice-presidency in the company, at least—power, authority, *prestige*. The company said no; Amadeus made the mistake of suing; the company's lawyers read the fine print into the court records and thereby ate him alive.

Amadeus's own lawyers dined well off the scraps that were left over, and the life of the Savior of the World wearied itself out in obscurity. It was true that there were statues of him in public places. Perhaps that was why it was generally assumed, by those who thought of it at all, that he was dead.

And ultimately, of course, he was. But just before that, while he was in the process of dying, an idle intern in his hospital, casting about for something to relieve the boredom of his three-hour work shift, decided to give the old man his third physical examination of the day. The intern found nothing that was not already recorded on the chart, of course, but when he looked more carefully at the chart the name lit a slow fuse. "Why, that's Amalfi Amadeus!" he cried, disturbing the other interns on his shift as they drowsed over their soap operas or card games. "Mr. Amadeus! You're the fellow who invented cheap fusion power and gave us all this prosperity!"

The old man pumped up breath for a moment, then got it out: "Goddamn right," he gasped weakly.

Another intern stretched, yawned, abandoned her book and came over. "Hey, you're right," she said. "Poor old guy."

"Why poor?"

She shrugged. "Well, the way my dad used to tell it, he never got much out of it, did he? They sort of froze him out—not counting money, of course, but what's the good of money?"

The male intern said stubbornly, "He's in all the history books. The whole human race knows his name."

"I don't think that makes up for being left on the shelf most of your life. If I were him I don't think I'd be that crazy about the human race—in fact, I think I might want to do it in the eye."

Amalfi Amadeus wheezed and lifted his head off the pillow, sucking in enough air for one supreme effort. The withered lips parted in a grin; the rheumy eyes brightened with delight.

"I already did," he cackled, and turned away, and died.

2

THE MIDAS PLAGUE

Scarcity ended, but young couples continued to fall in love. And so they were married.

The bride and groom made a beautiful couple, she in her twenty-yard frill of immaculate white, he in his formal gray ruffled blouse and pleated pantaloons.

It was a modest wedding, the best Morey Fry could afford. For guests, they had only the immediate family and a few close friends. And when the minister had performed the ceremony, Morey kissed his bride and they drove off to the reception. There were twenty-eight limousines in all (though it is true that twenty of them contained only the caterer's robots) and three flower cars. But they held their heads high.

"Bless you both," said old man Elon sentimentally. "You've got a fine girl in our Cherry, Morey." He blew his nose on a ragged square of cambric.

The old folks behaved very well, Morey thought. At the reception, surrounded by the enormous stacks of wedding gifts, they drank the champagne and ate a great many of the tiny, delicious canapés. They listened politely to the fifteen-piece orchestra, and Cherry's mother even danced one dance with Morey for sentiment's sake, though it was clear that dancing was far from the usual pattern of her life. They tried as hard as they could to blend into the gathering, but all the same, the two elderly figures in severely simple and probably rented garments were dismayingly conspicuous in the quarter-acre of tapestries and tinkling fountains that was the main ballroom of Morey's country home.

When it was time for the guests to go home and let the newlyweds begin their life together, Cherry's father shook Morey by the hand and Cherry's mother kissed him. But as they drove away in their tiny runabout their faces were full of foreboding.

It was nothing against Morey as a person, of course. But poor people should not marry wealth.

Morey and Cherry loved each other, certainly. That helped. They told each other so a dozen times an hour, all of the long hours they were together, for the first months of their marriage. Morey even took time off to go shopping with his bride, which endeared him to her enormously. They drove their shopping carts through the immense vaulted corridors of the supermarket, Morey checking off the items on the shopping list as Cherry picked out the goods. It was fun.

For a while.

Their first fight started in the supermarket, between breakfast foods and floor furnishings, just where the new precious stones department was being opened.

Morey called off from the list, "Diamond lavaliere, costume rings, earbobs."

Cherry said rebelliously, "Morey, I *have* a lavaliere. Please, dear!"

Morey folded back the pages of the list uncertainly. The lavaliere was on there, all right, and no alternative selection was shown.

"How about a bracelet?" he coaxed. "Look, they have some nice ruby ones there. See how beautifully they go with your hair, darling!" He beckoned a robot clerk, who bustled up and handed Cherry the bracelet tray. "Lovely," Morey exclaimed as Cherry slipped the largest of the lot on her wrist.

"And I don't have to have a lavaliere?" Cherry asked.

"Of course not." He peeked at the tag. "Same number of ration points exactly!" Since Cherry looked only dubious, not convinced, he said briskly, "And now we'd better be getting along to the shoe department. I've got to pick up some dancing pumps."

Cherry made no objection, neither then nor throughout the rest of their shopping tour. At the end, while they were sitting in the supermarket's ground-floor lounge waiting for the robot accountants to tote up their bill and the robot cashiers to affix the stamps in their ration books, Morey remembered to have the shipping department save out the bracelet.

"I don't want that sent with the other stuff, darling," he explained. "I want you to wear it right now. Honestly, I don't think I ever saw anything looking so *right* for you."

Cherry looked flustered and pleased. Morey was delighted with himself; it wasn't everybody who knew how to handle these little domestic problems just right!

He stayed self-satisfied all the way home, while Henry, their companion-robot, regaled them with funny stories of the factory in which it had been built and trained. Cherry wasn't used to Henry by a long shot, but it was hard not to like the robot. Jokes and funny stories when you needed amusement, sympathy when you were depressed, a never-failing supply of news and information on any subject you cared to name—Henry was easy enough to take. Cherry even made a special point of asking Henry to keep them company through dinner, and she laughed as thoroughly as Morey himself at its droll anecdotes.

But later, in the conservatory, when Henry had considerately left them alone, the laughter dried up.

Morey didn't notice. He was very conscientiously making the rounds: turning on the tri-D, selecting their after-dinner liqueurs, scanning the evening newspapers.

Cherry cleared her throat self-consciously, and Morey

stopped what he was doing. "Dear," she said tentatively, "I'm feeling kind of restless tonight. Could we—I mean do you think we could just sort of stay home and—well, relax?"

Morey looked at her with a touch of concern. She lay back wearily, eyes half closed. "Are you feeling all right?" he asked.

"Perfectly. I just don't want to go out tonight, dear. I don't feel up to it."

He sat down and automatically lit a cigarette. "I see," he said. The tri-D was beginning a comedy show; he got up to turn it off, snapping on the tape player. Muted strings filled the room.

"We had reservations at the club tonight," he reminded her.

Cherry shifted uncomfortably. "I know."

"And we have the opera tickets that I turned last week's in for. I hate to nag, darling, but we haven't used *any* of our opera tickets."

"We can see them right here on the tri-D," she said in a small voice.

"That has nothing to do with it, sweetheart. I—I didn't want to tell you about it, but Wainwright, down at the office, said something to me yesterday. He told me he would be at the circus last night and as much as said he'd be looking to see if we were there, too. Well, we weren't there. Heaven knows what I'll tell him next week."

He waited for Cherry to answer, but she was silent.

He went on reasonably, "So if you *could* see your way clear to going out tonight—"

He stopped, slack-jawed. Cherry was crying, silently and in quantity.

"Darling!" he said inarticulately.

He hurried to her, but she fended him off. He stood helpless over her, watching her cry.

"Dear, what's the matter?" he asked.

She turned her head away.

Morey rocked back on his heels. It wasn't exactly the first time he'd seen Cherry cry—there had been that poignant scene when they Gave Each Other Up, realizing that their backgrounds were too far apart for happiness, before the realization that they *had* to have each other, no matter what. . . . But it was the first time her tears had made him feel guilty.

And he did feel guilty. He stood there staring at her.

Then he turned his back on her and walked over to the bar. He ignored the ready liqueurs and poured two stiff highballs, brought them back to her. He set one down beside her, took a long drink from the other.

In quite a different tone, he said, "Dear, what's the *matter?*"

No answer.

"Come on. What is it?"

She looked up at him and rubbed her eyes. Almost sullenly, she said, "Sorry."

"I know you're sorry. Look, we love each other. Let's talk this thing out."

She picked up her drink and held it for a moment, before setting it down untasted. "What's the use, Morey?"

"Please. Let's try."

She shrugged.

He went on remorselessly, "You aren't happy, are you? And it's because of—well, all this." His gesture took in the richly furnished conservatory, the thick-piled carpet, the host of machines and contrivances for their comfort and entertainment that waited for their touch. By implication it took in twenty-six rooms, five cars, nine robots. Morey said, with an effort, "It isn't what you're used to, is it?"

"I can't help it," Cherry said. "Morey, you know I've tried. But back home—"

"Dammit," he flared, "*this* is your home. You don't

live with your father any more in that five-room cottage; you don't spend your evenings hoeing the garden or playing cards for matchsticks. You live here, with me, your husband! You knew what you were getting into. We talked all this out long before we were married—"

The words stopped, because words were useless. Cherry was crying again, but not silently.

Through her tears, she wailed: "Darling, I've tried. You don't *know* how I've tried! I've worn all those silly clothes and I've played all those silly games and I've gone out with you as much as I *possibly* could and—I've eaten all that terrible food until I'm actually getting fa-fa-*fat!* I thought I could stand it. But I just can't go on like this; I'm not used to it. I—I love you, Morey, but I'm going crazy, living like this. I can't help it, Morey—*I can't stand being poor!*"

Eventually the tears dried up, and the quarrel healed, and the lovers kissed and made up. But Morey lay awake that night, listening to his wife's gentle breathing from the suite next to his own, staring into the darkness as tragically as any pauper before him had ever done.

Blessed are the poor, for they shall inherit the Earth.

Blessed Morey, heir to more worldly goods than he could possibly consume.

Morey Fry, steeped in grinding poverty, had never gone hungry a day in his life, never lacked for anything his heart could desire in the way of food, or clothing or a place to sleep. In Morey's world, no one lacked for these things, no one could.

Malthus was right—for a civilization without machines, automatic factories, hydroponics and food synthesis, ocean-mining for metals and organics . . .

And a vastly increasing supply of labor . . .

And architecture that rose high in the air and dug deep

in the ground and floated far out on the water on piers and pontoons . . . architecture that could be poured one day and lived in the next . . .

And robots—robots to burrow and haul and smelt and fabricate, to build and farm and weave and sew . . .

And, above all, energy.

Energy! It was energy that made everything else go. Amalfi Amadeus, who taught the human race how to hold fusing hydrogen plasma in a cup of monopoles, gave mankind the gift of plenty.

What the land lacked in wealth, the sea was made to yield and the laboratory invented the rest . . . and the factories became a pipeline of plenty, churning out enough to feed and clothe and house a dozen worlds.

Limitless discovery, Amalfi's infinite fusion power, tireless labor of humanity and robots, mechanization that drove jungle and swamp and ice off the Earth, and put up office buildings and manufacturing centers and rocket ports in their place . . .

The pipeline of production spewed out riches that no king in the time of Malthus could have known.

But a pipeline has two ends. The invention and power and labor pouring in at one end must somehow be drained out at the other. . . .

Lucky Morey, blessed economic-consuming unit, drowning in the pipeline's flood, striving manfully to eat and drink and wear and wear out his share of the ceaseless tide of wealth.

Morey felt far from blessed, for the blessings of the poor are always best appreciated from afar.

Quotas worried his sleep until he awoke at eight o'clock the next morning, red-eyed and haggard, but inwardly resolved. He had reached a decision. He was starting a new life.

There was trouble in the morning mail. Under the

letterhead of the National Ration Board, it said:

"We regret to advise you that the following items returned by you in connection with your August quotas as used and no longer serviceable have been inspected and found insufficiently worn." The list followed—a long one, Morey saw to his sick disappointment. "Credit is hereby disallowed for these and you are therefore given an additional consuming quota for the current month in the amount of 435 points, at least 350 points of which must be in the textile and home-furnishing categories."

Morey dashed the letter to the floor. The valet picked it up emotionlessly, creased it and set it on his desk.

It wasn't fair! All right, maybe the bathing trunks and beach umbrellas hadn't been *really* used very much— though how the devil, he asked himself bitterly, did you go about using up swimming gear when you didn't have time for such leisurely pursuits as swimming? But certainly the hiking slacks were used! He'd worn them for three whole days and part of a fourth; what did they expect him to do, go around in *rags?*

Morey looked belligerently at the coffee and toast that the valet-robot had brought in with the mail, and then steeled his resolve. Unfair or not, he had to play the game according to the rules. It was for Cherry, more than for himself, and the way to begin a new way of life was to begin it.

Morey was going to consume for two.

He told the valet robot, "Take that stuff back. I want cream and sugar with the coffee—*lots* of cream and sugar. And besides the toast, scrambled eggs, fried potatoes, orange juice—no, make it half a grapefruit. *And* orange juice, come to think of it."

"Right away, sir," said the valet. "You won't be having breakfast at nine then, will you, sir?"

"I certainly will," said Morey virtuously. "Double portions!" As the robot was closing the door, he called after it, "Butter and marmalade with the toast!"

He went to the bath; he had a full schedule and no time to waste. In the shower, he carefully sprayed himself with lather three times. When he had rinsed the soap off, he went through the whole assortment of taps in order: three lotions, plain talcum, scented talcum and thirty seconds of ultra-violet. Then he lathered and rinsed again, and dried himself with a towel instead of using the hot-air drying jet. Most of the miscellaneous scents went down the drain with the rinse water, but if the Ration Board accused him of waste, he could claim he was experimenting. The effect, as a matter of fact, wasn't bad at all.

He stepped out, full of exuberance. Cherry was awake, staring in dismay at the tray the valet had brought. "Good morning, dear," she said faintly. "Ugh."

Morey kissed her and patted her hand. "Well!" he said, looking at the tray with a big, hollow smile. "Food!"

"Isn't that a *lot* for just the two of us?"

"Two of us?" repeated Morey masterfully. "Nonsense, my dear, I'm going to eat it all by myself!"

"Oh, Morey," gasped Cherry, and the adoring look she gave him was enough to pay for a dozen such meals.

Which, he thought as he finished his morning exercises with the sparring-robot and sat down to his *real* breakfast, it just about had to be, day in and day out, for a long, long time.

Still, Morey had made up his mind. As he worked his way through the kippered herring, tea and crumpets, he ran over his plans with Henry. He swallowed a mouthful and said, "I want you to line up some appointments for me right away. Three hours a week in an exercise gym— pick one with lots of reducing equipment, Henry. I think I'm going to need it. And fittings for some new clothes— I've had these for weeks. And, let's see, doctor, dentist—

say, Henry, don't I have a psychiatrist's date coming up?"

"Indeed you do, sir!" it said warmly. "This morning, in fact. I've already instructed the chauffeur and notified your office."

"Fine! Well, get started on the other things, Henry."

"Yes, sir," said Henry, and assumed the curious absent look of a robot talking on its TBR circuits—the Talk Between Robots radio—as it arranged the appointments for its master.

Morey finished his breakfast in silence, pleased with his own virtue, at peace with the world. It wasn't so hard to be a proper, industrious consumer if you *worked* at it, he reflected. It was only the malcontents, the ne'er-do-wells and the incompetents who simply could not adjust to the world around them. Well, he thought with distant pity, someone had to suffer; you couldn't break eggs without making an omelet. And his proper duty was not to be some sort of wild-eyed crank, challenging the social order and beating his breast about injustice, but to take care of his wife and his home.

It was too bad he couldn't really get right down to work on consuming today. But this was his one day a week to hold a *job*—the other six days were devoted to solid consuming—and, besides, he had a group therapy session scheduled as well. His analysis, Morey told himself, would certainly take a sharp turn for the better, now that he had faced up to his problems.

Morey was immersed in a glow of self-righteousness as he kissed Cherry good-bye (she had finally got up, all in a confusion of delight at the new regime) and walked out the door to his car. He hardly noticed the little man in enormous floppy hat and garishly ruffled trousers who was standing almost hidden in the shrubs.

"Hey, Mac." The man's voice was almost a whisper.

"Huh? What is it?"

The man looked around furtively. "Listen, friend," he said rapidly, "you look like an intelligent man who could use a little help. Times are tough; you help me, I'll help you. Want to make a deal on ration stamps? Six for one. One of yours for six of mine, the best deal you'll get anywhere in town. Naturally, my stamps aren't exactly the real McCoy, but they'll pass, friend, they'll pass—"

Morey blinked at him. "No!" he said violently, and pushed the man aside. Now it's racketeers, he thought bitterly. Slums and endless sordid preoccupation with rations weren't enough to inflict on Cherry; now the neighborhood was becoming a hangout for people on the shady side of the law. It was not, of course, the first time he had ever been approached by a counterfeit ration-stamp hoodlum, but never at his own front door!

Morey thought briefly, as he climbed into his car, of calling the police. But certainly the man would be gone before they could get there; and, after all, he had handled it pretty well as it was.

Of course, it would be nice to get six stamps for one.

But very far from nice if he got caught.

"Good morning, Mr. Fry," tinkled the robot receptionist. "Won't you go right in?" With a steel-tipped finger, it pointed to the door marked GROUP THERAPY.

Someday, Morey vowed to himself as he nodded and complied, he would be in a position to afford a private analyst of his own. Group therapy helped relieve the infinite stresses of modern living, and without it he might find himself as badly off as the hysterical mobs in the ration riots, or as dangerously anti-social as the counterfeiters. But it lacked the personal touch. It was, he thought, too public a performance of what should be a private affair, like trying to live a happy married life with an interfering, ever-present crowd of robots in the house—

Morey brought himself up in panic. How had *that* thought crept in? He was shaken visibly as he entered the room and greeted the group to which he was assigned.

There were eleven of them: four Freudians, two Reichians, two Jungians, a Gestalter, a shock therapist and the elderly and rather quiet Sullivanite. Even the members of the majority groups had their own individual differences in technique and creed, but, despite four years with this particular group of analysts, Morey hadn't quite been able to keep them separate in his mind. Their names, though, he knew well enough.

"Morning, Doctors," he said. "What is it today?"

"Morning," said Semmelweiss morosely. "Today you come into the room for the first time looking as if something is really bothering you, and yet the schedule calls for psychodrama. Dr. Fairless," he appealed, "can't we change the schedule a little bit? Fry here is obviously under a strain; *that's* the time to start digging and see what he can find. We can do your psychodrama next time, can't we?"

Fairless shook his gracefully bald old head. "Sorry, Doctor. If it were up to me, of course—but you know the rules."

"Rules, rules," jeered Semmelweiss. "Ah, what's the use? Here's a patient in an acute anxiety state if I ever saw one—and believe me, I saw plenty—and we ignore it because the *rules* say ignore it. Is that professional? Is that how to cure a patient?"

Little Blaine said frostily, "If I may say so, Dr. Semmelweiss, there have been a great many cures made without the necessity of departing from the rules. I myself, in fact—"

"You yourself!" mimicked Semmelweiss. "You yourself never handled a patient alone in your life. When you going to get out of a group, Blaine?"

Blaine said furiously, "Dr. Fairless, I don't think I have to stand for this sort of personal attack. Just because Semmelweiss has seniority and a couple of private patients one day a week, he thinks—"

"Gentlemen," said Fairless mildly. "Please, let's get on with the work. Mr. Fry has come to us for help, not to listen to us losing our tempers."

"Sorry," said Semmelweiss curtly. "All the same, I appeal from the arbitrary and mechanistic ruling of the chair."

Fairless inclined his head. "All in favor of the ruling of the chair? Nine, I count. That leaves only you opposed, Dr. Semmelweiss. We'll proceed with the psychodrama, if the recorder will read us the notes and comments of the last session."

The recorder, a pudgy, low-ranking youngster named Sprogue, flipped back the pages of his notebook and read in a chanting voice, "Session of twenty-fourth May, subject, Morey Fry; in attendance, Doctors Fairless, Bileck, Semmelweiss, Carrado, Weber—"

Fairless interrupted kindly, "Just the last page, if you please, Dr. Sprogue."

"Um—oh, yes. After a ten-minute recess for additional Rorschachs and an electroencephalogram, the group convened and conducted rapid-fire word association. Results were tabulated and compared with standard deviation patterns, and it was determined that the subject's major traumas derived from, respectively—"

Morey found his attention waning. Therapy was *good;* everybody knew that, but every once in a while he found it a little dull. If it weren't for therapy, though, there was no telling what might happen. Certainly, Morey told himself, he had been helped considerably—at least he hadn't set fire to his house and shrieked at the fire-robots, like Newell down the block when his eldest daughter divorced her husband and came back to live with him—bringing her ration quota along, of course. Morey hadn't even been *tempted* to do anything as outrageously, frighteningly immoral as *destroy* things or *waste* them—well, he admitted to himself honestly, perhaps a little tempted, once in a great while. But never anything important enough to worry about; he was sound, perfectly sound.

He looked up, startled. All the doctors were staring at him. "Mr. Fry," Fairless repeated, "will you take your place?"

"Certainly," Morey said hastily. "Uh—where?"

Semmelweiss guffawed. *"Told* you. Never mind, Morey; you didn't miss much. We're going to run through one of the big scenes in your life, the one you told us about last time. Remember? You were fourteen years old, you said. Christmas time. Your mother had made you a promise."

Morey swallowed. "I remember," he said unhappily. "Well, all right. Where do I stand?"

"Right here," said Fairless. "You're you, Carrado is your mother, I'm your father. Will the doctors not participating mind moving back? Fine. Now, Morey, here we are on Christmas morning. Merry Christmas, Morey!"

"Merry Christmas," Morey said halfheartedly. "Uh— Father dear, where's my—uh—my puppy that Mother promised me?"

"Puppy!" said Fairless heartily. "Your mother and I have something much better than a puppy for you. Just take a look under the tree there—it's a *robot!* Yes, Morey, your very own robot—a full-size thirty-eight-chip fully automatic companion-robot for you! Go ahead, Morey, go right up and speak to it. It's name is Henry. Go on, boy."

Morey felt a sudden, incomprehensible tingle inside the bridge of his nose. He said shakily, "But I—I didn't *want* a robot."

"Of course you want a robot," Carrado interrupted. "Go on, child, play with your nice robot."

Morey said violently, "I *hate* robots!" He looked around him at the doctors, at the gray-paneled consulting room. He added defiantly, "You hear me, all of you? I *still* hate robots!"

There was a second's pause, then the questions began.

It was half an hour before the receptionist came in and announced that time was up.

In that half hour, Morey had got over his trembling and lost his wild, momentary passion, but he had remembered what for thirteen years he had forgotten.

He hated robots.

The surprising thing was not that young Morey Fry had hated robots. The surprise was that they were not hated more than they were.

Everybody knew what was supposed to happen. Technological forecasters predicted it. Economic prognosticators confirmed the warnings. Politicians viewed with alarm. The displacement of flesh and blood workers by ugly, anthropomorphic machines meant violence! The Luddites would rise again, and the factory aisles would run sticky with lubricating oil.

But it didn't happen.

The Robot Riots, that ultimate outbreak of flesh against metal for which the whole human race was poised, the battle to the death between mankind and its machine heirs . . . never happened. A little boy hated robots. But the man he became worked with them, hand in hand.

And yet history held a warning. Always and always before, the new worker, the competitor for the jobs, was at once and inevitably outside the law. It had happened over and over again, for centuries. The waves of immigration swelled in—the Irish, the Negroes, the Jews, the Italians, the Poles, the Russians. They were squeezed into their

ghettoes and there they encysted, seethed and struck
back, until the blending of generations made them indis-
tinguishable. But for robots, such genetic relief was not in
sight.

And still the conflict never came. With Amalfi Amadeus's power and General Motors engineers and a handful
of chips from Silicon Valley, the robots clanked off the
assembly lines.

And they came bearing a gift; and its name was "plenty."

And by the time the gift had shown its unguessed
penalty, the time for a Robot Riot was past. Plenty is a
habit-forming drug. You do not cut the dosage down. You
kick it if you can; you stop the dose entirely. But the con-
vulsions that follow may wreck the body once and for all.

The addict craves the grainy white powder; he doesn't
hate it, or the runner who sells it to him. And if Morey as
a little boy could hate the robot that had deprived him of
his pup, Morey the man was perfectly aware that the
robots were his servants and his friends.

But the little Morey inside the man—*he* had never been
convinced.

Morey ordinarily looked forward to his work. The one
day a week at which he *did* anything was a wonderful
change from the dreary consume, consume, consume
grind. He entered the bright-lit drafting room of the Bradmoor Amusements Company with a feeling of uplift.

But as he was changing from street garb to his drafting
smock, Howland from Procurement came over with a
knowing look. "Wainwright's been looking for you,"
Howland whispered. "Better get right in there."

Morey nervously thanked him and got. Wainwright's office was the size of a phone booth and as bare as Antarctic
ice. Every time Morey saw it, he felt his insides churn
with envy. Think of a desk with nothing on it but work

surface—no calendar-clock, no twelve-color pen rack, no dictating machines!

He squeezed himself in and sat down while Wainwright finished a phone call. He mentally reviewed the possible reasons why Wainwright would want to talk to him in person instead of over the phone, or by dropping a word to him as he passed through the drafting room.

Very few of them were good.

Wainwright put down the phone and Morey straightened up. "You sent for me?" he asked.

Wainwright in a chubby world was aristocratically lean. As General Superintendent of the Design & Development Section of the Bradmoor Amusements Company, he ranked high in the upper section of the well-to-do. He rasped, "I certainly did. Fry, just what the hell do you think you're up to now?"

"I don't know what you m-mean, Mr. Wainwright," Morey stammered, reviewing his mental list of possible reasons for the interview and crossing off all of the good ones.

Wainwright snorted. "I guess you don't. Not because you weren't told, but because you don't want to know. Think back a whole week. What did I have you on the carpet for then?"

Morey said sickly, "My ration book. Look, Mr. Wainwright, I know I'm running a little bit behind, but—"

"But nothing! How do you think it looks to the Committee, Fry? They got a complaint from the Ration Board about you. Naturally they passed it on to me. And naturally I'm going to pass it right along to you. The question is, what are you doing to do about it? Good God, man, look at these figures—textiles, fifty-one per cent; food, sixty-seven per cent; amusements and entertainment, *thirty* per cent! You haven't come up to your ration in anything for months!"

Morey stared at the card miserably. "We—that is, my wife and I—just had a long talk about that last night, Mr. Wainwright. And, believe me, we're going to do better. We're going to buckle right down and get to work and— uh—do better," he finished weakly.

Wainwright nodded, and for the first time there was a note of sympathy in his voice. "Your wife. Judge Elon's daughter, isn't she? Good family. I've met the Judge many times." Then, gruffly, "Well, nevertheless, Fry, I'm warning you. I don't care how you straighten this out, but *don't let the Committee mention this to me again.*"

"No, sir."

"All right. Finished with the schematics on the new K-50?"

Morey brightened. "Just about, sir! I'm putting the first section on tape today. I'm very pleased with it, Mr. Wainwright, honestly I am." For a moment Morey almost forgot why he was in Wainwright's office, for Morey loved his work. Well, *everybody* loved his work, of course—that was why working hours were so hard to come by! But Morey's work was special. Games! Technologically brilliant devices to please people and charm away their time—and produce no tangible commodities at all! Morey combined the flexibility of video games with the rattle and roll of a pinball machine; and the results were spectacular. So his work was socially useful and, besides, Morey was very good at it. Though still only a detailer, his touch was beginning to be recognized. "I've got more than eighteen hundred moving parts in the new one," he boasted.

"Good. Good." Wainwright glanced down at his desk. "Get back to it. And straighten out this other thing. You can do it, Fry. Consuming is everybody's duty. Just keep that in mind."

Howland followed Morey out of the drafting room, down to the spotless shops. "Bad time?" he inquired solicitously. Morey grunted. It was none of Howland's business.

Howland looked over his shoulder as he was setting up the programming panel. Morey studied the matrices silently, then got busy reading the summary tapes, checking them back against the schematics, setting up the instructions on the programming board. Howland kept quiet as Morey completed the setup and ran off a test tape. It checked perfectly; Morey stepped back to light a cigarette in celebration before pushing the *start* button.

Howland said, "Go on, run it. I can't go until you put it in the works."

Morey grinned and pushed the button. The board lighted up; within it, a tiny metronomic beep began to pulse. That was all. At the other end of the quarter-mile shed, Morey knew, the automatic sorters and conveyers were fingering through the copper reels and steel ingots, measuring hoppers of plastic powder and colors, setting up an intricate weaving path for the thousands of individual components that would make up Bradmoor's new K-50 Spin-a-Game. But from where they stood, in the elaborately muraled programming room, nothing showed. Bradmoor was an ultra-modernized plant; in the manufacturing end, even robots had been dispensed with in favor of machines that guided themselves.

Morey glanced at his watch and logged in the starting time while Howland quickly counter-checked Morey's raw-material flow program.

"Checks out," Howland said solemnly, slapping him on the back. "Calls for a celebration. Anyway, it's your first design, isn't it?"

"Yes. First all by myself, at any rate."

Howland was already fishing in his private locker for the bottle he kept against emergency needs. He poured with a flourish. "To Morey Fry," he said, "our most favorite designer, in whom we are much pleased."

Morey drank. It went down easily enough. Morey had conscientiously used his liquor rations for years, but he had never gone beyond the minimum, so that although liquor was no new experience for him, the single drink immediately warmed him. It warmed his mouth, his throat, the hollows of his chest; and it settled down with a warm glow inside him. Howland, exerting himself to be nice, complimented Morey fatuously on the design and poured another drink. Morey didn't utter any protest at all.

Howland drained his glass. "You may wonder," he said formally, "why I am so pleased with you, Morey Fry. I will tell you why this is."

Morey grinned. "Please do."

Howland nodded. "I will. It's because I am pleased with the world, Morey. My wife left me last night."

Morey was as shocked as only a recent bridegroom can be by the news of a crumbling marriage. "That's too ba— I mean is that a fact?"

"Yes, she left my beds and board and five robots, and I'm happy to see her go." He poured another drink for both of them. "Women. Can't live with them and can't live without them. First you sigh and pant and chase after 'em—you like poetry?" he demanded suddenly.

Morey said cautiously, "Some poetry."

Howland quoted: "'How long, my love, shall I behold this wall between our gardens—yours the rose, and mine the swooning lily.' Like it? I wrote it for Jocelyn—that's my wife—when we were first going together."

"It's beautiful," said Morey.

"She wouldn't talk to me for two days." Howland drained his drink. "Lots of spirit, that girl. Anyway, I hunted her like a tiger. And then I caught her. *Wow!*"

Morey took a deep drink from his own glass. "What do you mean, *wow?*" he asked.

"Wow." Howland pointed his finger at Morey. *"Wow,* that's what I mean. We got married and I took her home to the dive I was living in, and *wow* we had a kid, and *wow* I got in a little trouble with the Ration Board—nothing serious, of course, but there was a mixup—and now fights.

"Everything was a fight," he explained. "She'd start with a little nagging, and naturally I'd say something or other back, and *bang* we were off. Budget, budget, budget; I hope to die if I ever hear the word 'budget' again. Morey, you're a married man; you know what it's like. Tell me the truth, weren't you just about ready to blow your top the first time you caught your wife cheating on the budget?"

"Cheating on the budget?" Morey was startled. "Cheating how?"

"Oh, lots of ways. Making your portions bigger than hers. Sneaking extra shirts for you on her clothing ration. You know."

"Damn it, I do *not* know!" cried Morey. "Cherry wouldn't do anything like that!"

Howland looked at him opaquely for a long second. "Of course not," he said at last. "Let's have another drink."

Ruffled, Morey held out his glass. Cherry wasn't the type of girl to *cheat.* Of course she wasn't. A fine, loving girl like her—a pretty girl, of a good family; she wouldn't know how to begin.

Howland was saying, in a sort of chant, "No more budget. No more fights. No more 'Daddy never treated me like this.' No more nagging. No more extra rations for household allowance. No more—Morey, what do you say we go out and have a few drinks? I know a place where—"

"Sorry, Howland," Morey said. "I've got to get back to the office, you know."

Howland guffawed. He held out his wristwatch. As Morey, a little unsteadily, bent over it, it tinkled out the hour. It was a matter of minutes before the office closed for the day.

"Oh," said Morey. "I didn't realize— Well, anyway, Howland thanks, but I can't. My wife will be expecting me."

"She certainly will." Howland snickered. "Won't catch *her* eating up your rations and hers tonight."

Morey said tightly, "Howland!"

"Oh, sorry, sorry." Howland waved an arm. "Don't mean to say anything against *your* wife, of course. Guess maybe Jocelyn soured me on women. But honest, Morey, you'd like this place. Name of Uncle Piggotty's, down in the Old Town. Crazy bunch hangs out there. You'd like them. Couple nights last week they had—I mean, you understand, Morey, I don't go there as often as all that, but I just happened to drop in and—"

Morey interrupted firmly. "Thank you, Howland. Must go home. Wife expects it. Decent of you to offer. Good night. Be seeing you."

He walked out, turned at the door to bow politely, and in turning back cracked the side of his face against the doorjamb. A sort of pleasant numbness had taken possession of his entire skin surface, though, and it wasn't until he perceived Henry chattering at him sympathetically that he noticed a trickle of blood running down the side of his face.

"Mere flesh wound," he said with dignity. "Nothing to cause you *least* conshter—consternation, Henry. Now kindly shut your ugly face. Want to think."

And he slept in the car all the way home.

It was worse than a hangover. The name is "holdover." You've had some drinks; you've started to sober up by catching a little sleep. Then you are required to be awake and to function. The consequent state has the worst features of hangover and intoxication; your head thumps and your mouth tastes like the floor of a bear-pit, but you are nowhere near sober.

There is one cure. Morey said thickly, "Let's have a cocktail, dear."

Cherry was delighted to share a cocktail with him before dinner. Cherry, Morey thought lovingly, was a wonderful, wonderful, wonderful—

He found his nead nodding in time to his thoughts and the motion made him wince.

Cherry flew to his side and touched his temple. "Is it bothering you, darling?" she asked solicitously. "Where you ran into the door, I mean?"

Morey looked at her sharply, but her expression was open and adoring. He said bravely, "Just a little. Nothing to it, really."

The butler brought the cocktails and retired. Cherry lifted her glass. Morey raised his, caught a whiff of the liquor and nearly dropped it. He bit down hard on his churning insides and forced himself to swallow.

He was surprised but grateful to find that it stayed down. In a moment, the curious phenomenon of warmth began to repeat itself. He swallowed the rest of the drink and held out his glass for a refill. He even tried a smile. Oddly enough, his face didn't fall off.

One more drink did the job. Morey felt happy and relaxed, but by no means drunk. They went in to dinner in fine spirits. They chatted cheerfully with each other and Henry, and Morey found time to feel sentimentally sorry for poor Howland, who couldn't make a go of his marriage, when marriage was obviously such an easy relationship, so beneficial to both sides, so warm and relaxing. . . .

Startled, he said, "What?"

Cherry repeated, "It's the cleverest scheme I ever heard of. Such a funny little man, dear. All kind of *nervous,* if you know what I mean. He kept looking at the door as if he was expecting someone, but of course that was silly. None of his friends would have come to *our* house to see him."

Morey said tensely, "Cherry, *please!* What was that you said about ration stamps?"

"But I told you, darling! It was just after you left this morning. This funny little man came to the door; the butler said he wouldn't give any name. Anyway, I talked to him. I thought he might be a neighbor and I certainly would *never* be rude to any neighbor who might come to call, even if the neighborhood was—"

"The ration stamps!" Morey begged. "Did I hear you say he was peddling phony ration stamps?"

Cherry said uncertainly, "Well, I suppose that in a *way* they're phony. The way he explained it, they weren't the regular official kind. But it was four for one, dear—four of his stamps for one of ours. So I just took out our household book and steamed off a couple of weeks' stamps and—"

"How many?" Morey bellowed.

Cherry blinked. "About—about two weeks' quota," she said faintly. "Was that wrong, dear?"

Morey closed his eyes dizzily. "A couple of weeks' stamps," he repeated. "Four for one—you didn't even get the regular rate."

Cherry wailed, "How was I supposed to know? I never had anything like this when I was *home!* We didn't have food riots and slums and all those horrible robots and filthy little revolting men coming to the door!"

Morey stared at her woodenly. She was crying again, but it made no impression on the case-hardened armor that was suddenly thrown around his heart.

Henry made a tentative sound that, in a human, would have been a preparatory cough, but Morey froze him with a white-eyed look.

Morey said in a dreary monotone that barely penetrated the sound of Cherry's tears, "Let me tell you just what it was you did. Assuming, at best, that these stamps you got are at least average good counterfeits, and not so bad that the best thing to do with them is throw them away before we get caught with them in our possession, you have approximately a two-month supply of funny stamps. In case you didn't know it, those ration books are not merely ornamental. They have to be turned in every month to prove that we have completed our consuming quota for the month.

"When they are turned in, they are spot-checked. Every book is at least glanced at. A big chunk of them are gone over very carefully by the inspectors, and a certain percentage are tested by ultraviolet, infra-red, X-ray, radioisotopes, bleaches, fumes, paper chromatography and every other damned test known to Man." His voice was rising to an uneven crescendo. "*If* we are lucky enough to get away with using any of these stamps at all, we daren't —we simply *dare* not— use more than one or two counterfeits to every dozen or more real stamps.

"That means, Cherry, that what you bought is not a two-month supply, but maybe a two-*year* supply—and since, as you no doubt have never noticed, the things have expiration dates on them, there is probably no chance in the world that we can ever hope to use more than half of them." He was bellowing by the time he pushed back his chair and towered over her. "Moreover," he went on, "right *now,* right as of this *minute,* we have to make up the stamps you gave away, which means that at the very best we are going to be on double rations for two weeks or so. And that won't do it. We'll have to—I'll have to—"

He stopped, thinking hard. There was no doubt they would "have to" do something, but what? "I don't know," he growled. "Maybe I'll have some cosmetic surgery, or get my teeth capped."

"Oh, please, Morey! Your beautiful teeth!"

"Yes!" he snapped savagely. "It's as bad as that! And that's saying nothing about the one feature of this whole grisly mess that you seem to have thought of least, namely that counterfeit stamps are against the *law!* I'm poor, Cherry. I live in a slum, and I know it. I've got a long way to go before I'm as rich or respected or powerful as your father, about whom I am beginning to get considerably tired of hearing. But, poor as I may be, I can tell you this for sure. Up until now, at any rate, I have always been *honest.*"

Cherry's tears had stopped entirely and she was bowed down, white-faced and dry-eyed, by the time Morey had finished. He had spent himself. There was no violence left in him.

He stared dismally at Cherry for a moment, then turned without another word and stamped out of the house. As he left he thought, *Marriage!*

He walked for hours, blind to where he was going.

What brought him back to awareness was a sensation he had not felt in a dozen years. It was not, Morey abruptly realized, the dying traces of his hangover that made his stomach feel so queer. It was empty. He was hungry—actually hungry!

He looked about him. He was in the Old Town, miles from home. That great somber windowless block had to be an Amadeus fusion plant, and the people were what you would expect in a decrepit industrial slum. Morey had never seen so many minks—in this weather, growing warmer every year! The street he was on was as conspicuously poverty-stricken as Morey had ever seen—Chinese pagodas stood next to rococo imitations of the chapels around Versailles; gingerbread marred every facade; no building was without its brilliant signs and flarelights.

He saw a blindingly overdecorated eating establishment called Billie's Budget Busy Bee and crossed the street toward it, dodging through the unending streams of traffic. It was a miserable excuse for a restaurant, but Morey was in no mood to care. He found a seat under a potted palm, as far from the tinkling fountains and robot string ensemble as he could manage, and ordered recklessly, paying no attention to the ration prices. As the waiter was gliding noiselessly away, Morey had a sickening realization: He'd come out without his ration book. He groaned out loud; it was too late to leave without causing a disturbance. But then, he thought rebelliously, what difference did one more unrationed meal make, anyhow?

Food made him feel a little better. He finished the last of his *profiterole au chocolat,* not even leaving on the plate the uneaten one-third that tradition permitted, and paid his check. The robot cashier reached automatically for his ration book. Morey had a moment of grandeur as he said simply, "No ration stamps."

Robot cashiers are not equipped to display surprise, but this one tried. The man behind Morey in line audibly caught his breath, and less audibly mumbled something about *slummers.* Morey took it as a compliment and strode outside feeling almost in good humor.

Good enough to go home to Cherry? Morey thought seriously of it for a second; but he wasn't going to pretend he was wrong and certainly Cherry wasn't going to be willing to admit that *she* was.

Besides, Morey told himself grimly, she was undoubtedly asleep. That was an annoying thing about Cherry at best: she never had any trouble getting to sleep. Didn't even use her quota of sleeping tablets, though Morey had spoken to her about it more than once. Of course, he reminded himself, he had been so polite and tactful about it, as befits a newlywed, that very likely she hadn't even understood that it was a complaint. Well, *that* would stop!

Man's man Morey Fry, wearing no collar ruff but his own, strode determinedly down the streets of the Old Town.

"Hey, Joe, want a good time?"

Morey took one unbelieving look. "You again!" he roared.

The little man stared at him in genuine surprise. Then a faint glimmer of recognition crossed his face. "Oh, yeah," he said. "This morning, huh?" He clucked commiseratingly. "Too bad you wouldn't deal with me. Your wife was a lot smarter. Of course, you got me a little sore, Jack, so naturally I had to raise the price a little bit."

"You skunk, you cheated my poor wife blind! You and I are going to the local station house and talk this over."

The little man pursed his lips. "We are, huh?"

Morey nodded vigorously. "Damn right! And let me tell you—" He stopped in the middle of a threat as a large hand cupped around his shoulder.

The equally large man who owned the hand said, in a mild and cultured voice, "Is this gentleman disturbing you, Sam?"

"Not so far," the little man conceded. "He might want to, though, so don't go away."

Morey wrenched his shoulder away. "Don't think you can strongarm me. I'm taking you to the police."

Sam shook his head unbelievingly. "You mean you're going to call the law in on this?"

"I certainly am!"

Sam sighed regretfully. "What do you think of that, Walter? Treating his wife like that. Such a nice lady, too."

"What are you talking about?" Morey demanded, stung on a peculiarly sensitive spot.

"I'm talking about your wife," Sam explained. "Of course, I'm not married myself. But it seems to me that if I was, I wouldn't call the police when my wife was engaged in some kind of criminal activity or other. No, sir, I'd try to settle it myself. Tell you what," he advised, "why don't you talk this over with her? Make her see the error of—"

"Wait a minute," Morey interrupted. "You mean you'd involve my wife in this thing?"

The man spread his hands helplessly. "It's not me that would involve her, Buster," he said. "She already involved her own self. It takes two to make a crime, you know. I sell, maybe; I won't deny it. But after all, I can't sell unless somebody buys, can I?"

Morey stared at him glumly. He glanced in quick speculation at the large-sized Walter; but Walter was just as big as he'd remembered, so that took care of that. Violence was out; the police were out; that left no really attractive way of capitalizing on the good luck of running into the man again.

Sam said, "Well, I'm glad to see that's off your mind. Now, returning to my original question, Mac, how would you like a good time? You look like a smart fellow to me; you look like you'd be kind of interested in a place I happen to know of down the block."

Morey said bitterly, "So you're a dive-steerer, too. A real talented man."

"I admit it," Sam agreed. "Stamp business is slow at night, in my experience. People have their minds more on a good time. And, believe me, a good time is what I can show 'em. Take this place I'm talking about, Uncle Piggotty's is the name of it. It's what I would call an unusual kind of place. Wouldn't you say so, Walter?"

"Oh, I agree with you entirely," Walter rumbled.

But Morey was hardly listening. He said, "Uncle Pig-gotty's, you say?"

"That's right," said Sam.

Morey frowned for a moment, digesting an idea. Uncle Piggotty's sounded like the place Howland had been talking about back at the plant; it might be interesting, at that.

While he was making up his mind, Sam slipped an arm through his on one side and Walter amiably wrapped a big hand around the other. Morey found himself walking.

"You'll like it," Sam promised comfortably. "No hard feelings about this morning, sport? Of course not. Once you get a look at Piggotty's, you'll get over your mad, anyhow. It's something special, I swear, on the stamps they give me for bringing in customers. I wouldn't do it unless I *believed* in it."

"Dance, Jack?" the hostess yelled over the noise at the bar. She stepped back, lifted her flounced skirts to ankle height and executed a tricky nine-step.

"My name is Morey," Morey yelled back. "And I don't want to dance, thanks."

The hostess shrugged, frowned meaningfully at Sam and danced away.

Sam flagged the bartender. "First round's on us," he explained to Morey. "Then we won't bother you any more. Unless you want us to, of course. Like the place?" Morey hesitated, but Sam didn't wait. "Fine place," he yelled, and picked up the drink the bartender left him. "See you around."

He and the big man were gone. Morey stared after them uncertainly, then gave it up. He was here, anyhow; might as well at least have a drink. He ordered and looked around.

Uncle Piggotty's was a third-rate dive disguised to look in parts of it at least, like one of the exclusive upper-class

country clubs. The bar, for instance, was treated to resemble the clean lines of nailed wood; but underneath the
surface treatment, Morey could detect the intricate lami-
nations of plyplastic. What at first glance appeared to be
burlap hangings were in actuality elaborately textured syn-
thetics. And all through the bar the motif was carried out.

A floor show of sorts was going on, but nobody seemed
to be paying much attention to it. Morey, straining briefly
to hear the master of ceremonies, gathered that the wit
was on a more than mildly vulgar level. There was a dispirited string of chorus beauties in long ruffled pantaloons
and diaphanous tops; one of them, Morey was almost
sure, was the hostess who had talked to him just a few
moments before.

Next to him a man was declaiming to a middle-aged
woman:

> *Smote I the monstrous rock, yahoo!*
> *Smote I the turgid tube, Bully Boy!*
> *Smote I the cankered hill—*

"Why, Morey!" he interrupted himself. "What are you
doing here?"

He turned farther around and Morey recognized him.
"Hello, Howland," he said. "I—uh—I happened to be
free tonight, so I thought—"

Howland snickered. "Well, guess your wife is more lib-
eral than mine was. Order a drink, boy."

"Thanks, I've got one," said Morey.

The woman, with a tigerish look at Morey, said, "Don't
stop, Everett. That was one of your most beautiful
things."

"Oh, Morey's heard my poetry," Howland said. "Morey, I'd like you to meet a very lovely and talented young
lady, Tanaquil Bigelow. Morey works in the office with
me, Tan."

"Obviously," said Tanaquil Bigelow in a frozen voice, and Morey hastily withdrew the hand he had begun to put out.

The conversation stuck there, impaled, the woman cold, Howland relaxed and abstracted, Morey wondering if, after all, this had been such a good idea. He caught the eye-cell of the robot bartender and ordered a round of drinks for the three of them. Since he didn't have his own ration book, he politely put them on Howland's. By the time the drinks had come and Morey had just got around to deciding that it wasn't a very good idea, the woman had all of a sudden become thawed.

She said abruptly, "You look like the kind of man who *thinks*, Morey, and I like to talk to that kind of man. Frankly, Morey, I just don't have any patience at all with the stupid, stodgy men who just work in their offices all day and eat all their dinners every night, and gad about and consume like mad and where does it all get them, anyhow? That's right, I can see you understand. Just one crazy rush of consume, consume from the day you're born *plop* to the day you're buried *pop!* And who's to blame if not the robots?"

Faintly, a tinge of worry began to appear on the surface of Howland's relaxed calm. "Tan," he chided, "Morey may not be very interested in politics."

Politics, Morey thought; well, at least that was a clue. He'd had the dizzying feeling, while the woman was talking, that he himself was the ball in the games machine he had designed for the shop earlier that day. Following the woman's conversation might, at that, give his next design some valuable pointers in swoops, curves and obstacles.

He said, with more than half truth, "No, please go on, Miss Bigelow. I'm very much interested."

She smiled; then abruptly her face changed to a frightening scowl. Morey flinched, but evidently the scowl wasn't meant for him. "Robots!" she hissed. "Supposed to work for us, aren't they? Hah! We're their slaves, slaves for every moment of every miserable day of our lives. Slaves! Wouldn't you like to join us and be free, Morey?"

Morey took cover in his drink. He made an expressive gesture with his free hand—expressive of exactly what, he didn't truly know, for he was lost. But it seemed to satisfy the woman.

She said accusingly, "Did you know that more than three-quarters of the people in this country have had a nervous breakdown in the past five years and four months? That more than half of them are under the constant care of psychiatrists for psychosis—not just plain ordinary neurosis like my husband's got and Howland here has got and you've got, but psychosis. Like I've got. Did you know that? Did you know that forty per cent of the population are essentially manic depressive, thirty-one per cent are schizoid, thirty-eight per cent have an assortment of other unfixed psychogenic disturbances and twenty-four—"

"Hold it a minute, Tan," Howland interrupted critically. "You've got too many per cents there. Start over again."

"Oh, the hell with it," the woman said moodily. "I wish my husband were here. He expresses it so much better than I do." She swallowed her drink. "Since you've wriggled off the hook," she said nastily to Morey, "how about setting up another round—on my ration book this time?"

Morey did; it was the simplest thing to do in his confusion. When that was gone, they had another on Howland's book.

As near as he could figure out, the woman, her husband and quite possibly Howland as well belonged to some kind of anti-robot group. Morey had heard of such things; they had a quasi-legal status, neither approved nor prohibited, but he had never come into contact with them before. Remembering the hatred he had so painfully relived at the psychodrama session, he thought anxiously that perhaps he belonged with them. But, question them though he might, he couldn't seem to get the principles of the organization firmly in mind.

The woman finally gave up trying to explain it, and went off to find her husband while Morey and Howland had another drink and listened to two drunks squabble over who bought the next round. They were at the Alphonse-Gaston stage of inebriation; they would regret it in the morning; for each was bending over backward to permit the other to pay the ration points. Morey wondered uneasily about his own points; Howland was certainly getting credit for a lot of Morey's drinking tonight. Served him right for forgetting his book, of course.

When the woman came back, it was with the large man Morey had encountered in the company of Sam, the counterfeiter, steerer and general man-about-Old-Town.

"A remarkably small world, isn't it?" boomed Walter Bigelow, only slightly crushing Morey's hand in his. "Well, sir, my wife has told me how interested you are in the basic philosophical drives behind our movement, and I should like to discuss them further with you. To begin with, sir, have you considered the principle of twoness?"

Morey said, "Why—"

"Very good," said Bigelow courteously. He cleared his throat and declaimed:

> *Han-headed Cathay saw it first,*
> *Bright as brightest solar burst;*
> *Whipped it into boy and girl,*
> *The blinding spiral-sliced swirl:*
> *Yang*
> *And Yin.*

He shrugged deprecatingly. "Just the first stanza," he said. "I don't know if you got much out of it."

"Well, no," Morey admitted.

"Second stanza," Bigelow said firmly:

> *Hegel saw it, saw it clear;*
> *Jackal Marx drew near, drew near:*
> *O'er his shoulder saw it plain,*
> *Turned it upside down again:*
> *Yang*
> *And Yin.*

There was an expectant pause. Morey said, "I—uh—"

"Wraps it all up, doesn't it?" Bigelow's wife demanded. "Oh, if only others could see it as clearly as you do! The robot peril *and* the robot savior. Starvation *and* surfeit. Always twoness, always!"

Bigelow patted Morey's shoulder. "The next stanza makes it even clearer," he said. "It's really very clever—I shouldn't say it, of course, but it's Howland's as much as it's mine. He helped me with the verses." Morey darted a glance at Howland, but Howland was carefully looking away. "Third stanza," said Bigelow. "This is a hard one, because it's long, so pay attention."

> *Justice, tip your sightless scales;*
> *One pan rises, one pan falls.*

"Howland," he interrupted himself, "are you *sure* about that rhyme? I always trip over it. Well, anyway:

> *Add to A and B grows less;*
> *A's B's partner, nonetheless.*
> *Next, the twoness that there be*
> *In even electricity.*
> *Chart the current as it's found:*

Sine the hot lead, line the ground.
The wild sine dances, soars and falls,
But only to figures the zero calls.
Sine wave, scales, all things that be
Share a reciprocity.
Male and female, light and dark:
Name the numbers of Noah's Ark!
Yang
And Yin!

"Dearest!" shrieked Bigelow's wife. "You've never done it better!" There was a spatter of applause, and Morey realized for the first time that half the bar had stopped its noisy revel to listen to them. Bigelow was evidently quite a well-known figure here.

Morey said weakly, "I've never heard anything like it."

He turned hesitantly to Howland, who promptly said, "Drink! What we all need right now is a drink."

They had a drink on Bigelow's book.

Morey got Howland aside and asked him, "Look, level with me. Are these people nuts?"

Howland showed pique. "No. Certainly not."

"Does that poem mean anything? Does this whole business of twoness mean anything?"

Howland shrugged. "If it means something to them, it means something. They're philosophers, Morey. They see deep into things. You don't know what a privilege it is for me to be allowed to associate with them."

They had another drink. On Howland's book, of course.

Morey eased Walter Bigelow over to a quiet spot. He said, "Leaving twoness out of it for the moment, what's this about the robots?"

Bigelow looked at him round-eyed. "Didn't you understand the poem?"

"Of course I did. But diagram it for me in simple terms so I can tell my wife."

Bigelow beamed. "It's about the dichotomy of robots," he explained. "Like the little salt mill that the boy wished for: it ground out salt and ground out salt and ground out salt. He had to have salt, but not *that* much salt. Whitehead explains it clearly—"

They had another drink on Bigelow's book.

Morey wavered over Tanaquil Bigelow. He said fuzzily, "Listen. Mrs. Walter Tanaquil Strongarm Bigelow. Listen."

She grinned smugly at him. "Brown hair," she said dreamily.

Morey shook his head vigorously. "Never mind hair," he ordered. "Never mind poem. Listen. In *pre-cise* and el-e-*men*-ta-ry terms, explain to me what is wrong with the world today."

"Not enough brown hair," she said promptly.

"Never mind hair!"

"All right," she said agreeably. "Too many robots. Too many robots make too much of everything."

"Ha! Got it!" Morey exclaimed triumphantly. "Get rid of robots!"

"Oh, no. No! No! No. We wouldn't eat. Everything is mechanized. Can't get rid of them, can't slow down production—slowing down is dying, stopping is quicker dying. Principle of twoness is the concept that clarifies all these—"

"No!" Morey said violently. "What should we *do?*"

"Do? I'll tell you what we should do, if that's what you want. I can tell you."

"Then tell me."

"What we should do is—" Tanaquil hiccuped with a look of refined consternation—"have another drink."

They had another drink. He gallantly let her pay, of

course. She ungallantly argued with the bartender about the ration points due her.

Though not a two-fisted drinker, Morey tried. He really worked at it.

He paid the price, too. For some little time before his limbs stopped moving, his mind stopped functioning. Blackout. Almost a blackout, at any rate, for all he retained of the late evening was a kaleidoscope of people and places and things. Howland was there, drunk as a skunk, disgracefully drunk, Morey remembered thinking as he stared up at Howland from the floor. The Bigelows were there. His wife, Cherry, solicitous and amused, was there. And, oddly enough, Henry was there.

It was very, very hard to reconstruct. Morey devoted a whole morning's hangover to the effort. It was *important* to reconstruct it, for some reason. But Morey couldn't even remember what the reason was; and finally he dismissed it, guessing that he had solved either the secret of twoness or the question of whether Tanaquil Bigelow's remarkable figure was natural.

He did, however, know that the next morning he had awakened in his own bed, with no recollection of getting there. No recollection of anything much, at least not of anything that fit into the proper chronological order or seemed to mesh with anything else, after the dozenth drink when he and Howland, arms around each other's shoulders, composed a new verse on twoness and, plagiarizing an old marching tune, howled it across the boisterous barroom:

> *A twoness on the scene much later*
> *Rests in your refrigerator.*
> *Heat your house and insulate it.*
> *Next your food: Refrigerate it.*

Frost will damp your Freon coils,
So flux in Nichrome till it boils.

See the picture? Heat in cold.
In heat in cold, the story's told!
Giant-writ the sacred scrawl:
Oh, the twoness of it all!
Yang
And Yin!

It had, at any rate, seemed to mean something at the time.

If alcohol opened Morey's eyes to the fact that there *was* a twoness, perhaps alcohol was what he needed. For there was.

Call it a dichotomy, if the word seems more couth. A kind of two-pronged struggle, the struggle of two unwearying runners in an immortal race. There is the refrigerator inside the house. The cold air outside, surrounding the bubble of heated air that is the house, surrounding the bubble of cooled air that is the refrigerator, surrounding the momentary bubble of heated air that defrosts it. Call the heat Yang, if you will. Call the cold Yin. Yang overtakes Yin. Then Yin passes Yang. Then Yang passes Yin. Then—

Give them other names. Call Yin a mouth; call Yang a hand.

If the hand rests, the mouth will starve. If the mouth stops, the hand will die. The hand, Yang, moves faster.

Yin may not lag behind.

Then call Yang a robot.

And remember that a pipeline has two ends.

Like any once-in-a-lifetime lush, Morey braced himself for the consequences—and found startledly that there were none.

Cherry was a surprise to him. "You were so funny," she giggled. "And, honestly, so *romantic.*"

He shakily swallowed his breakfast coffee.

The office staff roared and slapped him on the back. "Howland tells us you're living high, boy!" they bellowed more or less in the same words. "Hey, listen to what Morey did—went on the town for the night of a lifetime *and didn't even bring his ration book along to cash in!*"

They thought it was a wonderful joke.

But, then, everything was going well. Cherry, it seemed, had reformed out of recognition. True, she still hated to go out in the evening and Morey never saw her forcing herself to gorge on unwanted food or play undesired games. But moping into the pantry one afternoon, he found to his incredulous delight that they were well ahead of their ration quotas. In some items, in fact, they were *out*—a month's supply and more was gone ahead of schedule!

Nor was it the counterfeit stamps, for he had found them tucked behind a bain-marie and quietly burned them. He cast about for ways of complimenting her, but caution prevailed. She was sensitive on the subject; leave it be.

And virtue had its reward.

Wainwright called him in, all smiles. "Morey, great news! We've all appreciated your work here and we've been able to show it in some more tangible way than compliments. I didn't want to say anything till it was definite, but—your status has been reviewed by Classification and the Ration Board. You're out of Class Four Minor, Morey!"

Morey said tremulously, hardly daring to hope, "I'm a full Class Four?"

"Class Five, Morey. *Class Five!* When we do something, we do it right. We asked for a special waiver and got it—you've skipped a whole class." He added honestly, "Not that it was just our backing that did it, of course.

Your own recent splendid record of consumption helped a lot. I told you you could do it!"

Morey had to sit down. He missed the rest of what Wainwright had to say, but it couldn't have mattered. He escaped from the office, sidestepped the knot of fellow employees waiting to congratulate him, and got to a phone.

Cherry was as ecstatic and inarticulate as he. "Oh, darling!" was all she could say.

"And I couldn't have done it without you," he babbled. "Wainwright as much as said so himself. Said if it wasn't for the way we—well, *you* have been keeping up with the rations, it never would have got by the Board. I've been meaning to say something to you about that, dear, but I just haven't known how. But I do appreciate it. I—hello?" There was a curious silence at the other end of the phone. "Hello?" he repeated worriedly.

Cherry's voice was intense and low. "Morey Fry, I think you're mean. I wish you hadn't spoiled the good news." And she hung up.

Morey stared slack-jawed at the phone.

Howland appeared behind him, chuckling. "Women," he said. "Never try to figure them. Anyway, congratulations, Morey."

"Thanks," Morey mumbled.

Howland coughed and said, "Uh—by the way, Morey, now that you're one of the big shots, so to speak, you won't—uh—feel obliged to—well, say anything to Wainwright, for instance, about anything I may have said while we—"

"Excuse me," Morey said, unhearing, and pushed past him. He thought wildly of calling Cherry back, of racing home to see just what he'd said that was wrong. Not that there was much doubt, of course. He'd touched her on her sore point.

Anyhow, his wristwatch was chiming a reminder of the

fact that his psychiatric appointment for the week was coming up.

Morey sighed. The day gives and the day takes away. Blessed is the day that gives only good things.

If there ever are any.

The session went badly. Many of the sessions had been going badly, Morey decided; there had been more and more whispering in knots of doctors from which he was excluded, poking and probing in the dark instead of the precise psychic surgery he was used to. Something was wrong, he thought.

Something was. Semmelweiss confirmed it when he adjourned the group session. After the other doctor had left, he sat Morey down for a private talk. On his own time, too—he didn't ask for his usual ration fee. That told Morey how important the problem was.

"Morey," said Semmelweiss, "you're holding back."

"I don't mean to, Doctor," Morey said earnestly.

"Who knows what you 'mean' to do? Part of you 'means' to. We've dug pretty deep and we've found some important things. Now there's something I can't put my finger on. Exploring the mind, Morey, is like sending scouts through cannibal territory. You can't see the cannibals—until it's too late. But if you send a scout through the jungle and he doesn't show up on the other side, it's a fair assumption that something obstructed his way. In that case, we would label the obstruction 'cannibals.' In the case of the human mind, we label the obstruction a 'trauma.' What the trauma is, or what its effects on behavior will be, we have to find out once we know that it's there."

Morey nodded. All of this was familiar; he couldn't see what Semmelweiss was driving at.

Semmelweiss sighed. "The trouble with healing traumas

and penetrating psychic blocks and releasing inhibitions—
the trouble with everything we psychiatrists do, in fact, is
that we can't afford to do it too well. An inhibited man is
under a strain. We try to relieve the strain. But if we suc-
ceed completely, leaving him with no inhibitions at all, we
have an outlaw, Morey. Inhibitions are often socially necessary. Suppose, for instance, that an average man were
not inhibited against blatant waste. It could happen, you
know. Suppose that instead of consuming his ration quota
in an orderly and responsible way, he did such things as
set fire to his house and everything in it or dumped his
food allotment in the river.

"When only a few individuals are doing it, we treat the
individuals. But if it were done on a mass scale, Morey, it
would be the end of society as we know it. Think of the
whole collection of anti-social actions that you see in
every paper. Man beats wife; wife turns into a harpy;
junior smashes up windows; husband starts a black-
market stamp racket. And every one of them traces to a
basic weakness in the mind's defenses against the most
important single anti-social phenomenon—failure to consume."

Morey flared, "That's not fair, Doctor! That was weeks
ago! We've certainly been on the ball lately. I was just
commended by the Board, in fact—"

The doctor said mildly, "Why so violent, Morey? I only
made a general remark."

"It's just natural to resent being accused."

The doctor shrugged. "First, foremost and above all,
we do *not* accuse patients of things. We try to help you
find things out." He lit his end-of-session cigarette.
"Think about it, please. I'll see you next week."

Cherry was composed and unapproachable. She kissed
him remotely when he came in. She said, "I called Mother

and told her the good news. She and Dad promised to
come over here to celebrate."

"Yeah," said Morey. "Darling, what did I say wrong on
the phone?"

"They'll be here about six."

"Sure. But what did I say? Was it about the rations? If
you're sensitive, I swear I'll never mention them again."

"I *am* sensitive, Morey."

He said despairingly, "I'm sorry. I just—"

He had a better idea. He kissed her.

Cherry was passive at first, but not for long. When he
had finished kissing her, she pushed him away and actually giggled. "Let me get dressed for dinner."

"Certainly. Anyhow, I was just—"

She laid a finger on his lips.

He let her escape and, feeling much less tense, drifted
into the library. The afternoon papers were waiting for
him. Virtuously, he sat down and began going through
them in order. Midway through the *World-Telegram-Sun-
Post-and-News,* he rang for Henry.

Morey had read clear through to the drama section of
the *Times-Herald-Tribune-Mirror* before the robot appeared. "Good evening," it said politely.

"What took you so long?" Morey demanded. "Where
are all the robots?"

Robots do not stammer, but there was a distinct pause
before Henry said, "Belowstairs, sir. Did you want them
for something?"

"Well, no. I just haven't seen them around. Get me a
drink."

It hesitated. "Scotch, sir?"

"*Before* dinner? Get me a Manhattan."

"We're all out of vermouth, sir."

"All out? Would you mind telling me how?"

"It's all used up, sir."

"Now that's just ridiculous," Morey snapped. "We

have never run out of liquor in our whole lives and you know it. Good heavens, we just got our allotment in the other day and I certainly—"

He checked himself. There was a sudden flicker of horror in his eyes as he stared at Henry.

"You certainly what, sir?" the robot prompted.

Morey swallowed. "Henry, did I—did I do something I shouldn't have?"

"I'm sure I wouldn't know, sir. It isn't up to me to say what you should and shouldn't do."

"Of course not," Morey agreed grayly.

He sat rigid, staring hopelessly into space, remembering. What he remembered was no pleasure to him at all.

"Henry," he said. "Come along, we're going belowstairs. Right now!"

It had been Tanaquil Bigelow's remark about the robots. *Too many robots—make too much of everything.*

That had implanted the idea; it germinated in Morey's home. More than a little drunk, less than ordinarily inhibited, he had found the problem clear and the answer obvious.

He stared around him in dismal worry. His own robots, following his own orders, given weeks before . . .

Henry said, "It's just what you *told* us to do, sir."

Morey groaned. He was watching a scene of unparalleled activity, and it sent shivers up and down his spine.

There was the butler-robot, hard at work, his copper face expressionless. Dressed in Morey's own sports knickers and golfing shoes, the robot solemnly hit a ball against the wall, picked it up and teed it, hit it again, over and again, with Morey's own clubs. Until the ball wore ragged and was replaced; and the shafts of the clubs leaned out of true; and the close-stitched seams in the clothing began to stretch and abrade.

"My God!" said Morey hollowly.

There were the maid-robots, exquisitely dressed in Cherry's best, walking up and down in the delicate, slim shoes, sitting and rising and bending and turning. The cook-robots and the serving-robots were preparing Dionysian meals.

Morey swallowed. "You—you've been doing this right along," he said to Henry. "That's why the quotas have been filled."

"Oh, yes, sir. Just as you told us."

Morey had to sit down. One of the serving-robots politely scurried over with a chair, brought from upstairs for their new chores.

Waste.

Morey tasted the word between his lips.

Waste.

You never wasted things. You *used* them. If necessary, you drove yourself to the edge of breakdown to use them; you made every breath a burden and every hour a torment to use them, until through diligent consuming and/or occupational merit, you were promoted to the next higher class, and were allowed to consume less frantically. But you didn't wantonly destroy or throw out. You *consumed*.

Morey thought fearfully: When the Board finds out about this . . .

Still, he reminded himself, the Board hadn't found out. It might take some time before they did, for humans, after all, never entered robot quarters. There was no law against it, not even a sacrosanct custom. But there was no reason to. When breaks occurred, which was infrequently, maintenance robots or repair squads came in and put them back in order. Usually the humans involved didn't even know it had happened, because the robots used their own TBR radio circuits and the process was the next thing to automatic.

Morey said reprovingly, "Henry, you should have told—well, I mean reminded me about this."

"But, sir!" Henry protested. "'Don't tell a living soul,' you said. You made it a direct order."

"Umph. Well, keep it that way. I—uh—I have to go back upstairs. Better get the rest of the robots started on dinner."

Morey left, not comfortably.

The dinner to celebrate Morey's promotion was an ordeal. Morey liked Cherry's parents. Old Elon, after the premarriage inquisition that father must inevitably give to daughter's suitor, had buckled right down to the job of adjustment. The old folks were good about not interfering, good about keeping their superior social status to themselves, good about helping out on the budget—at least once a week, they could be relied on to come over for a hearty meal, and Mrs. Elon had more than once remade some of Cherry's new dresses to fit herself, even to the extent of wearing all the high-point ornamentation.

And they had been wonderful about the wedding gifts, when Morey and their daughter got married. The most any member of Morey's family had been willing to take was a silver set or a few crystal table pieces. The Elons had come through with a dazzling promise to accept a car, a birdbath for their garden and a complete set of living-room furniture! Of course, they could afford it—they had to consume so little that it wasn't much strain for them even to take gifts of that magnitude. But without their help, Morey knew, the first few months of matrimony would have been even tougher consuming than they were.

But on this particular night it was hard for Morey to like anyone. He responded with monosyllables; he barely grunted when Elon proposed a toast to his promotion and his brilliant future. He was preoccupied.

Rightly so. Morey, in his deepest, bravest searching, could find no clue in his memory as to just what the punishment might be for what he had done. But he had a sick certainty that trouble lay ahead.

Morey went over his problem so many times that an anesthesia set in. By the time dinner was ended and he and his father-in-law were in the den with their brandy, he was more or less functioning again.

Elon, for the first time since Morey had known him, offered him one of *his* cigars. "You're Grade Five—can afford to smoke somebody else's now, hey?"

"Yeah," Morey said glumly.

There was a moment of silence. Then Elon, as punctilious as any companion-robot, coughed and tried again. "Remember being peaked till I hit Grade Five," he reminisced meaningfully. "Consuming keeps a man on the go, all right. Things piled up at the law office, couldn't be taken care of while ration points piled up, too. And consuming comes first, of course—that's a citizen's prime duty. Mother and I had our share of grief over that, but a couple that wants to make a go of marriage and citizenship just pitches in and does the job, hey?"

Morey repressed a shudder and managed to nod.

"Best thing about upgrading," Elon went on, as if he had elicited a satisfactory answer, "don't have to spend so much time consuming, give more attention to work. Greatest luxury in the world, work. Wish I had as much stamina as you young fellows. Five days a week in court are about all I can manage. Hit six for a while, relaxed first time in my life, but my doctor made me cut down. Said we mustn't overdo pleasures. You'll be working two days a week now, hey?"

Morey produced another nod.

Elon drew deeply on his cigar, his eyes bright as they watched Morey. He was visibly puzzled, and Morey, even in his half-daze, could recognize the exact moment at which Elon drew the wrong inference. "Ah, everything okay with you and Cherry?" he asked diplomatically.

"Fine!" Morey exclaimed. "Couldn't be better!"

"Good, good." Elon changed the subject with almost an audible wrench. "Speaking of court, had an interesting case the other day. Young fellow—year or two younger than you, I guess—came in with a Section Ninety-seven on him. Know what that is? Breaking and entering!"

"Breaking and entering," Morey repeated wonderingly, interested in spite of himself. "Breaking and entering what?"

"Houses. Old term; law's full of them. Originally applied to stealing things. Still does, I discovered."

"You mean he *stole* something?" Morey asked in bewilderment.

"Exactly! He *stole*. Strangest thing I ever came across. Talked it over with one of his bunch of lawyers later; new one on him, too. Seems this kid had a girl friend, nice kid but a little, you know, plump. She got interested in art."

"There's nothing wrong with that," Morey said.

"Nothing wrong with her, either. She didn't do anything. She didn't like him too much, though. Wouldn't marry him. Kid got to thinking about how he could get her to change her mind and—well, you know that big Mondrian in the Museum?"

"I've never been there," Morey said, somewhat embarrassed.

"Um. Ought to try it some day, boy. Anyway, comes closing time at the Museum the other day, this kid sneaks in. He steals the painting. That's right—*steals* it. Takes it to give to the girl."

Morey shook his head blankly. "I never heard of anything like that in my life."

"Not many have. Girl wouldn't take it, by the way. Got scared when he brought it to her. She must've tipped off the police, I guess. Somebody did. Took 'em three hours to find it, even when they knew it was hanging on a wall. Pretty poor kid. Forty-two-room house."

"And there was a *law* against it?" Morey asked. "I mean it's like making a law against breathing."

"Certainly was. Old law, of course. Kid got set back two grades. Would have been more but, my God, he was only a Grade Three as it was."

"Yeah," said Morey, wetting his lips. "Say, Dad—"

"Um?"

Morey cleared his throat. "Uh—I wonder—I mean what's the penalty, for instance, for things like—well, misusing rations or anything like that?"

Elon's eyebrows went high. "Misusing rations?"

"Say you had a liquor ration, it might be, and instead of drinking it, you—well, flushed it down the drain or something . . ."

His voice trailed off. Elon was frowning. He said, "Funny thing, seems I'm not as broadminded as I thought I was. For some reason, I don't find that amusing."

"Sorry," Morey croaked.

And he certainly was.

It might be dishonest, but it was doing him a lot of good, for days went by and no one seemed to have penetrated his secret. Cherry was happy. Wainwright found occasion after occasion to pat Morey's back. The wages of sin were turning out to be prosperity and happiness.

There was a bad moment when Morey came home to find Cherry in the middle of supervising a team of packing-robots; the new house, suitable to his higher grade, was ready, and they were expected to move in the next day. But Cherry hadn't been belowstairs, and Morey had his household robots clean up the evidences of what they had been doing before the packers got that far.

The new house was, by Morey's standards, pure luxury.

It had only fifteen rooms. Morey had shrewdly retained one more robot than was required for a Class Five, and had been allowed a compensating deduction in the size of his house.

The robot quarters were less secluded than in the old house, though, and that was a disadvantage. More than once Cherry had snuggled up to him in the delightful intimacy of their one bed in their single bedroom and said, with faint curiosity, "I wish they'd stop that noise." And Morey had promised to speak to Henry about it in the morning. But there was nothing he could say to Henry, of course, unless he ordered Henry to stop the tireless consuming through each of the day's twenty-four hours that kept them always ahead, but never quite far enough ahead, of the inexorable weekly increment of ration quotas.

But, though Cherry might once in a while have a moment's curiosity about what the robots were doing, she was not likely to be able to guess at the facts. Her upbringing was, for once, on Morey's side—she knew so little of the grind, grind, grind of consuming that was the lot of the lower classes that she scarcely noticed that there was less of it.

Morey almost, sometimes, relaxed.

He thought of many ingenious chores for robots, and the robots politely and emotionlessly obeyed.

Morey was a success.

It wasn't all gravy. There was a nervous moment for Morey when the quarterly survey report came in the mail. As the day for the Ration Board to check over the degree of wear on the turned-in discards came due, Morey began to sweat. The clothing and furniture and household goods the robots had consumed for him were very nearly in shreds. It had to look plausible, that was the big thing— no normal person would wear a hole completely through the knee of a pair of pants, as Henry had done with his dress suit before Morey stopped him. Would the Board question it?

Worse, was there something about the *way* the robots consumed the stuff that would give the whole show away? Some special wear point in the robot anatomy, for instance, that would rub a hole where no human's body could, or stretch a seam that should normally be under no strain at all?

It was worrisome. But the worry was needless. When the report of survey came, Morey let out a long-held breath. *Not a single item disallowed!*

Morey was a success—and so was his scheme!

To the successful man come the rewards of success. Morey arrived home one evening after a hard day's work at the office and was alarmed to find another car parked in his drive. It was a tiny two-seater, the sort affected by top officials and the very well-to-do.

Right then and there Morey learned the first half of the embezzler's lesson: Anything different is dangerous. He came uneasily into his own home, fearful that some high officer of the Ration Board had come to ask questions.

But Cherry was glowing. "Mr. Porfirio is a newspaper feature writer and he wants to write you up for their 'Consumers of Distinction' page! Morey, I *couldn't* be more proud!"

"Thanks," said Morey glumly. "Hello."

Mr. Porfirio shook Morey's hand warmly. "I'm not exactly from a newspaper," he corrected. "Trans-Video Press is what it is, actually. We're a news wire service; we supply forty-seven hundred papers with news and feature material. Every one of them," he added complacently, "on the required consumption list of Grades One through Six inclusive. We have a Sunday supplement self-help feature on consuming problems and we like to—well, give credit where credit is due. You've established an enviable record, Mr. Fry. We'd like to tell our readers about it."

"Um," said Morey. "Let's go in the drawing room."

"Oh, no!" Cherry said firmly. "I want to hear this. He's so modest, Mr. Porfirio, you'd really never know what kind of a man he is just to listen to him talk. Why, my goodness, I'm his wife and I swear *I* don't know how he does all the consuming he does. He simply—"

"Have a drink, Mr. Porfirio," Morey said, against all etiquette. "Rye? Scotch? Bourbon? Gin and tonic? Brandy Alexander? Dry Manha—I mean what would you like?" He became conscious that he was babbling like a fool.

"Anything," said the newsman. "Rye is fine. Now, Mr. Fry, I notice you've fixed up your place very attractively here and your wife says that your country home is just as nice. As soon as I came in, I said to myself, 'Beautiful home. Hardly a stick of furniture that isn't absolutely necessary. Might be a Grade Six or Seven.' And Mrs. Fry says the other place is even barer."

"She does, does she?" Morey challenged sharply. "Well, let me tell you, Mr. Porfirio, that every last scrap of my furniture allowance is accounted for! I don't know what you're getting at, but—"

"Oh, I certainly didn't mean to imply anything like *that!* I just want to get some information from you that I can pass on to our readers. You know, to sort of help them do as well as yourself. How *do* you do it?"

Morey swallowed. "We—uh—well, we just keep after it. Hard work, that's all."

Porfirio nodded admiringly. "Hard work," he repeated, and fished a triple-folded sheet of paper out of his pocket to make notes on. "Would you say," he went on, "that anyone could do as well as you simply by devoting himself to it—setting a regular schedule, for example, and keeping to it very strictly?"

"Oh, yes," said Morey.

"In other words, it's only a matter of doing what you have to do every day?"

"That's it exactly. I handle the budget in my house—

more experience than my wife, you see—but no reason a woman can't do it."

"Budgeting," Porfirio recorded approvingly. "That's our policy, too."

The interview was not the terror it had seemed, not even when Porfirio tactfully called attention to Cherry's slim waistline ("So many housewives, Mrs. Fry, find it difficult to keep from being—well, a little plump") and Morey had to invent endless hours on the exercise machines, while Cherry looked faintly perplexed, but did not interrupt.

From the interview, however, Morey learned the second half of the embezzler's lesson. After Porfirio had gone, he leaped in and spoke more than a little firmly to Cherry. "That business of exercise, dear. We really have to start doing it. I don't know if you've noticed it, but you *are* beginning to get just a trifle heavier and we don't want that to happen, do we?"

In the following grim and unnecessary sessions on the mechanical horses, Morey had plenty of time to reflect on the lesson. Stolen treasures are less sweet than one would like, when one dare not enjoy them in the open.

But some of Morey's treasures were fairly earned.

The new Bradmoor K-50 Spin-a-Game, for instance, was his very own. His job was design and creation, and he was a fortunate man in that his efforts were permitted to be expended along the line of greatest social utility— namely, to increase consumption.

The Spin-a-Game was a well-nigh perfect machine for the purpose. "Brilliant," said Wainwright, beaming, when the pilot machine had been put through its first tests. "Guess they don't call me the talent-picker for nothing. I knew you could do it, boy!"

Even Howland was lavish in his praise. He sat munching on a plate of petits-fours (he was still only a Grade

Three) while the tests were going on, and when they were over, he said enthusiastically, "It's a beauty, Morey. That series-corrupter—sensational! Never saw a prettier piece of machinery."

Morey flushed gratefully.

Wainwright left, exuding praise, and Morey patted his pilot model affectionately and admired its polychrome gleam. The looks of the machine, as Wainwright had lectured many a time, were as important as its function: "You have to make them *want* to play it, boy! They won't play it if they don't *see* it!" And consequently the whole K series was distinguished by flashing rainbows of light, provocative strains of music, haunting scents that drifted into the nostrils of the passerby with compelling effect.

Morey had drawn heavily on all the old masterpieces of design—the one-arm bandit, the pinball machine, the jukebox. You put your ration book in the hopper. You spun the wheels until you selected the game you wanted to play against the machine. You punched buttons or spun dials or, in any of 325 different ways, you pitted your human skill against the magnetic-tape skills of the machine.

And you lost. You had a chance to win, but the inexorable statistics of the machine's setting made sure that if you played long enough, you had to lose.

That is to say, if you risked a ten-point ration stamp—showing, perhaps, that you had consumed three six-course meals—your statistical return was eight points. You might hit the jackpot and get a thousand points back, and thus be exempt from a whole freezerful of steaks and joints and prepared vegetables; but it seldom happened. Most likely you lost and got nothing.

Got nothing, that is, in the way of your hazarded ration stamps. But the beauty of the machine, which was Morey's main contribution, was that, win or lose, you *always* found a pellet of vitamin-drenched, sugar-coated antibiotic hormone gum in the hopper. You played your game, won or lost your stake, popped your hormone gum into your mouth and played another. By the time that game was ended, the gum was used up, the coating dissolved; you discarded it and started another.

"That's what the man from the NRB liked," Howland told Morey confidentially. "He took a set of schematics back with him; they might install it on *all* new machines. Oh, you're the fair-haired boy, all right!"

It was the first Morey had heard about a man from the National Ration Board. It was good news. He excused himself and hurried to phone Cherry the story of his latest successes. He reached her at her mother's, where she was spending the evening, and she was properly impressed and affectionate. He came back to Howland in a glowing humor.

"Drink?" said Howland diffidently.

"Sure," said Morey. He could afford, he thought, to drink as much of Howland's liquor as he liked; poor guy, sunk in the consuming quicksands of Class Three. Only fair for somebody a little more successful to give him a hand once in a while.

And when Howland, learning that Cherry had left Morey a bachelor for the evening, proposed Uncle Piggotty's again, Morey hardly hesitated at all.

The Bigelows were delighted to see him. Morey wondered briefly if they *had* a home; certainly they didn't seem to spend much time in it.

It turned out they did, because when Morey indicated virtuously that he'd only stopped in at Piggotty's for a single drink before dinner and Howland revealed that he was free for the evening, they captured Morey and bore him off to their house.

Tanaquil Bigelow was haughtily apologetic. "I don't

suppose this is the kind of place Mr. Fry is used to," she observed to her husband, right across Morey, who was standing between them. "Still, we call it home."

Morey made an appropriately polite remark. Actually, the place nearly turned his stomach. It was an enormous glaringly new mansion, bigger even than Morey's former house, stuffed to bursting with bulging sofas and pianos and massive mahogany chairs and tri-D sets and bedrooms and drawing rooms and breakfast rooms and nurseries.

The nurseries were a shock to Morey; it had never occurred to him that the Bigelows had children. But they did and, though the children were only five and eight, they were still up, under the care of a brace of robot nursemaids, doggedly playing with their overstuffed animals and miniature trains.

"You don't know what a comfort Tony and Dick are," Tanaquil Bigelow told Morey. "They consume *so* much more than their rations. Walter says that every family ought to have at least two or three children to, you know, help out. Walter's so intelligent about these things, it's a pleasure to hear him talk. Have you heard his poem, Morey? The one he calls *The Twoness of—*"

Morey hastily admitted that he had. He reconciled himself to a glum evening. The Bigelows had been eccentric but fun back at Uncle Piggotty's. On their own ground, they seemed just as eccentric, but painfully dull.

They had a round of cocktails, and another, and then the Bigelows no longer seemed so dull. Dinner was ghastly, of course; Morey was nouveau riche enough to be a snob about his relatively Spartan table. But he minded his manners and sampled, with grim concentration, each successive course of chunky protein and rich marinades. With the help of the endless succession of table wines and liqueurs, dinner ended without destroying his evening or his strained digestive system.

And afterward, they were a pleasant company in the Bigelows' ornate drawing room. Tanaquil Bigelow, in consultation with the children, checked over their ration books and came up with the announcement that they would have a brief recital by a pair of robot dancers, followed by string music by a robot quartet. Morey prepared himself for the worst, but found before the dancers were through that he was enjoying himself. Strange lesson for Morey: when you didn't *have* to watch them, the robot entertainers were fun!

"Good night, dears," Tanaquil Bigelow said firmly to the children when the dancers were done. The boys rebelled, naturally, but they went. It was only a matter of minutes, though, before one of them was back, clutching at Morey's sleeve with a pudgy hand.

Morey looked at the boy uneasily, having little experience with children. He said, "Uh—what is it, Tony?"

"Dick, you mean," the boy said. "Gimme your autograph." He poked an engraved pad and a vulgarly jeweled pencil at Morey.

Morey dazedly signed and the child ran off, Morey staring after him. Tanaquil Bigelow laughed and explained, "He saw your name in Porfirio's column. Dick *loves* Porfirio, reads him every day. He's such an intellectual kid, really. He'd always have his nose in a book if I didn't keep after him to play with his trains and watch tri-D."

"That was quite a nice write-up," Walter Bigelow commented—a little enviously, Morey thought. "Bet you make Consumer of the Year. I wish," he sighed, "that we could get a little ahead on the quotas the way you did. But it just never seems to work out. We eat and play and consume like crazy, and somehow at the end of the month we're always a little behind. Everything keeps piling up somewhere. And then the Board sends us a warning, and they call me down and, first thing you know, I've got a couple of hundred added penalty points and we're worse off than before."

"Never you mind," Tanaquil replied staunchly. "Consuming isn't everything in life. You have your work."

Bigelow nodded judiciously and offered Morey another drink. Another drink, however, was not what Morey needed. He was sitting in a rosy glow, less of alcohol than of sheer contentment with the world.

He said suddenly, "Listen."

Bigelow looked up from his own drink. "Eh?"

"If I tell you something that's a *secret,* will you keep it that way?"

Bigelow rumbled, "Why, I guess so, Morey."

But his wife cut in sharply, "Certainly we will, Morey. Of course! What is it?" There was a gleam in her eye, Morey noticed. It puzzled him, but he decided to ignore it.

He said, "About that write-up. I—I'm not such a hotshot consumer, really, you know. In fact—" All of a sudden, everyone's eyes seemed to be on him. For a tortured moment, Morey wondered if he was doing the right thing. A secret that two people know is compromised, and a secret known to three people is no secret. Still—

"It's like this," he said firmly. "You remember what we were talking about at Uncle Piggotty's that night? Well, when I went home I went down to the robot quarters, and I—well—I decided to let the robots help me out. Help me consume, I mean." And he went on from there, the whole story.

Tanaquil Bigelow said triumphantly, "I *knew* it!"

Walter Bigelow gave his wife a mild, reproving look. He declared soberly, "You've done a big thing, Morey. A mighty big thing. God willing, you've pronounced the death sentence on our society as we know it. Future generations will revere the name of Morey Fry." He solemnly shook Morey's hand.

Morey said dazedly, "I *what?*"

Walter nodded. It was a valedictory. He turned to his wife. "Tanaquil, we'll have to call an emergency meeting."

"Of course, Walter," she said devotedly.

"And Morey will have to be there. Yes, you'll have to, Morey; no excuses. We want the Brotherhood to meet you. Right, Bigelow?"

Bigelow coughed uneasily. He nodded noncommittally and took another drink.

Morey demanded desperately, "What are you talking about? Bigelow, you tell me!"

Bigelow fiddled with his drink. "Well, he said, "it's like Tan was telling you that night. A few of us, well, politically mature persons have formed a little group. We—"

"*Little* group!" Tanaquil Bigelow said scornfully. "Bigelow, sometimes I wonder if you really catch the spirit of the thing at all! It's everybody, Morey, everybody in the world who really *counts*. Why, there are eighteen of us right here in Old Town! There are *scores more* all over the world! I knew you were up to something like this, Morey. I told Walter so the morning after we met you. I said, 'Walter, mark my words, that man Morey is up to something.' But I must say," she admitted worshipfully, "I didn't know it would have the *scope* of what you're proposing now! Imagine—a whole world of consumers, rising as one man, shouting the name of Morey Fry, fighting the Ration Board with the Board's own weapon—the robots. What poetic justice!"

Bigelow nodded enthusiastically. "Call Uncle Piggotty's, dear," he ordered. "See if you can round up a quorum right now! Meanwhile, Morey and I are going belowstairs. Let's go, Morey—let's get the new world started!"

Morey sat there, openmouthed. He closed it with a snap. "Bigelow," he whispered, "do you mean to say that you're going to spread this idea around through some kind of subversive organization?"

"Subversive?" Bigelow repeated stiffly. "My dear man, *all* creative minds are subversive, whether they operate singly or in such a group as the Brotherhood of Freemen. I scarcely like your choice of words."

"Never mind what you like," Morey insisted. "You're going to call a meeting of this Brotherhood and you want *me* to tell them what I just told you. Is that right?"

"Well—yes."

Morey got up. "I wish I could say it's been nice, but it hasn't. Good night!"

And he stormed out before they could stop him.

Out on the street, he hailed a robot cab and ordered the driver to take him on the traditional time-killing ride through the park while he thought things over.

The fact that he had left, of course, was not going to keep Bigelow from going through with his announced intention. Morey remembered, now, fragments of conversation from Bigelow and his wife at Uncle Piggotty's, and cursed himself. They had, it was perfectly true, said and hinted enough about politics and purposes to put him on his guard. All that nonsense about twoness had diverted him from what should have been perfectly clear: They were subversives indeed.

He glanced at his watch. Late, but not too late; Cherry would still be at her parents' home.

He leaned forward and gave the driver their address. It was like beginning the first of a hundred-shot series of injections: You know it's going to cure you, but it hurts just the same.

Morey said manfully: "And that's it, sir. I know I've been a fool. I'm willing to take the consequences."

Old Elon rubbed his jaw thoughtfully. "Um," he said.

Cherry and her mother had long passed the point where they could say anything at all; they were seated side by side on a couch across the room, listening with expressions of strain and incredulity.

Elon said abruptly, "Excuse me. Phone call to make." He left the room to make a brief call and returned. He said over his shoulder to his wife, "Coffee. We'll need it. Got a problem here."

Morey said, "Do you think it's serious? What should I do?"

Elon shrugged, then, surprisingly, grinned. "What can you do?" he demanded cheerfully. "Done plenty already, I'd say. Drink come coffee. Call I made," he explained, "was to Jim, my law clerk. He'll be here in a minute. Get some dope from Jim, then we'll know better."

Cherry came over to Morey and sat beside him. All she said was, "Don't worry," but to Morey it conveyed all the meaning in the world. He returned the pressure of her hand with a feeling of deepest relief. Hell, he said to himself, why *should* I worry? Worst they can do to me is drop me a couple of grades and what's so bad about that?

He grimaced involuntarily. He had remembered his own early struggles as a Class One and what *was* so bad about that.

The law clerk arrived, a smallish robot with a battered stainless-steel hide and dull coppery features. Elon took the robot aside for a terse conversation before he came back to Morey.

"As I thought," he said in satisfaction. "No precedent. No laws prohibiting. Therefore no crime."

"Thank heaven!" Morey said in ecstatic relief.

Elon shook his head. "They'll probably give you a reconditioning and you can't expect to keep your Grade Five. Probably call it anti-social behavior. Is, isn't it?"

Dashed, Morey said, "Oh." He frowned briefly, then

looked up. "All right, Dad, if I've got it coming to me, I'll take my medicine."

"Way to talk," Elon said approvingly. "Now go home. Get a good night's sleep. First thing in the morning, go to the Ration Board. Tell 'em the whole story, beginning to end. They'll be easy on you." Elon hesitated. "Well, fairly easy," he said, and then amended, "I hope."

The condemned man ate a hearty breakfast.

He had to. That morning, as Morey awoke, he had the sick certainty that he was going to be consuming triple rations for a long, long time to come.

He kissed Cherry good-bye and took the long ride to the Ration Board in silence. He even left Henry behind.

At the Board, he stammered at a series of receptionist robots and was finally brought into the presence of a mildly supercilious young man named Hachette.

"My name," he started, "is Morey Fry. I—I've come to—talk over something I've been doing with—"

"Certainly, Mr. Fry," said Hachette. "I'll take you in to Mr. Newman right away."

"Don't you want to know what I did?" demanded Morey.

Hachette smiled. "What makes you think we don't know?" he said, and left.

That was surprise number one.

Newman explained it. He grinned at Morey and ruefully shook his head. "All the time we get this sort of ignorance from the public," he complained. "People just don't take the trouble to learn anything about the world around them. Son," he demanded, "what do you think a robot is?"

Morey said, "Huh?"

"I mean how do you think it operates? Do you think it's just a kind of man with a tin skin and wire nerves?"

"Why, no. It's a machine, of course. It isn't *human.*"

Newman beamed. "Fine!" he said. "It's a machine. It hasn't got flesh or blood or intestines—or a brain. Oh"— he held up a hand—"robots are *smart* enough. I don't mean that. But an electronic thinking machine, Mr. Fry, takes about as much space as the chair you're sitting in. It has to. Robots don't carry brains around with them; brains are too heavy and much too bulky."

"Then how do they think?"

"With their brains, of course."

"But you just said—"

"I said they didn't *carry* them. Each robot is in constant radio communication with the Master Control on its TBR circuit—the Talk Between Robots radio. Master Control gives the answer, the robot acts."

"I see," said Morey. "Well, that's very interesting, but—"

"But you still don't see," said Newman. "Figure it out. If the robot gets information from Master Control, do you see that Master Control in return necessarily gets information from the robot?"

"Oh," said Morey. Then, louder, "Oh! You mean that all my robots have been—" The words wouldn't come.

Newman nodded in satisfaction. "Every bit of information of that sort comes to us as a matter of course. Why, Mr. Fry, if you hadn't come in today, we would have been sending for you within a very short time."

That was the second surprise. Morey bore up under it bravely. After all, it changed nothing, he reminded himself.

He said, "Well, be that as it may, sir, here I am. I came in of my own free will. I've been using my robots to consume my ration quotas—"

"Indeed you have," said Newman.

"—and I'm willing to sign a statement to that effect any

time you like. I don't know what the penalty is, but I'll take it. I'm guilty; I admit my guilt."

Newman's eyes were wide. "Guilty?" he repeated. "Penalty?"

Morey was startled. "Why, yes," he said. "I'm not denying anything."

"Penalty," repeated Newman musingly. Then he began to laugh. He laughed, Morey thought, to considerable excess; Morey saw nothing he could laugh at, himself, in the situation. But the situation, Morey was forced to admit, was rapidly getting completely incomprehensible.

"Sorry," said Newman at last, wiping his eyes, "but I couldn't help it. Penalties! Well, Mr. Fry, let me set your mind at rest. I wouldn't worry about the penalties if I were you. As soon as the reports began coming through on what you had done with your robots, we naturally assigned a special team to keep observing you, and we forwarded a report to the national headquarters. We made certain—ah—recommendations in it and—well, to make a long story short, the answers came back yesterday.

"Mr. Fry, the National Ration Board is delighted to know of your contribution toward improving our distribution problem. Pending a further study, a tentative program has been adopted for setting up consuming-robot units all over the country based on your scheme. Penalties? Mr. Fry, you're a *hero!*"

A hero has responsibilities. Morey's were quickly made clear to him. He was allowed time for a brief reassuring visit to Cherry, a triumphal tour of his old office, and then he was rushed off to Washington to be quizzed. He found the National Ration Board in a frenzy of work.

"The most important job we've ever done," one of the high officers told him. "I wouldn't be surprised if it's the last one we ever have! Yes, sir, we're trying to put ourselves out of business for good and we don't want a single thing to go wrong."

"Anything I can do to help—" Morey began diffidently.

"You've done fine, Mr. Fry. Gave us just the push we've been needing. It was there all the time for us to see, but we were too close to the forest to see the trees, if you get what I mean. Look, I'm not much on rhetoric and this is the biggest step mankind has taken in centuries and I can't put it into words. Let me show you what we've been doing."

He and a delegation of other officials of the Ration Board and men whose names Morey had repeatedly seen in the newspapers took Morey on an inspection tour of the entire plant.

"It's a closed cycle, you see," he was told, as they looked over a chamber of industriously plodding con- sumer-robots working off a shipment of shoes. "Nothing is permanently lost. If you want a car, you get one of the newest and best. If not, your car gets driven by a robot until it's ready to be turned in and a new one gets built for next year. We don't lose the metals—they can be sal- vaged. All we lose is a little power and labor. And Amalfi Amadeus's fusion-power generators give us all the power we need, and the robots give us more labor than we can use. Same thing applies, of course, to all products."

"But what's in it for the robots?" Morey asked.

"I beg your pardon?" one of the biggest men in the country said uncomprehendingly.

Morey had a difficult moment. His analysis had con- ditioned him against waste and this decidedly was sheer destruction of goods, no matter how scientific the jargon might be.

"If the consumer is just using up things for the sake of using them up," he said doggedly, realizing the danger he was inviting, "we could use wear-and-tear machines in- stead of robots. After all why waste *them?*"

They looked at each other worriedly.

"But that's what *you* were doing," one pointed out with a faint note of threat.

"Oh, no!" Morey quickly objected. "I built in satisfaction circuits—my training in design, you know. Adjustable circuits, of course."

"Satisfaction circuits?" he was asked. "Adjustable?"

"Well, sure. If the robot gets no satisfaction out of using up things—"

"Don't talk nonsense," growled the Ration Board official. "Robots aren't human. How do you make them feel satisfaction? And adjustable satisfaction at that!"

Morey explained. It was a highly technical explanation, involving the use of great sheets of paper and elaborate diagrams. But there were trained men in the group and they became even more excited than before.

"Beautiful!" one cried in scientific rapture. "Why, it takes care of every possible moral, legal and psychological argument!"

"What does?" the Ration Board official demanded. "How?"

"You tell him, Mr. Fry."

Morey tried and couldn't. But he could *show* how his principle operated. The Ration Board lab was turned over to him, complete with more assistants than he knew how to give orders to, and they built satisfaction circuits for a squad of robots working in a hat factory.

Then Morey gave his demonstration. The robots manufactured hats of all sorts. He adjusted the circuits at the end of the day and the robots began trying on the hats, squabbling over them, each coming away triumphantly with a huge and diverse selection. Their metallic features were incapable of showing pride or pleasure, but both were evident in the way they wore their hats, their fierce possessiveness . . . and their faster, neater, more intensive, more *dedicated* work to produce a still greater quantity of hats . . . which they also were allowed to own.

"You see?" an engineer exclaimed delightedly. "They can be adjusted to *want* hats, to wear them lovingly, to wear the hats to pieces. And not just for the sake of wearing them out—the hats are an incentive for them!"

"But how can we go on producing just hats and more hats?" the Ration Board man asked puzzledly. "Civilization does not live by hats alone."

"That," said Morey modestly, "is the beauty of it. Look."

He set the adjustment of the satisfaction circuit as porter robots brought in skids of gloves. The hat-manufacturing robots fought over the gloves with the same mechanical passion as they had for hats.

"And that can apply to anything we—or the robots—produce," Morey added. "Everything from pins to yachts. But the point is that they get satisfaction from possession, and the craving can be regulated according to the glut in various industries, and the robots show their appreciation by working harder." He hesitated. "That's what I did for my servant-robots. It's a feedback, you see. Satisfaction leads to more work—and *better* work—and that means more goods, which they can be made to want, which means incentive to work, and so on, all around."

"Closed cycle," whispered the Ration Board man in awe. "I must give debit where debit is due, Mr. Fry. You've given us a *real* closed cycle this time!"

And so the inexorable laws of supply and demand were irrevocably repealed. No longer was mankind hampered by inadequate supply or drowned by overproduction. What mankind needed was there. What the race did not require passed into the insatiable—and adjustable—robot maw. Nothing was wasted.

For a pipeline has two ends.

Morey was thanked, complimented, rewarded, given a ticker-tape parade through the city, and put on a plane

back home. By that time, the Ration Board had liq-
uidated itself.

Cherry met him at the airport. They jabbered excitedly at
each other all the way to the house.

In their own living room, they finished the kiss they had
greeted each other with. At last Cherry broke away,
laughing.

Morey said, "Did I tell you I'm through with Bradmoor? *And,*" he added impressively, "starting right away,
I'm a Class Eight!"

"My!" gasped Cherry, so worshipfully that Morey felt a
twinge of conscience.

He said honestly, "Of course, if what they were saying
in Washington is so, the classes aren't going to mean
much pretty soon. Still, it's quite an honor."

"It certainly is," Cherry said staunchly. "Why, Dad's
only a Class Eight himself, and he's been a judge for I
don't know *how* many years."

Morey pursed his lips. "We can't all be fortunate," he
said generously. "Of course, the classes still will count for
something—that is, a Class One will have so much to consume in a year, a Class Two will have a little less, and so
on. But each person in each class will have robot help,
you see, to do the actual consuming. The way it's going to
be, special facsimile robots will—"

Cherry flagged him down. "I know, dear. Each family
gets a robot duplicate of every person in the family."

"Oh," said Morey, slightly annoyed. "How did you
know?"

"Ours came yesterday," she explained. "The man from
the Board said we were the first in the area—because it
was your idea, of course. They haven't even been activated yet. I've still got them in the Green Room. Want to
see them?"

"Sure," said Morey buoyantly. He dashed ahead of

Cherry to inspect the results of his own brainstorm. There they were, standing statue-still against the wall, waiting to be energized to begin their endless tasks.

"Yours is real pretty," Morey said gallantly. "But—say, is that thing supposed to look like me?" He inspected the chromium face of the man-robot disapprovingly.

"Only roughly, the man said." Cherry was right behind him. "Notice anything else?"

Morey leaned closer, inspecting the features of the facsimile robot at a close range. "Well, no," he said. "It's got a kind of a squint that I don't like, but—Oh, you mean *that!*" He bent over to examine a smaller robot, half hidden between the other pair. It was less than two feet high, big-headed, pudgy-limbed, thick-bellied. In fact, Morey thought wonderingly, it looked almost like—

"My God!" Morey spun around, staring wide-eyed at his wife. "You mean—"

"I mean," said Cherry, blushing slightly.

Morey reached out to grab her in his arms.

"Darling!" he cried. "Why didn't you *tell* me?"

3

THE SERVANT
OF THE PEOPLE

There were things that robots could do as well as people. But there were also, Congressman Fiorello Delano Fitzgerald O'Hare believed with pride, things that required the special human touch. One of them was sitting in the House of Representatives. For him, every election year, the campaign started on the Tuesday after Labor Day. It was a tradition. It was traditional for the Congressman, anyway, feisty little seventy-plus-year-old who liked his own traditions and didn't much care what anyone else's were. The summer was his own and his lady wife's, and when he started to press the flesh and hunt the votes was at the League of Women Voters televised debate and not a minute before. So at six o'clock on the evening of the eighth of September there was Carrie O'Hare one more time, straightening the fidgeting Congressman's tie, dabbing a blob of the Congressman's shaving cream off the lobe of the Congressman's fuzzy pink ear and reassuring the Congressman that he was wiser, juster and, above all, far more beloved by his constituents than that brash new interloper of an opponent, the Mayor of Elk City, could ever hope to be. "Quit fussing," said the Congressman, with his famous impudent elf's smile. "The voters don't mind if a candidate looks a little messy."

"Hold still a minute, hon."

"What for? It all has to come off again for the doctor, maybe."

"Or maybe he'll just take your pulse, so hold still. And listen. Please don't tell them about game-hunting in the Sahara tonight."

"Now, Carrie"—twinkling grin—"we leave the speeches to me and everything else to you, right? They're going to want to know what their Congressman did over the summer, aren't they?"

Carrie sighed and released him. It had been a successful safari—the Congressman had photographed dozens of mules, and even one actual live camel—but what did it have to do with the Congressman's qualifications for one more term in the United States House of Representatives? "Hold it a minute," she said as an afterthought, sent one of the household robots for a fresh pocket handkerchief, repinned the American flag button in his lapel and let it go at that. She needed all the rest of the time available on the larger task of herself. Voters might forgive a Congressman for looking rumpled, true enough, but a Congressman's wife never.

She sat before her mirror and reviewed all the things she had to do. There were plenty, not made easier by the little knot of worry in her stomach. Well, not worry. Normal nervousness, maybe, but not real *worry*. The Congressman was a winner and always had been. Fiorello Delano Fitzgerald O'Hare, servant of the people for half a century plus one year, eight months and a week, might have been custom-built for politics, as well designed as any robot, and with the further advantage (she thought guiltily that you shouldn't call it an "advantage") of being human. He had the name for it. He had the friendly and trustworthy look, with enough leprechaun mischief to make him interesting. He had the manner that caused each of thirty thousand voters to think himself personally known to the Congressman, and above all he had the disposition. He actually enjoyed such things as eating rubber chicken at a dinner for the B'nai B'rtih, square-dancing at fireman's fair, joining the Policemen's Benevolent Association for a communion breakfast. He even liked getting up at five A.M. to get to a factory gate to shake the hands of nine hundred workers on the early shift. All of these things were a lot less enjoyable for the Congressman's wife, but what she unfailingly enjoyed was the Congressman himself. For he was a sweet man.

Carrie Madeleine O'Hare was quite a sweet woman, too. You could tell that by the way she spoke to the maid tidying up behind her. Carrie had had that same maid since her marriage, forty years before. The Congressman had been thirty-five years old, Carrie herself twenty-two and the maid a wedding present, fresh off the assembly line, an old-style robot with all its brains in some central computation facility—no personality, no feelings to hurt. But Carrie treated the robot just as she would a human being—or one of the new Josephson-junction machines, so close to human that they even had voting rights . . . for which they had to thank in very large part the Congressman himself and damn well, Carrie thought, better remember it come November.

Carrie's preparations only went as far as makeup, hair and underwear—there was no point in putting on the dress until they were ready to go, and the Congressman's doctor hadn't even arrived yet for his traditional last-minute medical check. So she pulled on a robe and descended the back stairs to the big screened porch for a breath of air. The house was ancient and three stories high. It stood on a little hill in the bend of the river, water on two sides. It would have been a fine house to raise children in—but there hadn't been any children—and it was a first-rate house for a Congressman even without children. All through the years when small was status, the Congressman had stuck to his sixteen rooms because they were so fine for parties, so fine for entertaining delegations of voters and putting up visiting political VIPs and all the other functions of political power. Carrie sat on the porch swing, and found herself shivering. It wasn't the temperature. That had to be at least seventy-five degrees, in the old Fahrenheit system Carrie still used inside her head. It was still summer. But the wind made her feel cold. And that was strange, when you came to think of it. When had the TV weathermen started talking about wind-chill factors even in July and September? Why was it always so windy these days? Was it just because of the simple fact that, without ever willing it to happen, Carrie herself had somehow become sixty-two years old?

And then her husband's angry bellow from inside the house: "Carrie! Where are you? What's this damn thing doing here?"

Carrie ran inside the house. There was her husband, flushed and angry, with that ruffled-sparrow look he got when he was excited, facing down a stranger. The doctor had arrived when she wasn't looking, and it was a new model.

If you looked at the doctor what you saw was a sandy-haired man of youthful maturity, with little laugh wrinkles at the corners of his eyes and the expression of smiling competence that doctors cultivated. If you touched him, his handshake was firm and warm. If you listened to his voice, that was also warm—it was only if you went so far as to sniff him that you could notice a possible lack. There was no human scent of body and sweat. That meant a very recent shower, a foolproof deodorant—or a robot.

And, of course, a robot was what it was. "Oh, come on, Fee," she coaxed, anxiously good-humored, "you know it's just a doctor come to check your blood pressure and so on."

"It's not my *regular* doctor!" roared the Congressman, standing as tall and strong as possible for a man who, after all, was a shade shorter than Carrie herself. "I want *my* doctor! I've had the same doctor for thirty-five years, and that's the one I want now!"

It was so bad for him to get upset right before the kickoff debate! "Now, Fee," Carrie scolded humorously, trying to soothe him down, "you know that old dented wreck was due for the scrap heap. I'm sure that Dr.— uh—" She looked at the new robot for a name, and it supplied it, smilingly self-assured.

"I am Dr. William," it said. "I am a fully programmed Josephson-junction autonomous-intellect model robot, Mr. Congressman, with core storage for diagnostics, first aid and general internal medicine, and of course I carry data-chip memory for most surgical procedures and test functions."

The Congressman's cheeks had faded from red to pink; he was not generally an irascible man. "All the same," he began, but the robot was still talking.

"I'm truly sorry if I've caused you any concern, Mr. Congressman. Not only for professional reasons," it added warmly, "but because I happen to be one of your strongest supporters. I haven't yet had the privilege of voting in a congressional election, I'm sorry to say, because I was only activated last week, but I certainly intend to vote for you when I do."

"Huh," said O'Hare, looking from the robot to his wife. And then the reflexes of half a century took over. "Well, your time's valuable, Dr. William," he said, "so why don't we just get on with this examination? And we can talk about the problems of this district while we do. As I guess you know, I've always been a leader in the fight for robot rights—" And Carrie slipped gratefully away.

Fiorello O'Hare's vote-getting skills had been tested in more than two dozen elections, from his first runs for the

school board and then the county commission—a decade
before Carrie had been old enough to vote—through
twenty-two terms in the Congress of the United States.
Twenty-two terms: from the old days when a congressman
actually had to get in a plane or a car and go to Washington, D.C., to do his job, instead of the interactive-elec-
tronics sessions that had made the job attractive again.
And against twenty-two opponents. The opponents had
come in all shapes and sizes, pompous old has-beens when
O'Hare was a crusading youth, upstart kids as he grew
older. Male or female, black or white, peaceniks and pro-
lifers, spenders and budget-balancers—O'Hare had
beaten them all. He had, at least, beaten every one of
them who dared contest the Twenty-Third Congressional
District, anyway. He had not done as well the time he
made the mistake of trying for Governor (fortunately in
an off year, so his House seat was safe), and not well at all
the time when he had hopes for the Senate, even once for
the vice-presidency. The primaries had ended one of those
dreams. The national convention slew the other. O'Hare
learned his lesson. If he stayed in Congress he was safe,
and so were his committee chairmanships and his powerful seniority.

After all these years, Caroline O'Hare could no longer
remember all the opponents her husband had faced by
name. If she could dredge them out of her recollections at
all, it was by a single mnemonic trait. This one was Mean.
That one was Hairy. There was a Big and a Scared and a
Dangerous. Classified in those terms, Carrie thought as
they swept into the underground garage of the Shriner's
Auditorium, this year's opponent was a Neat. He wore a
neat brown suit with a neatly tied brown scarf and neatly
shined brown shoes. He was chatting, neatly, with a small
and self-assured group of his supporters as the O'Hares
got out of their car and approached the elevator, and

when he saw O'Hare he gave his opponent a neat, restrained smile of welcome.

The neat opponent was riding on a record of six years as the very successful mayor of a small city in the district. Mayor Thom had been quite a vote-getter in the home town, according to the data-file printout Carrie had ordered. Her husband disdained such things—"I'm a *personal* man, Carrie, and I deal with the voters *personally,* and I don't want to hit key issues or play to the demographics; I want them to know *me.*" But he must have retained a little bit of the data, for, when he saw the other group, he hurried over, smile flashing, speech ready on his lips. "A great pleasure to see you here, Mr. Mayor," he cried, pumping the Mayor's hand, "and to congratulate you again on the fine job you've been doing in Elk City!"

"You're very kind." Mayor Thom smiled, nodding politely to Carrie—neat nod, neat smile, neat and pleasant voice.

"Only truthful," O'Hare insisted as the elevator door opened for them. "Well, it's time to do battle, I guess, and may the best man win!"

"Oh, I hope not," the Mayor said politely. "For in that case, as I am mechanical, it would surely be you."

O'Hare blinked, then grinned ruefully at his wife. Cordiality toward his opponents was an O'Hare trademark. It cost nothing, and who knew but what it might soften them up? Not many opponents had played that back to O'Hare. Carrie saw him pat the Mayor's arm, stand courteously aside as they reached the auditorium floor and bow the other party out. But his expression had suddenly become firm. He was like a current breaker that had felt a surge of unexpected and dangerous power. It had opened unaware, but now it had reset itself. It would be ready for the next surge.

*   *   *

But actually, when the surge came, O'Hare wasn't.

The first rounds of the debate went normally. It wasn't really a true debate, of course. It was more like a virtuoso-piece ballet, with two prima ballerinas each showing off her own finest bits. A couple of perfect *entrechats* matched by a string of double *fouettés*. a marvelous *grand jeté* countered by a superb *pas en l'air*. O'Hare went first. His greatest strengths were the battles he had won, the fights he had led, the famous figures he had worked with. Not just politicians. O'Hare had been the intimate of ambassadors and corporation tycoons and scientists—he had even known Amalfi Amadeus himself, the man whose hydrogen fusion power had made the modern Utopia possible. O'Hare got an ovation after his first seven-minute performance. But so did his opponent. The Mayor was a modest and appealing figure; how handsome they made robots these days! The Mayor, talking about its triumphs in Elk City, had every name right, every figure detailed; how precise they made them! What O'Hare offered in glamour, the Mayor made up in encyclopedic competence . . . and then Carrie saw how the trick was done.

Against all advice, the Congressman in his second session was telling the audience about the highlights of their summer photo safari along the Nile. Against Carrie's expectations, the audience was enjoying it. Even the Mayor. As O'Hare described how they had almost, but not quite, seen a living crocodile and the actual place where a hippopotamus had once been sighted, the Mayor was chuckling along with everyone else. But while it was chuckling it was reaching for its neat brown attaché case; opened it, pulled out a module of data-store microchips, opened what looked like a pocket in the side of its jacket, removed one set of chips and replaced them with another.

It was plugging in a new set of memories! How very unfair. Carrie glanced around the crowded audience to see if any of the audience were as outraged as she, but if they were they didn't show it. They were intent on the Congressman's words, laughing with him, nodding with interest, clapping when applause was proper. They were a model audience, except that they did not seem to notice, or to care about, the unfairness of the Mayor. But why not? They certainly looked normal and decent enough, so friendly and so amiable and—

So neat.

Carrie's hand flew to her mouth. She gazed beseechingly at her husband, but he was too wily a campaigner to have failed to read the audience. Without a hitch, husbanding his time to spend it where it would do the most good, he swung from the pleasures of the summer holiday to the realities of his political life. "And now," he said, leaning forward over the lectern to beam at the audience, "it's back to work, to finish the job you've been electing me for. As you know, I was one of the sponsors of the Robot ERA. A lot of voters were against that, in the old days. Even my friends in political office advised me to leave that issue alone. They said I was committing political suicide, because the voters felt that if the amendment passed there would be no way anybody could tell the difference between a human and a mechanical any more, and the country would go to the dogs. Well, it passed— and I say the country's better off than ever, and I say I'm proud of what I did and anxious to go back and finish the job!" And he beamed triumphantly at his opponent as the applause swelled and he relinquished the floor.

But the Mayor was not in the least disconcerted. In fact, it led the clapping. When it reached the podium it cried, "I really thank you, Congressman O'Hare, and I believe that now every voter in the district, organic and mechanical alike, knows just how right you were! That amendment did not only give us mechanicals the vote. It not only purged from all the data stores any reference to the origins of any voter, mechanical or organic, but it also did the one great thing that remained to do. It freed human beings from one more onerous and difficult task—namely, the job of selecting their elected officials. What remains? Just one thing, I say—the task of carrying this one step further, by electing mechanicals to the highest offices in the land, so that human life can be pure pleasure!"

And the ovation was just as large. The Mayor waited it out, smiling gratefully toward O'Hare, and when the applause had died away it went on to supply specifics to back up its stand, all dredged, Carrie was sure, out of the store of chips she had seen it plug in.

On the stage, her husband's expression did not change, but Carrie saw the eyes narrow again. The relay had popped open once more and reset itself, *snick-snick;* O'Hare knew that this opponent was a cut above the others. This campaign was not going to be quite like those that had gone before.

And indeed it wasn't, although for the first few weeks it looked as though it would have the same sure outcome.

By the first of October the Congressman was hitting his stride. Three kaffeeklatsches a day, at least one dinner every evening—he had long ago learned how to push the food around his plate to disguise the fact that he wasn't eating. And all the hundreds of block parties and TV spots and news conferences and just strolling past the voters. The weather turned cooler, but it was still muggy, and the outdoor appearances every day began to worry Carrie. The Congressman's feet would never give out, or his handshake, or his smile muscles. What was vulnerable was his voice. Up on a street-corner platform her enemies were the damp wind and the sooty air. Walking along a shopping block, the same—plus the quiches and pitas, the ravioli and the dim sum, the kosher hot dogs and the sushi—the whole spectrum of ethnic foods that an ethnic-wooing candidate traditionally had to seem to enjoy. "The tradition's out of date," Carrie told him crossly, throat lozenges in one hand and anti-acid pills in the other as he gamely tried to recuperate before going to bed, "when half the voters are robots anyway!"

Her husband sat on the edge of their bed, rubbing his throat and his feet alternately. "It's the organics I need, love. The robots know where I stand!"

They also knew, Carrie thought but did not say, that his opponent was one of them. . . . But robots were programmed to be fair! Poring over the daily polls after her husband had gone to sleep, Carrie almost felt confidence that they were. The Congressman's reliable old polling service was also his driver, Martin, an antique remote-intelligence robot that needed only to query the central computation faculty to get the latest data on elections moods. Or indeed on anything else; and it was the robot's custom to lay a printout of the last polling data on Carrie's dressing table every night. Indeed the graphs did not look bad: 38 per cent for her husband, only 19 per cent for Mayor Thom—

But what they also showed was a whopping 43 per cent undecided, and the fly in the ointment was that the "undecideds" were overwhelmingly robots. Carrie understood why this was so; it had been so ever since her husband's Robot ERA passed and the autonomous-intelligence models got the vote. Robots did not like to hurt anyone's feelings. When robots were required to make a choice that might displease someone, they postponed it as long as they could. For robots were also programmed to be polite.

And if all that forty-three per cent came down for Mayor Thom—

Carrie simply would not face that possibility. Her husband was *happy* in his job. The Congress of the United States was an honorable career, and an easy one, too, not a small consideration for a man in his seventies who was now coughing fitfully in his sleep. In the old days it had been a mankiller. There was always so much to do, worrying about foreign powers, raising taxes, trying to give every citizen a fair share of the nation's prosperity—when there was any prosperity—at least, trying to give each one enough of a constant and never adequate supply of the available wealth to keep them from rioting in the streets. But since Amadeus' gift of power, with all the limitless wealth it made available to everyone, a Congressman could take pleasure in what he did, and if he chose not to do it for a while—to take a summer off for a photo safari along the Nile, for instance—why, where was the harm?

She slept uneasily that night.

Where the Congressman went, Carrie went too, even to a factory district far out of town, even when greeting the early shift meant being there at five-thirty in the morning. The sign over the chain-link fence said:

AMALFI ELECTRIC, INC.
A DIVISION OF MIDWEST POWER & TOOL CORP.

And as they approached, the managing director hurried out to greet them. "Congressman O'Hare!" he fawned. "And, yes, your lovely lady—what an honor!" He was a nervous, rabbity little man, obviously human; his name, Carrie knew from the briefing Marty had provided as they turned into the parking lot, was Robert Meacham. The briefing also said that he was the kind who could keep you talking while the whole shift passed by on the other side of the fence, so Carrie moved forward to distract him even while the Congressman was still pumping his hand.

It was no trick for Carrie to find things to talk about while the Congressman wooed Meacham's workers, not with Carrie's photographic—really more than photographic, almost robotic—memory for the names of wives, children and pets. By the time she had finished discussing Meacham's two spaniels, the Congressman had finished with his workers and the alert Marty was moving the car in to pick them up. Meacham detained Carrie a moment longer. "Mrs. O'Hare, can I ask you something?"

"Of course, Mr. Meacham," she said, wishing he wouldn't.

"Well—I can see why your husband goes after the late-model robots. They've got the vote. Besides, it's not that easy to tell them from real people anyway. But there's a lot of pre-Josephson models working on our line. They don't have any individual intelligence—they're radio-linked to the central computers, you know, like your driver. And they don't even have a vote!"

"I can see," said Carrie benignly, trying not to lose his vote but unwilling to refrain from setting him straight, "that you don't know the Congressman very well. He doesn't do this just for votes. He does it for love."

And indeed that was true. And as October dwindled toward Halloween what dampened the sparkle in the Congressman's eye was the first hint—not really a hint, hardly more than a suspicion—of love unrequited. For the polls were turning, like the autumn leaves, as the "undecideds" began to decide. He began to consult Marty's data-link reports more and more frequently, and the more he studied them, the more a trend was clear. Every day the Congressman picked up some small fraction of a percentage point, it was true. But the Mayor picked up a larger one.

As Marty drove them to yet another factory it extruded a hard-copy of the latest results from the tiny printer in its chest and passed it back to the Congressman wordlessly. O'Hare studied the printout morosely. "I didn't think it was going to work out this way," he admitted at last. "It seems—it actually seems as though the enfranchised mechanicals are bloc-voting."

"You'd think they'd do their bloc-voting for the man who gave them the Robot ERA," Carrie said bitterly, and bit her tongue. But O'Hare only sighed and stared out at the warm, smoggy air. His wife thought dismally that the Congressman was at last beginning to show his age.

That morning's factory was a robot robot-assembly plant. Robots were the workers, and robots were the products. Some of the production bays were a decade old and more, and the workers were CIMs—central intelligence mechanicals, like their old driver Marty. Their dented old skulls housed sensors and communications circuits, but no thought. The thinking took place in an air-conditioned, vibration-proof and lightless chamber in the bedrock under the factory floor, where a single giant computer ran a hundred and ninety robots. But if the bulk of the workers were ancient, what they produced was sparkling new. As the car drove up Carrie saw a big flatbed truck hauling away. It was furnished with what looked like pipe racks bolted to the bed, and in each niche in the pipes a shiny new Josephson-junction autonomous-intellect robot had harnessed itself to the rack and lapsed into power-down mode for the trip to the distribution center. There were more than a hundred of them in a single truckload. A hundred votes, Carrie thought longingly, assuming they would all stay in the Twenty-Third Congressional District . . . but she was not surprised, all the same, when she observed that the Congressman was not thinking along precisely those strategic lines.

She sighed fondly, watching him as he did what she knew he was going to do. He limped down the line of CIMs, with a word and a smile and a handshake for each . . . and not a vote in the lot of them. It was not a kindly place for a human being to be, noisy with the zap of welding sparks, hot, dusty. This was where the torsos were assembled and the limbs attached and the effector motors emplaced. The growing, empty robot bodies swung down the line like beefs at a meat-packer's. Fortunately, the

CIMs had only limited capacity for small talk, and so the Congressman was soon enough in the newer, cleaner detailing bays. The finishing touches were applied here. The empty skulls were filled with the Josephson-junction data processors that were their "brains." The freezer units that kept the cryo-circuits working were installed, and into the vacant torsos went the power units that held hydrogen-fusion reactors contained in a nest of monopoles the size of a thimble. The Congressman's time was not wasted here. All these workers were voters, enfranchised robots as new and remarkable as the ones they made. Along that line the robots being finished began to twist and move and emit sounds, as their circuits went through quality-control testing, until at the end of the line they unhooked themselves from the overhead cable, stepped off, blinked, stood silent for a moment while their internal scanners told them who and what they were, and why. . . .

And the Congressman's eyes gleamed, as he perceived them the way they perceived themselves. New beings. New voters!

It was the right place for the Congressman to be, a greeting for each new voter, a handshake . . . a vote. Carrie hated to try to pull him away, but Martin was looking worried and the schedule had to be met. "Oh, Carrie," he whispered as she tugged at his sleeve, "they're *imprinting* on me! Just like the ducklings in *King Solomon's Ring!* I'm the first thing they see, so naturally they're going to remember me forever!"

He was not only happy, he was flushed with pleasure. Carrie hoped that was what it was—pleasure, and not something more worrisome. His eyes were feverishly bright, and he talked so rapidly he was tripping over his words. She was adamant; and then, once she got him into the car, less sure. "Dear," she ventured, as Martin closed the door behind them, "do you suppose you could possibly cancel the Baptist Men's Prayer Breakfast?"

"Certainly not," he said inevitably.

"You really do need a rest—"

"It's only a week till the election," he pointed out reasonably, "and then we'll rest as much as you like—maybe even back to the Sahara for a few days in the sun. Now, what are you going to do?"

She stared at him uncertainly. "Do when?"

"Do now, while I go see the Baptists—it's a *men's* breakfast, you know."

For once he had caught Carrie unprepared. Gender-segregated events were so rare that she had simply forgotten about this one. "Martin can drop me off and take you home, if you like," her husband supplied, "but of course it's going the wrong way—"

"No." She opened the door on her side, kissed her husband's warm cheek—too warm? she wondered—and got out. "I'll take a cab. You go ahead."

And she watched her husband pull out of one end of the parking lot just as the six-car procession she had seen coming down the far side of the fence entered at the other.

The Mayor.

It was the old days all over again, the next thing to a circus parade. Six cars! And not just cars, but bright-orange vehicles, purpose-built for nothing but campaigning. The first was an open car with half a dozen pretty young she-robots—no! They were human, Carrie was sure!—with pretty girls tossing pink and white carnations to the passersby. There were not many passersby, at that hour of the morning, but the Mayor's parade was pulling out all the stops. Next another open car, with the neat, smiling figure of the Mayor bestowing waves and nods on all sides. Next a PA car, with a handsome male singer and a beautiful female alternating to sing all the traditional political campaign numbers, "Happy Days Are Here Again" and Schiller's "Ode to Joy" and "God Bless America" with an up-tempo beat. And then two more flower-girl cars, surrounding a vehicle that was nothing more than a giant animated electronic display showing the latest and constantly changing poll results and extrapolations. All, of course, favoring the Mayor. How gross! And how very effective, Carrie conceded dismally to herself. . . . "You the lady that wants the taxi?" someone called behind her, and she turned to see a cab creeping up toward her. Reliable Martin had sent for it, of course. She sighed and turned to go inside it, and then paused, shaking her head.

"No, not now. I'll stay here a while."

"Whatever you say, lady," the driver agreed, gazing past her at the Mayor's procession. It was only a central-intelligence mechanical, but Carrie was sure she saw admiration in its eyes.

The Mayor had not noticed her. Carrie devoted herself to noticing it, as inconspicuously as she could. It was repeating her husband's tour of the plant—fair enough—but then she saw that it was not fair at all, for the Mayor had a built-in advantage. It too was a robot. In her husband's tour of the plant he had given each worker a minute's conversation. The Mayor gave each worker just as much conversation, but both it and the workers had their communications systems in fast mode. The sound of their voices was like the sonar squeaks of bats, the pumping of arms in the obligatory handshake like the flutter of hummingbird wings, too fast for Carrie's eyes to follow.

A voice from behind her said, "I know who you are, Mrs. O'Hare, but would you like a carnation anyhow?"

It was one of the flower girls—not, however, one of the human ones from the first car, for human girls did not have liquid-crystal readouts across their foreheads that said *Vote for Thom!*

There was no guile in its expression, no hidden photographer waiting to sneak a tape of the Congressman's wife accepting a flower from the opponent. It seemed to be simple courtesy, and Carrie O'Hare responded in kind. "Thank you. You're putting on a really nice show," she said, her heart envious but her tone, she hoped, only admiring. "Could you tell me something?"

"Of course, Mrs. O'Hare!"

Carrie hesitated; it was her instinct to be polite to everyone, robots included—her own programming, of course. How to put what she wanted to know? "I notice," she said delicately, "that Mayor Thom is spending time even with the old-fashioned mechanicals that don't have a vote. Can you tell me why?"

"Certainly, Mrs. O'Hare," the flower girl said promptly. "There are three reasons. The first is that it looks good, so when he goes to the autonomous-intellect mechanicals they're disposed in his favor. The second is that the Mayor is going to sponsor a bill to give the CIMs a fractional vote, too—did you know that?"

"I'm afraid I didn't," Carrie confessed. "But surely they can't be treated the way humans or Josephson-junction mechanicals are?"

"Oh, no, not at all," it agreed, smiling. "That's why it's only a fractional vote. You see, each of the CIMs is controlled by a central computer that is quite as intelligent as any of us, perhaps even more so; the central intelligence has no vote at all. So what Mayor Thom proposes is that each of the CIMs will have a fraction of a vote—one one-hundred-and-ninetieth of a vote, in the case of the workers here, since that's how many of them the plant computer runs. So if they all vote, the central computer will in effect have the chance to cast a ballot on its own—you know the old slogan, Mrs. O'Hare: One intelligence, one vote!"

Carrie nodded unhappily. It made sense—it was exactly the sort of thing her husband would have done himself, if he had thought of it. But he hadn't. Maybe he was getting past the point of thinking up the really good political ideas. Maybe— "You said there were three reasons."

"Well, just the obvious one, Mrs. O'Hare. The same

reason as your husband does it. It's not just for votes with the Mayor. It's love." Then she hesitated, then confided, "I don't know whether you know this or not, Mrs. O'Hare, but autonomous-intellect mechanicals like Mayor Thom and I have a certain discretion in our behavior patterns. One of the first things we do is study the available modes and install the ones we like best. I happen to have chosen nearly twenty per cent you, Mrs. O'Hare. And the Mayor—he's nearly three-quarters your husband."

There is a time for all things, thought Carrie O'Hare as she walked over to the Mayor's procession to ask them to call her a cab. There is a time to stay, and a time to go, and maybe the time to stay in office was over for Fiorello Delano Fitzgerald O'Hare. Some of the robots her husband had greeted as they came off the assembly line were standing in a clump, waiting, no doubt, for the arrival of the next truck to bear them away. They waved to Carrie. She responded with a slight decrease of worry—they were sure votes, anyway. Unless—

She stopped short. What was the Mayor doing with them? She gazed incredulously at the scene, like a high-speed film, the Mayor thrusting a hand into a pouch, jerking it out, swiftly passing something that shone dully to the robot it was talking to and moving briskly to the next. . . . And then, without willing it, Carrie herself was in high-speed mode, almost running toward the Mayor, her face crimson with rage. The Mayor looked up as she approached and politely geared down. "Mrs. O'Hare," it murmured, "how nice to see you here."

"I'm *shocked!*" she cried. "You're *brainwashing* them!"

The mobile robot face registered astonishment and what was almost indignation. "Why, certainly not, Mrs. O'Hare! I assure you I would never do such a thing."

"I saw you, Mayor Thom. You're reprogramming the robots with data chips!"

Comprehension broke over the Mayor's face, and it

gestured to the she-robot who had given Carrie the
flower. "Ah, the chips, yes. I see." It pulled a chip out of
the pouch and passed it to the she with a burst of high-
speed squeaks—"Oh, I beg your pardon, Mrs. O'Hare.
Let me repeat what I just said in normal mode. I simply
asked Millicent here to display the chip contents for you."

"Sure thing, Mayor." Millicent smiled, tucking the chip
under the strap of its halter top. The running message on
Millicent's forehead disappeared, and the legend appeared:

The Constitution
of the United States of America

We the people of the United States, in order to
form a more perfect Union, establish justice, insure
domestic tranquility, provide for the common de-
fence—

"Move it on, please," ordered the Mayor. "Search
'O'Hare.' Most of it," he added to Carrie, "is only the
basic legislation, the Constitution, the election laws and so
on. We don't get to your husband until—ah, here it is!"
And the legend read:

H.R. 29038. An Act to Propose a Constitutional
Amendment to grant equal voting rights and other
civil rights to citizens of mechanical origin which satisfy certain requirements as to autonomy of intellect
and judgment.

"The Robot ERA," Carrie said.
"That's right, Mrs. O'Hare, and of course your husband's name is on it. Then there's nothing about him until—advance search, please, Millicent—yes. Until we
come to his basic biographical information. Birth place,
education, voting record, medical reports and so on—"

"Medical reports! That's confidential material!"

The Mayor looked concerned. "Confidential, Mrs. O'Hare? But I assure you, the data on myself is just as complete—"

"It's *different* with human beings! Fiorello's doctor had no business releasing that data!"

"Ah, I see," said the Mayor, nodding in comprehension. "Yes, of course, that is true for his present doctor, Mrs. O'Hare. But previously the Congressman made use of a CIM practitioner—a robot whose central processing functions took place in the general data systems, and of course all of that is public information. I'm sorry. I assumed you knew that. Display the Congressman's medical history," it added to the she, and Carrie gazed at the moving line of characters through tear-blurred eyes. It was all there. His mild tachycardia, the arthritis that kicked up every winter, the asthma, even the fact that now and then the Congressman suffered from occasional spells of constipation. "It's disgusting to use his illnesses against him, Mayor Thom! Half of his sickness was on behalf of you robots!"

"Why, that's true, yes." The Mayor nodded. "It is largely tension-induced, and much of it undoubtedly occurred during the struggle for robot rights. If you'll look at the detailed record—datum seventy-eight, line four, please, Millicent—you'll see that his hemorrhoidectomy was definitely stress-linked, and moreover occurred just after the Robot ERA debate." The expression on the Mayor's face was no longer neat and self-assured, it was beginning to be worried. "I don't understand why you are upset, Mrs. O'Hare," Thom added defensively.

"It's a filthy trick, that's why!" Carrie could feel by the dampness on her cheeks that she was actually weeping now, and mostly out of helpless frustration. It was the one political argument her husband could never answer. It was obvious that the strain of the Robot ERA had cost Congressman O'Hare physical damage. The robots would understand that, and would behave as programmed. They served human beings. They spared them drudgery and pain. They would, therefore, remove him from a task that might harm him—not out of dislike, but out of love. "Don't you see it's not like that any more?" she blazed. "There's no strain to being in Congress any more—no tax bills to pass, no foreign nations to arm against, no subversives to control—why, if you look at the record you'll see that his doctor *urged* Fiorello to run again!"

"Ah, yes." The Mayor nodded. "But one never knows what may come up in the future—"

"One damn well does," she snapped. "One knows that it'll break Fee's heart to lose this election!"

The Mayor glanced at the she-robot, then returned to Carrie. Its neat, concerned face was perplexed and it was silent for a moment in thought.

Then it spoke in the bat-squeak triple time to the she, which pulled the chip out of its scanning slot, handed it to the Mayor and departed on a trot for the van with the poll displays. "One moment, please, Mrs. O'Hare," said the Mayor, tucking the chip into its own scanner. "I've asked Millicent to get me a data chip on human psychogenic medicine. I must study this." And it closed its eyes for a moment, opening them only to receive and insert the second chip from the she.

When the Mayor opened its eyes its expression was— regret? Apology? Neither of those, Carrie decided. Possibly compassion. It said, "Mrs. O'Hare, my deepest apologies. You're quite right. It would cause the Congressman great pain to be defeated by me, and I will make sure that every voting mechanical in the district knows this by this time tomorrow morning."

There had to be right words to say, but Carrie O'Hare couldn't find them. She contented herself with "Thank you," and then realized that those had been the right words after all . . . but was unable to leave it at that. "Mayor Thom? Can I ask you something?"

"Of course, Mrs. O'Hare."

"It's just—well, I'm sure you realize that you people could easily beat my husband if you stuck together. You could probably do that in nearly every election in the country. You could rule the nation—and yet you don't seem to go after that power."

The Mayor frowned. "Power, Mrs. O'Hare? You mean the chance to make laws and compel others to do what you want them to? Why, good heavens, Mrs. O'Hare, who in his right mind would want that?" He paused for a moment, looking into space. "Still," he said thoughtfully, "given the right circumstances, I suppose we could learn."

4

THE MAN WHO ATE THE WORLD

It is possible to be brutalized by poverty, and in the long, cruel history of the human race that has been done to tens of billions. But not after Amalfi Amadeus lit his fires. Then it became the burden of wealth, not poverty, that crushed spirit and soul out of its victims. Morey Fry helped lift that load . . . but not in time for everyone.

Especially, it was not in time for one little boy.

He had a name—it was Anderson Trumie—but at home he was called Sonny, and he was almost always at home. He hated it. Other boys his age went to school. Sonny would have done anything to go to school, but his family was, to put it mildly, not well off. It was not Sonny's fault that his father was a failure. Many children grow up poorest on the block. They are not to blame. But it meant no school for Sonny, no boys of his own age for Sonny to play with. All childhoods are tragic (as all adults forget), but Sonny's was misery all the way through.

The worst time was at night, when the baby sister was asleep and the parents were grimly eating and reading and dancing and drinking, until they were ready to drop. And of all bad nights, the night before his twelfth birthday was perhaps Sonny's worst. He lay awake dreading it, watching children's stories on television without seeing them, for he was old enough to know what a birthday party was like.

It would be cake and candy, shows and games.

It would be presents, presents, presents.

It would be a terrible, endless day.

He switched off the color-D television and the recorded tapes of sea chanteys and, with an appearance of absent-mindedness, walked toward the door of his playroom. Davey Crockett got up from beside the model rocket field and said, "Hold on thar, Sonny. Mought take a stroll with you." Davey, with a face as serene and strong as a Tennessee crag, swung its long huntin' rifle under one arm and put its other arm around Sonny's shoulders. "Where you reckon the two of us ought to head?"

Sonny shook Davey Crockett's arm off. "Get lost," he said petulantly. "Who wants you around?"

Long John Silver came out of the closet, hobbling on its wooden leg, crouched over its knobby cane. "Ah, young master," it said reproachfully, "you shouldn't ought to talk to old Davey like that! He's a good friend to you, Davey is. Many's the weary day Davey and me has been a-keepin' of your company. I asks you this, young master: Is it fair and square that you should be a-tellin' him to get lost? Is it fair, young master? Is it square?"

Sonny looked at the floor stubbornly and didn't answer. What was the use of answering dummies like them? He stood rebelliously silent and still until he just felt like saying something. And then he said: "You go in the closet, both of you. I don't want to play with you. I'm going to play with my trains."

Long John said unctuously: "Now there's a good idea, that is! You just be a-havin' of a good time with your trains and old Davey and me'll—"

"Go ahead!" shouted Sonny. He kept stamping his foot until they were out of sight.

His fire truck was in the middle of the floor; he kicked at it, but it rolled quickly out of reach and slid into its little garage under the tanks of tropical fish.

He scuffed over to the model railroad layout and glared

at it. As he approached, the Twentieth Century Limited came roaring out of a tunnel, sparks flying from its stack. It crossed a bridge, whistled at a grade crossing, steamed into the Union Station. The roof of the station glowed and suddenly became transparent, and through it Sonny saw the bustling crowds of redcaps and travelers—

"I don't want that kind of baby stuff," he said disagreeably. "Casey, crack up old Number Ninety-Nine again."

Obediently the layout quivered and revolved a half-turn. Old Casey Jones, one and an eighth inches tall, leaned out of the cab of the S.P. locomotive and waved good-bye to Sonny. The locomotive whistled shrilly twice and picked up speed—

It was a good crackup. Little old Casey's body, thrown completely free, developed real blisters from the steam and bled real blood. But Sonny turned his back on it. He had liked that crackup for a long time—longer than he liked almost any other toy he owned. But he was tired of it.

He looked around the room.

Tarzan of the Apes, leaning against a foot-thick tree trunk, one hand on a vine, lifted its head and looked at him; but Tarzan was clear across the room. The others were in the closet.

Sonny ran out and slammed the door. He saw Tarzan start to come after him, but even before Sonny was out of the room, Tarzan slumped and stood stock-still.

It wasn't fair, Sonny thought angrily. They wouldn't even *chase* him, so that at least he could have some kind of chance to get away by himself. They'd just talk to each other on their little radios, and in a minute one of the tutors, or one of the maids, or whatever else happened to be handy would vector in on him—

But, for the moment, he was free.

He slowed down and walked along the Great Hall toward his baby sister's room. The fountains began to splash as he entered the hall; the mosaics on the wall began to tinkle music and sparkle with moving colors.

"Now, chile, whut you up to?"

He turned around, but he knew it was Mammy coming toward him. It was slapping toward him on big, flat feet, its pink-palmed hands lifted to its shoulders. The face under the red bandanna was frowning, its gold tooth sparkling as Mammy scolded: "Chile, you is got us'ns so worried, we's fit to *die!* How you 'speck us to take good keer of you efn you run off lak that? Now you jes come on back to your nice room with Mammy an' we'll see if there ain't some real nice program on the TV."

Sonny stopped and waited for it, but he wouldn't give it the satisfaction of looking at it. *Slap-slap,* the big feet waddled cumbersomely toward him; but he didn't have any illusions. Waddle, big feet, three hundred pounds and all, Mammy could catch him in twenty yards with a ten-yard start. Any of them could.

He said in his best icily indignant voice: "I was just going in to look at my baby sister."

Pause. "You was?" The plump black face looked suspicious.

"Yes, I was. Doris is my own sister and I love her."

Pause—long pause. "Dat's nice," said Mammy, but its voice was still doubtful. "I 'speck I better come 'long with you. You wouldn't want to wake your li'l baby sister up. Ef I come, I'll he'p you keep real quiet."

Sonny shook free of it—they were always putting their hands on kids! "I don't *want* you to come with me, Mammy!"

"Aw, now, honey! Mammy ain't gwine bother nothin', you knows that!"

Sonny turned his back on it and marched grimly toward his sister's room. If only they would leave him *alone!* But they never did.

It was always that way, always one darn old robot—yes, *robot,* he thought, savagely tasting the naughty word. Always one darn *robot* after another. Why couldn't Daddy be like other daddies, so they could live in a decent little house and get rid of those darn *robots*—so he could go to a real school and be in a class with other boys, instead of being taught at home by Miss Brooks and Mr. Chips and all those other *robots?*

They spoiled everything. And they would spoil what he wanted to do now. But he was going to do it all the same, because there was something in Doris's room that he wanted very much.

It was probably the only tangible thing he wanted in the world.

As he and Mammy passed the imitation tumbled rocks of the Bear Cave, Mama Bear poked its head out and growled: "Hello, Sonny. Don't you think you ought to be in bed? It's nice and warm in our bear bed, Sonny."

He didn't even look at it. Time was when he had liked that sort of thing, too, but he wasn't a four-year-old like Doris any more. All the same, there was one thing a four-year-old had—

He stopped at the door of her room. "Doris?" he whispered.

Mammy scolded: "Now, chile, you knows that li'l baby is asleep! How come you tryin' to wake her up?"

"I won't wake her up." The farthest thing from Sonny's mind was to wake his sister up. He tiptoed into the room and stood beside the little girl's bed. *Lucky kid!* he thought enviously. Being four, she was allowed to have a tiny little room and a tiny bed—while Sonny had to wallow around in a forty-foot bedchamber and a bed eight feet long.

He looked down at his sister. Behind him, Mammy clucked approvingly. "Dat's nice when chilluns loves each other lak you an' that li'l baby," it whispered.

Doris was sound asleep, clutching her teddy bear. It wriggled slightly and opened an eye to look at Sonny, but it didn't say anything.

Sonny took a deep breath, leaned forward and gently slipped the teddy bear out of the bed.

It scrambled pathetically, trying to get free.

Mammy whispered urgently: "Sonny! Now you let dat old teddy bear alone, you heah me?"

Sonny whispered: "I'm not hurting anything. Leave me alone, will you?"

"Sonny!"

He clutched the little furry robot desperately around its middle. The stubby arms pawed at him, the furred feet scratched against his arms. It growled a tiny doll-bear growl, and whined, and suddenly his hands were wet with its real salt tears.

"Sonny! Come on now, honey, you knows that's Doris's Teddy. Aw, chile!"

He said: "It's mine!" It wasn't his. He knew it wasn't. His was long gone, taken away from him when he was six because it was *old,* and because he had been six, and six-year-olds had to have bigger, more elaborate companion-robots. It wasn't even the same color as his—it was brown and his had been black and white. But it was cuddly and gently warm and he had heard it whispering little bedtime stories to Doris. And he wanted it very much.

Footsteps in the hall outside. A low-pitched pleading voice from the door: "Sonny, you must not interfere with your sister's toys. One has obligations."

He stood forlornly, holding the teddy bear. "Go away, Mr. Chips!"

"Really, Sonny! This isn't proper behavior. Please return the toy."

"I won't!"

Mammy, dark face pleading in the shadowed room, leaned toward him and tried to take it away from him. "Aw, honey, now you know that's not—"

"Leave me alone!" he shouted. There was a gasp and a little whimper from the bed, and Doris sat up and began to cry.

The little girl's bedroom was suddenly filled with robots—and not only robots, for in a moment the butler appeared, leading Sonny's actual flesh-and-blood mother and father.

Sonny made a terrible scene. He cried, and he swore at them childishly for being the unsuccessful clods they were, and they nearly wept, too, because they were aware that their lack of standing was bad for the children. But he couldn't keep Teddy.

They marched him back to his room, where his father lectured him while his mother stayed behind to watch Mammy comfort the little girl.

His father said: "Sonny, you're a big boy now. We aren't as well off as other people, but you have to help us. Don't you know that, Sonny? We all have to do our part. Your mother and I'll be up till midnight now, consuming, because you've made this scene. Can't you at least *try* to consume something bigger than a teddy bear? It's all right for Doris because she's so little, but a big boy like you—"

"I hate you!" cried Sonny, and he turned his face to the wall.

They punished him, naturally. The first punishment was that they give him an extra birthday party the week following.

The second punishment was even worse.

II

The sins of the parents are visited upon the children, but the punishments of the children, unfortunately, are passed on to everyone within reach. And the reach of Sonny Trumie was great.

So later—much, much later, nearly a score of years—a man named Roger Garrick in a place named Fisherman's Island walked into his hotel room. It was Garrick's job to repair the damage of, among other things, anti-social behavior. He was a troubleshooter, and on Fisherman's Island there was plenty of trouble.

To begin with, the light didn't go on.

The bellhop apologized. "We're sorry, sir. We'll have it attended to, if possible."

"If possible?" Garrick's eyebrows went up. The bellhop made putting in a new light tube sound like a major industrial operation. "All right." He waved the bellhop out of the room. It bowed and closed the door.

Garrick looked around him, frowning. One light tube more or less didn't make a lot of difference; there was still the light from the sconces at the walls, from the reading lamps at the chairs and chaise lounge and from the photomural on the long side of the room—to say nothing of the fact that it was broad, hot daylight outside and light poured through the windows. All the same, it was a new sensation to be in a room where the central lighting wasn't on. He didn't like it. It was—creepy.

A rap on the door. A girl was standing there, young, attractive, rather small. But a woman grown, it was apparent. "Mr. Garrick? Mr. Roosenburg is expecting you on the sun deck."

"All right." He rummaged around in the pile of luggage, looking for his briefcase. It wasn't even sorted out! The bellhop had merely dumped the stuff and left.

The girl said: "Is that what you're looking for?" He
looked where she was pointing; it was his briefcase, behind another bag. "You'll get used to that around here.
Nothing in the right place, nothing working right. We've
all gotten used to it."

We. He looked at her sharply, but she was no robot;
there was life, not the glow of electronic tubes, in her
eyes. "Pretty bad, is it?"

She shrugged. "Let's go see Mr. Roosenburg. I'm Kathryn Pender, by the way. I'm his statistician."

He followed her into the hall, blinking. Roosenburg
was a district manager, and of course he would have need
of statistical advice. But—from this girl? This *human* girl?
"Statistician, did you say?"

She turned and smiled—a tight, grim smile of annoyance. "That's right. Surprised?"

Garrick said uneasily, "Well, it's more a robot job, you
know. Of course, I'm not familiar with the practice in this
sector—"

"You will be," she promised bluntly. "The nice, orderly
procedures you're used to—they've broken down here.
We all do everything. As a matter of fact, I was even getting tutoring in your own subject—" Garrick stiffened.
"Oh, not now. Before we realized that this was not something an amateur could handle. So we called for help—
don't go in there! We aren't taking the elevator. Mr.
Roosenburg's in too much of a hurry to see you."

Garrick paused at the lift door, his eyebrows framing a
question. She glared back at him. "Don't you understand?
Day before yesterday, I took the elevator and I was hung
up between floors for an hour and a half. Something was
going on at North Guardian and it took all the power in
the lines. Would it happen again today? I don't know.
But, believe me, an hour and a half is a long time to be
stuck in an elevator."

She turned and led him to the fire stairs. Over her

shoulder, she said: "Get it straight once and for all, Mr. Garrick. You're in a disaster area here. . . . Anyway, it's only ten more flights."

Ten flights. *Nobody* climbed ten flights of stairs voluntarily! Garrick was huffing and puffing before they were halfway, but the girl kept on ahead, light as a gazelle. Her skirt reached between hip and knees, and Garrick had plenty of opportunity to observe that her legs were attractively tanned. Embarrassed, he looked around him.

It was a robot's-eye view of the hotel that he was getting; this was the bare wire armature that held up the confectionery suites and halls where the humans went. Garrick knew, as everyone absently knew, that there were places like this behind the scenes everywhere. Belowstairs, the robots worked; behind scenes, they moved about their errands and did their jobs. But nobody *went* there.

It was funny about the backs of this girl's knees. They were paler than the rest of the leg—

Garrick wrenched his mind back to his surroundings. Take the guardrail along the steps, for instance. It was wire-thin, frail-looking. No doubt it could bear any weight it was required to, but why couldn't it *look* that strong?

The answer, obviously, was that robots did not have humanity's built-in concepts of how strong a rail should look before they could believe it really was strong. If a robot should be in any doubt—and how improbable that a robot should be in doubt!—it would perhaps reach out a sculptured hand and test it. Once. And then it would remember, and never doubt again, and it wouldn't be continually edging toward the wall, away from the spider-strand between it and the vertical drop—

He conscientiously took the middle of the steps all the rest of the way up.

Of course, that merely meant a different distraction, when he really wanted to do some thinking. But it was a pleasurable distraction. And by the time they reached the top, he had solved the problem. The pale spots at the back of Miss Pender's knees meant she had got her tan the hard way—walking in the Sun, perhaps working in the Sun, so that the bending knees kept the Sun from the patches at the back; not, as anyone else would acquire a tan, by lying beneath a normal, healthful sunlamp held by a robot masseur.

He wheezed: "You don't mean we're all the way up!"

"All the way up," she said, and looked at him closely. "Here, lean on me if you want to."

"No, thanks!" He staggered over to the door, which opened naturally enough as he approached it, and stepped out into the flood of sunlight on the roof, to meet Mr. Roosenburg, a small man with a huge voice who amiably poured Garrick a drink before saying hello. Then he sat back in the sunshine that flooded his roof and waved at the horizon. "There's the problem," he said. "This is the best place to see it from."

All Garrick could see was a distant island. What he felt was more vivid. Garrick wasn't a medical doctor, but he remembered enough of his basic pre-specialization to know there had been something special in that fizzy golden drink. It tasted perfectly splendid—just cold enough, just fizzy enough, not quite too sweet. And after two sips of it, he was buoyant with strength and well-being.

He put the glass down and said: "Thank you for whatever it was. Now let's talk."

"Gladly, gladly!" boomed Mr. Roosenburg. "Kathryn, the files!"

Garrick looked after her, shaking his head. Not only was she a statistician, which was robot work, she was also a file clerk—and that was barely robot work. It was the kind of thing handled by a semisentient microchip in a decently run sector.

Roosenburg said sharply: "Shocks you, doesn't it? But that's why you're here." He was a slim, fair little man and he wore a golden beard cropped square.

Garrick took another sip of the fizzy drink. It was good stuff; it didn't intoxicate, but it cheered. He said: "I'm glad to know why I'm here."

The golden beard quivered. "Area Control sent you down and didn't tell you this was a disaster area?"

Garrick put down the glass. "I'm a psychist. Area Control said you needed a psychist. From what I've seen, it's more of a supply problem, but—"

"Here are the files," said Kathryn Pender, and stood watching him.

Roosenburg took the spools of tape from her and dropped them in his lap. He asked tangentially: "How old are you, Roger?"

Garrick was annoyed. "I'm a qualified psychist! I happen to be assigned to Area Control and—"

"How old are you?"

Garrick scowled. "Twenty-four."

Roosenburg nodded. "Umm. Rather young," he observed. "Maybe you don't remember how things used to be."

Garrick said dangerously: "All the information I need is on that tape. I don't need any lectures from you."

Roosenburg pursed his lips and got up. "Come here a minute, will you?"

He moved over to the rail of the sun deck and pointed. "See those things down there?"

Garrick looked. Twenty stories down, the village straggled off toward the sea in a tangle of pastel oblongs and towers. Over the bay, the hills of the mainland were faintly visible through mist and, riding the bay, the flat white floats of the power plant.

"It's an Amalfi fusion-power generating plant. Is that what you mean?"

Roosenburg boomed, "A fusion-power plant. Yes! All the power the world can ever use, out of this one and all the others, all over the world." He peered out at the bobbing floats, with their squat, pale buildings atop them. "And did you know that people used to try to wreck them?" he added.

Garrick said stiffly: "I may only be twenty-four years old, Mr. Roosenburg, but I *have* completed school."

"Oh, yes. Of course you have, Roger. But maybe schooling isn't the same thing as living through a time like that. I grew up in the Era of Plenty, when the law was *Consume!* My parents were poor and I still remember the misery of my childhood. Eat and consume, wear and use. I never had a moment's peace, Roger! For the very poor, it was a treadmill; we had to consume so much that we could never catch up, and the farther we fell behind, the more the Ration Board forced on us—"

"That's ancient history, Mr. Roosenburg. Morey Fry liberated us from all that."

The girl said softly: "Not all of us."

The man with the golden beard nodded. "Not all of us—as you should know, Roger, being a psychist."

Garrick, who was not fond of being told what he ought to know, sat up straight, but Roosenburg didn't give him a chance to speak. "Fry showed us that the robots could help at both ends—by both producing and consuming. But the Fry breakthrough came a little too late for some of us. The patterns of childhood do linger on, and adults get crippled by them."

Kathryn Pender leaned impatiently toward Garrick. "What he's trying to say, Mr. Garrick, is that we've got a compulsive consumer on our hands."

III

The home of the compulsive consumer, whose name was Anderson Trumie, was on North Guardian Island, nine miles away. It wasn't as much as a mile wide and not much more than that in length, but it had its city and its bathing beaches, its parks and its theaters. It was possibly the most densely populated island in the world . . . for the number of its inhabitants.

It was also the only spot on the face of the Earth that was at war.

So the President of the Military Council of the Sovereign State of North Guardian Island convened their afternoon meeting. It was held in a large and lavish room. There were nineteen councilmen seated around a lustrous mahogany table. Over the President's shoulder, the others could see the situation map, wide as the hall, tall as floor to ceiling, showing all of North Guardian and the waters surrounding it. North Guardian Island glowed blue, cold, impregnable. The sea was misty green. The intruding edges of the mainland, Fisherman's Island, South Guardian and the rest of the little archipelago were hot, hostile red, and spearheads and serpents of red and blue showed where engagements were being fought.

The war was going badly. Since none of the councilmen had played any part in deciding their war objectives, or had any very clear idea of what those objectives were, it was not easy for them to know what steps to take. It was a consideration for them—though not an important one—that if they took the wrong steps they probably would not survive to take any others. Anderson Trumie, warlord of North Guardian Island, did not forgive mistakes.

So they watched the changing situation board with interest. Little flickering fingers of red were attacking the blue. Flick, and a ruddy flame wiped out a corner of a beach. Flick, and a red spark appeared in the middle of the city, to grow and blossom, and then to die. Each little red whip-flick was a point where, momentarily, the defenses of the island were down; but always and always, the cool blue brightened around the red and drowned it.

The President was tall, stooped, old. It wore glasses, though robot eyes saw well enough without. It said, in a voice that throbbed with power and pride: "The first item of the order of business will be a report of the Defense Secretary."

The Defense Secretary rose to its feet, hooked a thumb in its vest and cleared its throat. "Mr. President—"

"Excuse me, sir." A whisper from the sweet-faced young blonde taking down the minutes of the meeting. "Mr. Trumie has just left Bowling Green, heading north."

The whole council turned to glance at the situation map, where Bowling Green had just flared red.

The President nodded stiffly, like the crown of an old redwood nodding. "You may proceed, Mr. Secretary," it said after a moment.

"Our invasion fleet," began the Secretary, in its high, clear voice, "is ready for sailing on the first suitable tide. Certain units have been, ah, inactivated, at the, ah, instigation of Mr. Trumie. But on the whole, repairs have been completed and the units will be serviceable within the next few hours." Its lean, attractive face turned solemn. "I am afraid, however, that the Air Command has sustained certain, ah, increments of attrition—due, I should emphasize, to chances involved in certain calculated risks—"

"Question! Question!" It was the Commissioner of Public Safety, small, dark, fire-eyed, angry.

"Mr. Commissioner?" the President began, but it was interrupted again by the soft whisper of the recording stenographer, listening intently to the earphones that brought news from outside.

"Mr. President," it whispered, "Mr. Trumie has passed the Navy Yard."

The robots turned to look at the situation map. Bowling Green, though it smoldered in spots, had mostly gone back to blue. But the jagged oblong of the Yard flared red and bright. There was a faint electronic hum in the air, almost a sigh.

The robots turned back to face each other. "Mr. President! I demand that the Defense Secretary explain the loss of the *Graf Zeppelin* and the 456th Bomb Group!"

The Defense Secretary nodded to the Commissioner of Public Safety. "Mr. Trumie threw them away," it said sorrowfully.

Once again, that sighing electronic drone from the assembled robots.

The Council fussed and fiddled with its papers, while the situation map on the wall flared and dwindled, flared and dwindled.

The Defense Secretary cleared its throat again. "Mr. President, there is no question that the, ah, absence of an effective air component will seriously hamper, not to say endanger, our prospects of a suitable landing. Nevertheless—and I say this, Mr. President, in full knowledge of the conclusions that may—indeed, should!—be drawn from such a statement—nevertheless, Mr. President, I say that our forward elements will successfully complete an assault landing—"

"Mr. President!" The breathless whisper of the blonde stenographer again. "Mr. President, Mr. Trumie is in the building!"

On the situation map behind it, the Pentagon—the building they were in—flared scarlet.

The Attorney General, nearest the door, leaped to its feet. "Mr. President, I hear him!"

And they could all hear now. Far off, down the long corridors, a crash. A faint explosion, and another crash, and a raging, querulous, high-pitched voice. A nearer crash, and a sustained, smashing, banging sound, coming toward them.

The oak-paneled doors flew open with a crash, splintering.

A tall, dark male figure in gray leather jacket, rocket-gun holsters swinging at its hips, stepped through the splintered doors and stood surveying the Council. Its hands hung just below the butts of the rocket guns.

It drawled: "Mistuh Anderson Trumie!"

It stepped aside. Another male figure—shorter, darker, hobbling with the aid of a stainless-steel cane that concealed a ray-pencil, wearing the same gray leather jacket and the same rocket-gun holsters—entered, stood for a moment, and took position on the other side of the door.

Between them, Mr. Anderson Trumie shambled ponderously into the Council Chamber to call on his Council.

And there was Sonny Trumie, come of age, now playing with larger toys. He wasn't much more than five feet tall, but his weight was close to 400 pounds. He stood there in the door, leaning against the splintered oak, quivering jowls obliterating his neck, his eyes nearly swallowed in the fat that swamped his skull, his thick legs trembling as they tried to support him.

"You're all under arrest!" he screeched. "Traitors! Traitors!"

He panted ferociously, glowering at them. They waited with bowed heads. Beyond the ring of councilmen, the situation map slowly blotted out the patches of red as the repair-robots worked feverishly to fix what Sonny Trumie had destroyed.

"Mr. Crockett!" Sonny cried shrilly. "Slay me these traitors!"

Wheep-wheep, and the guns whistled out of their holsters into the tall bodyguard's hands. *Rata-tat-tat*, and two by two, the nineteen councilmen leaped, clutched at air and fell as the rocket pellets pierced them through.

"That one, too!" Mr. Trumie pointed at the sweet-faced blonde.

Bang. The sweet young face convulsed and froze; it fell, slumping across its little table.

On the wall, the situation map flared red again, but only faintly—for what were twenty robots?

Sonny gestured curtly to his other bodyguard. It leaped forward, tucking the stainless steel cane under one arm, putting the other around the larded shoulders of Sonny Trumie. "Ah, now, young master," it crooned. "You just get ahold o' Long John's arm now—"

"Get them fixed," Sonny ordered abruptly. He pushed the President of the Council out of its chair and, with the robot's help, sank into it himself. "Get them fixed *right*, you hear? I've had enough traitors! I want them to do what I tell them!"

"Sartin sure, young master. Long John'll be pleased to—"

"Do it *now*! And you, Davey, I want my lunch!"

"Reckoned you would, Mistuh Trumie. It's right hyar." The Crockett robot kicked the fallen councilmen out of the way as a procession of waiters filed in from the corridor.

Sonny Trumie sat down, with his faithful companions in attendance, in the imperial splendor of the smallest empire the world had ever known, and did the thing he did best. He consumed. He ate.

He ate until eating was pain, and then he sat there sobbing, his arms braced against the tabletop, until he could eat more.

The Crockett robot said worriedly: "Mistuh Trumie, moughtn't you rear back a mite? Old Doc Aeschylus, he don't hold with you eatin' too much, you know."

"I hate Doc!" Trumie said bitterly.

He pushed the plates off the table. They fell with a rattle and a clatter, and they went spinning away as he heaved himself up and lurched alone over to the window.

"I hate Doc!" he brayed again, sobbing, staring through tears out the window at his kingdom with its hurrying throngs and marching troops and roaring waterfront. The tallow shoulders tried to shake with pain. He felt as though hot cinder blocks were being thrust down his throat, the ragged edges cutting, the hot weight crushing.

"Take me back," he wept to the robots. "Take me away from these traitors. Take me to my Private Place!"

IV

"As you can understand," Roosenburg finished, "the man is dangerous."

Garrick looked out over the water, toward North Guardian. The concept of a "dangerous" human being was hard to assimilate. "And this has been going on for years?"

"Long enough," said Roosenburg. "At first we just left him alone. What harm could he do? Waste a few resources is all—we thought—and who cares about that? Then it got worse." He tugged at his pale beard, frowning toward the island. "He sends out raiding parties."

Garrick jumped. *"Raiding* parties?"

"Oh, he doesn't harm human beings, of course—so far, anyway. But we can't keep a Josephson-junction robot here. His machines destroy them. And that whole generating plant's output gets drawn off for his needs!"

Garrick had heard enough. "I'd better study his personal history," he said.

The girl said, "Of course," and produced a set of data chips. While she was getting ready to display them, Garrick was facing up to the fact that there was a real challenge to his abilities as a healer of minds. This Trumie indeed was dangerous. Dangerous to the balanced, stable world, for it might take only one Trumie to topple its stability. It had taken thousands and thousands of years for society to learn its delicate tightrope walk. It was a matter for a psychist, all right.

And Garrick was uncomfortably aware that he was only twenty-four.

"Here you are," said the girl.

"Look them over," Roosenburg suggested. "Then, after you've studied the tapes on Trumie, we've got something else. One of his robots. But you'll need the tapes first."

"Let's go," said Garrick.

The girl flicked a switch and the life of Anderson Trumie appeared before them, in color, in three dimensions—in miniature.

Robots had eyes; and where the robots went the eyes of Robot Central went with them. And the robots went everywhere. From the stored files of Robot Central came the spool of tape that was the frightful life story of Sonny Trumie.

The tapes played into the globe-shaped viewer, ten inches high, a crystal ball that looked back into the past. First, from the recording eyes of the robots in Sonny Trumie's nursery. The lonely little boy, twenty years before, lost in the enormous nursery.

"Disgusting!" breathed Kathryn Pender, wrinkling her nose. "How could people live like that?"

Garrick said: "Please, let me watch this. It's important."

In the gleaming globe, the little boy kicked at his toys, threw himself across his huge bed, sobbed. Garrick squinted, frowned, reached out, tried to make contact. It was hard. The tapes showed the objective facts, but for a psychist, it was the subjective reality behind the facts that mattered.

Kicking at his toys. Yes, but why? Because he was tired of them—and why was he tired? Because he feared them? *Kicking at his toys.* Because—because they were the wrong toys? *Kicking—hate them! Don't want them! Want—*

A bluish flare in the viewing globe. Garrick blinked and jumped, and that was the end of that section.

The colors flowed and suddenly jelled into bright life. Garrick recognized the scene after a moment—it was right there in Fisherman's Island, some pleasure spot overlooking the water. A bar, and at the end of it was Anderson Trumie at twenty, staring somberly into an empty glass. The view was through the eyes of the robot bartender.

Anderson Trumie was weeping.

Once again, there was the objective fact—but the fact behind the fact, what was it? Trumie had been drinking, drinking. Why?

Drinking, drinking.

With a sudden sense of shock, Garrick saw what the drink was—the golden, fizzy liquor. Not intoxicating. Not habit-forming! Trumie had become no alcoholic. It was something else that kept him *drinking, drinking, must drink, must keep on drinking, or else—*

And again the bluish flare.

There was more—Trumie feverishly collecting objects of art, Trumie decorating a palace, Trumie on a world tour, and Trumie returned to Fisherman's Island.

And then there was no more.

"That," said Roosenburg, "is the file. Of course, if you

want the raw, unedited tapes, we can try to get them from Robot Central, but—"

"No." The way things were, it was best to stay away from Robot Central; there might be more breakdowns and there wasn't much time. Besides, something was beginning to suggest itself.

"Run the first one again," said Garrick. "I think maybe I'll find something there."

Garrick made out a quick requisition slip and handed it to Kathryn Pender, who looked at it, raised her eyebrows, shrugged and went off to have it filled.

By the time she came back, Roosenburg had escorted Garrick to the room where the captured Trumie robot lay chained.

"He's cut off from Robot Central," Roosenburg was saying. "I suppose you figured that out. Imagine! Not only has Trumie built a whole city for himself—but even his own Robot Central!"

Garrick looked at the robot. It was a fisherman, or so Roosenburg had said. It was small, dark, black-haired. Possibly the hair would have been curly, if the seawater hadn't plastered the curls to the scalp. It was still damp from the tussle that had landed it in the water and eventually into Roosenburg's hands.

Roosenburg was already at work. Garrick tried to think of the robot as a machine, but it wasn't easy. The thing looked very nearly human—except for the crystal and copper that showed where the back of its head had been removed.

"It's as bad as a brain operation," said Roosenburg, working rapidly without looking up. "I've got to short out the input leads without disturbing the electronic balance—"

Snip, snip. A curl of copper fell free, to be grabbed by Roosenburg's tweezers. The fisherman's arms and legs kicked sharply like a dissected, galvanized frog's.

Kathryn Pender said: "They found him this morning, casting nets into the bay and singing '*O Sole Mio.*' He's from North Guardian, all right."

Abruptly the lights flickered and turned yellow, then slowly returned to normal brightness. Roger Garrick got up and walked over to the window. North Guardian was a haze of light in the sky, across the water.

Click, *snap*. The fisherman robot began to sing:

> *Tutte le sere, dopo quel fanal,*
> *Dietro la caserma, ti starò ed—*
> *Click.*

Roosenburg muttered under his breath and probed further. Kathryn Pender joined Garrick at the window.

"Now you see," she said.

Garrick shrugged. "You can't blame him."

"*I* blame him!" she said hotly. "I've lived here all my life. Fisherman's Island used to be a tourist spot—why, it was lovely here. And look at it now. The elevators don't work. The lights don't work. Practically all of our robots are gone. Spare parts, construction material, everything— it's all gone to North Guardian! There isn't a day that passes, Garrick, when half a dozen bargeloads of stuff don't go north, because *he* requisitioned them. Blame him? I'd like to kill him!"

Snap. Sputter*snap*. The fisherman lifted its head and caroled:

> *Forse domani, piangerai,*
> *E dopo tu, sorriderai—*

Kathryn was staring at the singing thing on the table. "I think I've seen that one before," she said. "Around here,

I mean, long ago—but he wasn't a fisherman then. That's another little trick of Trumie's, he steals our old centrally controlled robots and changes them around."

"It's an obsolete one, all right," Roosenburg grunted as his probe encountered a flat black disk. "Kathryn, look this up, will you?" He read the serial number from the disk and then put down the probe. He stood flexing his fingers, looking irritably at the motionless figure.

Garrick joined him. Roosenburg jerked his head at the fisherman.

"That's robot repair work, trying to tinker with their insides. Trumie has his own Robot Central, as I told you. What I have to do is recontrol this one from the substation on the mainland, but keep its receptor circuits open to North Guardian on the symbolic level. You understand what I'm talking about? It'll think from North Guardian, but act from the mainland."

"Sure," said Garrick.

"And it's damned close work. There isn't much room inside one of those things—" He stared at the figure and picked up the probe again.

Kathryn Pender came back with a printout in her hand. "It was one of ours, all right. Used to be a busboy in the cafeteria at the beach club." She scowled, "That Trumie!"

"You can't blame him," Garrick said reasonably. "He's only trying to be good."

She looked at him queerly. "He's only—"

Roosenburg interrupted with an exultant cry. "Got it! Okay, you—sit up and start telling us what Trumie's up to now!"

The fisherman figure said obligingly, "Yes, boss. What you wanna know?"

What they wanted to know, they asked; and what they asked, it told them, volunteering nothing, concealing nothing.

There was Anderson Trumie, king of his island, the compulsive consumer.

It was like an echo of the bad old days of the Age of Plenty, when the world was smothering under the endless, pounding flow of goods from the robot factories and the desperate race between consumption and production strained the whole society. But Trumie's orders came not from society, but from within. *Consume!* commanded something inside him, and *Use!* it cried, and *Devour!* it ordered. And Trumie obeyed, heroically.

They listened to what the fisherman robot had to say, and the picture was dark. Armies had sprung up on North Guardian; navies floated in its waters. Anderson Trumie stalked among his creations like a blubbery god, wrecking and ruling. Garrick could see the pattern in what the fisherman had to say. In Trumie's mind, he was dictator, building a war machine. He was supreme engineer, constructing a mighty state. He was warrior.

"He was playing tin soldiers," said Roger Garrick, and Roosenburg and the girl nodded.

"The trouble is," Roosenburg said, "he has stopped playing. Invasion fleets, Garrick! He isn't content with North Guardian any more. He wants the rest of the country, too!"

"You can't blame him," said Roger Garrick for the third time, and stood up. "The question is, what do we do about it?"

"That's what you're here for," Kathryn told him.

"All right. We can forget about the soldiers—as soldiers, that is. They won't hurt anyone. Robots can't."

"I know that," Kathryn snapped.

"The problem is what to do about Trumie's drain on the world's resources." Garrick pursed his lips. "According to my directive from Area Control, the first plan was to let him alone—there is still plenty of everything for anyone, so why not let Trumie enjoy himself? But that didn't work out too well."

"Didn't work out too well," repeated Kathryn Pender bitterly.

"No, no—not on your local level," Garrick explained quickly. "After all, what are a few thousand robots, a few hundred million dollars' worth of equipment? We could resupply this area in a week."

"And in a week," said Roosenburg, "Trumie would have us cleaned out again!"

"*That's* the trouble," Garrick declared. "He doesn't seem to have a stopping point. Yet we can't *refuse* his orders. Speaking as a psychist, that would set a very bad precedent. It would put ideas in the minds of a lot of persons—minds that, in some cases, might not prove stable in the absence of a completely reliable source of everything they need, on request. If we say no to Trumie, we open the door on some mighty dark corners of the human mind. Covetousness. Greed. Pride of possession—"

"So what are you going to do?" demanded Kathryn Pender.

Garrick said resentfully, "The only thing there is to do. I'm going to look over Trumie's file again. And then I'm going to North Guardian Island."

"I'll go with you," said the girl. Garrick hesitated.

"You could be very useful," he admitted, "but the danger—"

"I'll go," she said, and that was that.

V

Roger Garrick was all too aware of the fact that he was only twenty-four. But his age couldn't make a great deal of difference. The oldest and wisest psychist in Area Control's wide sphere might have been doubtful of success in as thorny a job as the one ahead.

He and Kathryn Pender warily started out at daybreak. Vapor was rising from the sea about them, and the little battery motor of their launch whined softly beneath the keelson. Garrick sat patting the little box that contained their invasion equipment, while the girl steered.

The workshops of Fisherman's Island had been all night making some of the things in that box—not because they were so difficult to make, but because it had been a bad night. Big things were going on at North Guardian; twice, the power had been out entirely for an hour, while the demand on the lines from North Guardian took all the power the system could deliver.

The Sun was well up as they came within hailing distance of the Navy Yard.

Robots were hard at work; the Yard was bustling with activity. An overhead traveling crane, eight feet tall, laboriously lowered a prefabricated fighting top onto an eleven-foot aircraft carrier.

A motor torpedo boat—full-sized, this one was, not to scale—rocked at anchor just before the bow of their launch. Kathryn steered around it, ignoring the hail from the robot lieutenant-j.g. at its rail.

She glanced at Garrick over her shoulder, her face taut. "It's—it's all mixed up."

Garrick nodded. The battleships were model-sized, the small boats full-scale. In the city beyond the Yard, the pinnacle of the Empire State Building barely cleared the Pentagon, right next door. A soaring suspension bridge leaped out from the shore a quarter of a mile away and stopped short a thousand yards out, over empty water.

It was easy to understand—even for a psychist just out of school, on his first real assignment. Trumie was trying to run a world singlehanded, and where there were gaps in his conception of what his world should be, the results showed.

"Get me battleships!" he ordered his robot supply clerks, and they found the only battleships there were in the world to copy, the child-sized, toy-scaled play battleships that still delighted kids.

"Get me an Air Force!" And a thousand model bombers were hastily put together.

"Build me a bridge!" But perhaps he had forgotten to say to where.

Garrick shook his head and focused on the world around him. Kathryn Pender was standing on a gray steel stage, the mooring line from their launch secured to what looked like a coast-defense cannon—but only about four feet long. Garrick picked up the little box and leaped up to the stage beside her. She turned to look at the city.

"Hold on a second." He was opening the box, taking out two little cardboard placards. He turned her by the shoulder and, with pins from the box, attached one of the cards to her back. "Now me," he said, turning his back to her.

She read the placard dubiously.

```
    I
  AM A
  SPY!
```

"Garrick," she said, "you're sure you know what you're doing?"

"I'm not a bit sure," he said fretfully, "but in order to deal with him I have to get close to him, and in order to get close to him I have to play in his game. *We* have to. So put it on!" She shrugged and pinned it to the back of his jacket.

Side by side, they entered the citadel of the enemy.

According to the fisherman robot, Trumie lived in a gingerbread castle south of the Pentagon. Most of the robots got no chance to enter it. The city outside the castle was Trumie's kingdom, and he roamed about it, overseeing, changing, destroying, rebuilding. But inside the castle was his Private Place; the only robots that had both an inside- and outside-the-castle existence were the two bodyguards of his youth, Davey Crockett and Long John Silver.

"That," said Garrick, "must be the Private Place."

It was decidedly a gingerbread castle. The "gingerbread" was stonework, gargoyles and columns; there were a moat and a drawbridge, and there were robot guards with crooked little rifles, wearing scarlet tunics and fur shakos three feet tall. The drawbridge was up and the guards stood at stiff attention.

"Let's reconnoiter," said Garrick. He was unpleasantly conscious of the fact that every robot they passed—and they had passed thousands—had turned to look at the signs on their backs.

Yet the plan was going right, wasn't it? There was no hope of avoiding observation in any event. The only hope was to fit somehow into the pattern—and spies would certainly be a part of the military pattern.

Wouldn't they?

Garrick turned his back on doubts and led the way around the gingerbread palace.

The only entrance was the drawbridge.

They stopped out of sight of the ramrod-stiff guards. Garrick said: "We'll go in. As soon as we can get close to him, you find some way to get into your costume." He handed her the box that Roosenburg had—oh, so dubiously—provided. "You know what to do after that. All you have to do is keep him quiet for a while and let me talk to him."

"Garrick, will this work?"

Garrick exploded: "How the devil do I know? I had Trumie's dossier to work with. I know everything that happened to him when he was a kid—when this trouble started. But to reach him takes a long time, Kathryn. And we don't have a long time. So—"

He took her elbow and marched her toward the guards. "So you know what to do," he said.

"I hope so," breathed Kathryn Pender, looking very small and very young.

They marched down the wide white pavement, past the motionless guards—

Something was coming toward them. Kathryn held back.

"Come on!" Garrick muttered.

"No, look!" she whispered. "Is that—is that Trumie?"

He looked, then stared.

It was Trumie, larger than life. It was Anderson Trumie, the entire human population of the most-congested-island-for-its-population in the world. On one side of him was a tall dark figure, on the other side a squat dark figure, helping him along. His face was a horror, drowned in fat. The bloated cheeks shook damply, wet with tears. The eyes squinted out with fright on the world he had made.

Trumie and his bodyguards rolled up to them and past. And then Anderson Trumie stopped.

He turned the blubbery head and read the sign on the back of the girl. I AM A SPY. Panting heavily, clutching the shoulder of the Crockett robot, he gaped wildly at her.

Garrick cleared his throat. This far his plan had gone, and then there was a gap. There had to be a gap. Trumie's history, in the folder that Roosenburg had supplied, had told him what to do with Trumie; and Garrick's own ingenuity had told him how to reach the man. But a link was missing. Here was the subject, and here was the psychist who could cure him, and it was up to Garrick to start the cure.

Trumie cried out in a staccato bleat: "You! What are you? Where do you belong?"

He was talking to the girl. Beside him, the Crockett robot murmured: "Reckon it's a spy, Mistuh Trumie. See thet sign a-hangin' on its back?"

"Spy? Spy?" The quivering lips pouted. "Curse you, are you Mata Hari? What are you doing out here? It's changed its face," Trumie complained to the Crockett robot. "It doesn't belong here. It's supposed to be in the harem. Go on, Crockett, put it back!"

"Wait!" said Garrick, but the Crockett robot was ahead of him. It took Kathryn Pender by the arm.

"Come along thar," it said soothingly, and urged her across the drawbridge. She glanced back at Garrick, and for a moment it looked as though she were going to speak. Then she shook her head, as if giving an order.

"Kathryn!" yelled Garrick. "Trumie, wait a minute! That isn't Mata Hari!"

No one was listening. Kathryn Pender disappeared into the Private Place. Trumie, leaning heavily on the hobbling Long John Silver robot, followed.

Garrick, coming back to life, leaped after them.

The scarlet-coated guards jumped before him, their shakos bobbing precariously, their twisty little rifles crossed to bar his way.

What an indignity! He ordered: "One side! Get out of my way! I'm a human, can't you see that? You've got to let me pass!"

They didn't even look at him. Trying to get by them was like trying to walk through a wall of moving, thrusting steel. He shoved, and they pushed him back. He tried to dodge, and they were before him.

But robots did not act like that! It made nonsense of his

plan, and it meant terrible danger for Kathryn Pender. He could not leave her to carry out the fragile scheme by herself! He tried once more to break through, and once more was stopped by the silent, thrusting robot bodies that interposed themselves.

It was hopeless.

And then it was hopeless indeed, because the drawbridge had gone up. The entrance was out of reach.

VI

Sonny Trumie collapsed into a chair like a mound of blubber falling to the deck of a whaler.

Though he made no signal, the procession of serving robots started at once. In minced the maitre d', bowing and waving its graceful hands. In marched the sommelier, clanking its necklace of keys, bearing its wines in their buckets of ice. In came the lovely waitress robots and the sturdy steward robots, with the platters and tureens, the plates and bowls and cups.

They spread a meal—a dozen meals—before him, and he began to eat.

He ate as a penned pig eats, gobbling until it chokes, forcing the food down because there is nothing to do *but* eat. He ate, with a sighing accompaniment of moans and gasps, and some of the food was salted with the tears of pain he wept into it, and some of the wine was spilled by his shaking hand. But he ate. Not for the first time that day, and not for the tenth.

Sonny Trumie wept as he ate. He no longer even knew he was weeping. There was the gaping void inside him that he had to fill, had to fill; there was the gaping world about him that he had to people and build and furnish . . . and *use*.

He moaned to himself. Four hundred pounds of meat and lard, and he had to lug it from end to end of his island, every hour of the day, never resting, never at peace! There should have been a place somewhere, there should have been a time, when he could rest. When he could sleep without dreaming, sleep without waking after a few scant hours with the goading drive to eat and to use, to use and to eat. . . .

And it was all so *wrong!*

The robots didn't understand. They didn't try to understand; they didn't think for themselves. Let him take his eyes from any one of them for a single day and everything went *wrong.* It was necessary to keep after them, from end to end of the island, checking and overseeing and ordering—yes, and destroying to rebuild, over and over!

He moaned again and pushed the plate away.

He rested, with his tallow forehead flat against the table, waiting, while inside him the pain ripped and ripped, and finally became bearable again. And slowly he pushed himself up, and rested for a moment, and pulled a fresh plate toward him, and began again to eat.

After a while, he stopped. Not because he didn't want to go on, but because he absolutely couldn't.

He was bone-tired, but something was bothering him— one more detail to check, one more thing that was *wrong.* Mata Hari. The houri at the drawbridge. It shouldn't have been out of the Private Place. It should have been in the harem, of course. Not that it mattered, except to Sonny Trumie's never-resting sense of what was right.

Time was when the houris of the harem had their uses, but that time was long and long ago; now they were property, to be fussed over and made to be *right,* to be replaced if they were worn, destroyed if they were *wrong.*

But only property, as all of North Guardian was property—as all of the world would be his property, if only he could manage it.

But property shouldn't be *wrong*.

He signaled to the Crockett robot and, leaning on it, walked down the long terrazzo hall toward the harem. He tried to remember what the houri had looked like. The face didn't matter; he was nearly sure it had changed it. It had worn a sheer red blouse and a brief red skirt, he was almost certain, but the face—

It had had a face, of course. But Sonny had lost the habit of faces. This one had been somehow different, but he couldn't remember just why. Still—the blouse and skirt were red, he was nearly sure. And it had been carrying something in a box. And that was odd, too.

He waddled a little faster, for now he was positive it was *wrong*.

"Thar's the harem, Mistuh Trumie," said the robot at his side. It disengaged itself gently, leaped forward and held the door to the harem for him.

"Wait for me," Sonny commanded, and waddled forward into the harem halls.

Once he had so arranged the harem that he needed no help to get around inside it; the halls were railed, at a height where it was easy for a pudgy hand to grasp the rail; the distances were short, the rooms close together.

He paused and called over his shoulder: "Stay where you can hear me." It had occurred to him that if the houri robot was *wrong,* he would need Crockett's guns to make it right.

A chorus of female voices sprang into song as he entered the main patio. They were a bevy of beauties, clustered around a fountain, diaphanously dressed, languorously glancing at Sonny Trumie as he waddled inside.

"Shut up!" he shrieked. "Go back to your rooms!"

They bowed their heads and, one by one, slipped into the cubicles.

No sign of the red blouse and the red skirt. He began the rounds of the cubicles, panting, peering into them.

"Hello, Sonny," whispered Theda Bara, lithe on a leopard rug, and he passed on. "I love you!" cried Nell Gwynn, and "Come to me!" commanded Cleopatra, but he passed them by. He passed Du Barry and Marilyn Monroe, he passed Moll Flanders and he passed Troy's Helen. No sign of the houri in red—

Yes, there was. He didn't see the houri, but he saw the signs of the houri's presence: the red blouse and the red skirt, lying limp and empty on the floor.

Sonny gasped: "Where are you? Come out here where I can see you!"

Nobody answered Sonny.

"Come out!" he bawled.

And then he stopped. A door opened and someone came out; not an houri, not female; a figure without sex but loaded with love, a teddy-bear figure, as tall as pudgy Sonny Trumie himself, waddling as he waddled, its stubby welcoming arms stretched out to him.

He could hardly believe his eyes. Its color was a little darker than Teddy. It was a good deal taller than Teddy. But unquestionably, undoubtedly, in everything that mattered, it was—

"Teddy," whispered Sonny Trumie, and let the furry arms go around his four hundred pounds.

Twenty years disappeared. "They wouldn't let me have you," Sonny told the teddy bear.

It said, in a voice musical and warm: "It's all right, Sonny. You can have me now, Sonny. You can have everything, Sonny."

"They took you away," he whispered, remembering.

They took the teddy bear away; he had never forgotten.

They took it away and Mother was wild and Father was furious. They raged at the little boy and scolded him and threatened him. Didn't he know they were *poor,* and Did he want to ruin them all, and What was wrong with him, anyway, that he wanted his little sister's silly stuffed robots when he was big enough to use nearly grown-up goods?

The night had been a terror, with the frowning, sad robots ringed around, and the little girl crying; and what had made it terror was not the scolding—he'd had scoldings—but the *worry,* the *fear* and almost the *panic* in his parents' voices. For what he did, he came to understand, was no longer a childish sin. It was a *big* sin, a failure to consume his quota—

And it had to be punished.

The first punishment was the extra birthday party.

The second was—shame.

Sonny Trumie, not quite twelve, was made to feel shame and humiliation. Shame is only a little thing, but it makes the victim of it little, too.

Shame.

The robots were reset to scorn him. He woke to mockery and went to bed with contempt. Even his little sister lisped the catalog of his failures.

You aren't trying, Sonny, and You don't care, Sonny, and You're a terrible disappointment to us, Sonny.

And finally all the things were true, because Sonny at twelve was what his elders made him.

And they made him . . . "neurotic" is the term; a pretty-sounding word that means ugly things like fear and worry and endless self-reproach. . . .

"Don't worry," whispered the Teddy. "Don't worry, Sonny. You can have me. You can have what you want. You don't have to have anything else."

VII

There had to be some other entrance to Anderson Trumie's inner lair and there was, but it took Garrick an hour to find it. An hour of worry and fury, and then he raged like a tiger through the halls of the Private Place. "Kathryn!" he shouted. "Kathryn Pender!"

The place was the playroom for a child. A demented child! Quarter-size model cars spun underfoot, tiny model aircraft hissed or droned past his ears. He batted them out of the way, shouting Kathryn's name. The robots peeped out at him worriedly and sometimes they got in his way and he bowled them aside. Inside the Private Place the orders that had made them form a wall against him no longer applied. They didn't fight back, naturally—what robot would hurt a human, or even inconvenience him without the most urgent of commands? But sometimes they spoke to him, pleading, for it was not according to the wishes of Mr. Trumie that anyone but him rage destroying through North Guardian Island. Garrick passed them by.

"Kathryn!" he called. "Kathryn!"

He told himself fiercely: Trumie was *not* physically dangerous. Trumie was laid bare in the data profile that Roosenburg had supplied, and he couldn't be blamed; he meant no harm. He had once been a little boy who was trying to be good by consuming, consuming, and he wore himself into neurosis doing it; and then they changed the rules on him. End of the ration, end of forced consumption, as the robots took over for mankind at the other end of the farm-and-factory cornucopia. It wasn't necessary to struggle to consume, so the rules were changed.

And maybe Trumie knew that the rules had been

changed, but Sonny didn't. It was Sonny, the little boy trying to be good, who had made North Guardian Island. And it was Sonny who owned the Private Place and all it held—including Kathryn Pender.

Garrick called hoarsely: "Kathryn! If you hear me, *answer me!*"

It had seemed so simple. The fulcrum on which the weight of Trumie's neurosis might move was a teddy bear. Give him a teddy bear—or, perhaps, a teddy-bear suit, made by night in the factories of Fisherman's Island, with a girl named Kathryn Pender inside—and let him hear, from a source he could trust, the welcome news that it was no longer necessary to struggle, that compulsive consumption could have an end. Then Garrick or any other psychist would clear it all up, but only if Trumie would listen.

"Kathryn!" roared Roger Garrick, racing through a room of mirrors and carved statues. Because, just in case Trumie didn't listen, just in case the folder was wrong and Teddy wasn't the key—

Why, then, Teddy to Trumie would be only a robot. And Trumie destroyed them by the score.

"Kathryn!" bellowed Roger Garrick, trotting through the silent palace, and at last he heard what might have been an answer. At least it was a voice—a girl's voice, at that. He was before a passage that led to a room with a fountain and silent female robots, standing and watching him. The voice came from a small room. He ran to the door.

It was the right door.

There was Trumie, four hundred pounds of lard, lying on a marble bench with a foam-rubber cushion, the jowled head in the small lap of—

Teddy. Or Kathryn Pender in the teddy-bear suit, the sticklike legs pointed straight out, the sticklike arms clumsily patting him. She was talking to him, gently and reassuringly. She was telling him what he needed to know—that he had eaten *enough,* that he had used *enough,* that he had consumed *enough* to win the respect of all, and an end to consuming.

The six years of technical training as a psychist were matched by simple understanding and human compassion. Garrick himself could not have done better.

It was a sight from Mother Goose, the child being soothed by his toy. But it was not a sight that fitted in well with its surroundings, for the seraglio was upholstered in mauve and pink, and the paintings that hung about were wicked.

Sonny Trumie rolled the pendulous head and looked squarely at Garrick. The worry was gone from the fear-filled little eyes.

Garrick stepped back.

No need for him just at this moment. Let Trumie relax for a while, as he had not been able to relax for a score of years. Then the psychist could pick up where the girl had been unable to proceed, but in the meantime, Trumie was finally at rest.

The Teddy looked up at Garrick and in its bright blue eyes, the eyes that belonged to the girl named Kathryn, he saw a queer tincture of triumph and compassion.

Garrick nodded, and left, and went out to the robots of North Guardian and started them clearing away the monstrous child's-eye conception of an empire.

Sonny Trumie nestled his head in the lap of the teddy bear. It was talking to him nicely, so nicely. It was droning away: "Don't worry, Sonny. Don't worry. Everything's all right. Everything's all right." Why, it was almost as though it were real.

It had been, he calculated with the part of his mind that was razor-sharp and never relaxed, nearly two hours since he had eaten. Two hours! And he felt as though he could go another hour at least, maybe two. Maybe—maybe even not eat at all again that day. Maybe even learn to live on three meals. Perhaps two. Perhaps—

He wriggled—as well as four hundred greasy pounds can wriggle—and pressed against the soft warm fur of the teddy bear. It was so soothing.

"You don't have to eat so much, Sonny. You don't have to drink so much. No one will mind. Your father won't mind, Sonny. Your mother won't mind . . ."

It was very comfortable to hear the teddy bear telling him those things. It made him drowsy. So deliciously drowsy! It wasn't like going to sleep, as Sonny Trumie had known going to sleep for a dozen or more years, the bitterly fought surrender to the anesthetic weariness. It was just drowsy.

And he did want to go to sleep.

And finally he slept. All of him. Not just the four hundred pounds of blubber and the little tormented eyes, but even the razor-sharp-mind Trumie that lived in the sad, obedient hulk.

It slept as it had not slept all these twenty years.

5

THE FARMER ON THE DOLE

Limitless energy eased the grinding pain of human poverty and the psychists healed humanity's inner woes. But there was still pain in the world. It simply took newer forms. As humans began to forget suffering, others began to learn.

Zeb was learning, as he stared about. Stretching east to the horizon, a thousand acres, was all soybeans; across the road to the west, another thousand acres, all corn. Zeb kicked the irrigation valve moodily and watched the meter register the change in flow. Dem weather! Why didn't it rain? He trudged down between the rows, lifting a leaf with the toe of his boot to peer under it for bugs, snapping a bean off the stalk to judge its nearing ripeness. As he straightened and mopped his brow he was hailed from the cornfield across the road: "Evenin', Zeb."

Zeb tucked the bandanna back in his hip pocket before he nodded to his neighbor. "Evenin', Wally," he said. He didn't go beyond that. He had nothing against the other farmer, but Wally was corn and Zeb was soy and they didn't, really, have that much in common. So it bothered Zeb, some, that as he turned to walk down the clear stretch along the irrigation pipes Wally paced him, silently watching him from the other side of the road.

It made Zeb nervous. He turned away and bent down to scoop up a clod of soil. He crumbled it thoughtfully between his fingers, eyes closed. Then he raised it to his nose and then to his mouth.

"How's it look, Zeb?" Wally called. His voice was a little thin, as though he was nervous too.

Zeb stood up, crunching the soil for a moment between his teeth before depositing it in his palm and dropping it back onto the ground. "Cobalt's a tetch low," he said, "and, 'course, it's runnin' pretty dry. Seems like you no sooner run some water in than it steams right out again. Probably got to rise up the flow, oh, I'd say another eighteen hundred liters a day."

"Same thing in the corn," Wally declared, leaning on the fence. Since he weighed nearly two hundred kilos, the bobwire sagged under him. He raised his head and sniffed the air. "Good CO_2, though. S'pose we'll get good carbon fixing."

Zeb nodded, looking carefully at his neighbor. They did not know each other very well. They met, of course, at the hoedowns and revival meetings, and they naturally went caroling together at Christmas, and trick-or-treating with the little ones at Halloween—that sort of thing—but corn didn't usually get *close* with soy. Wasn't natural.

But, this time, corn seemed to want to. "All right, then," Zeb said, "you got suthin' on your mind, Wally. Out with it!"

Pause. "You ain't heard nothin'?"

"'Bout what?"

"'Bout—oh, anythin', you know?"

Zeb said steadily, "You mean I ain't heard no dumb gossip that says they're gone close down the farms, when everybody knows they can't never do that? That what you mean?"

Wally scowled without answering, and Zeb went on. "'Cause if that's what you mean, no, I ain't. Not to pay attention to, anyway. An' another thing I ain't, I ain't got

time to spend makin' no sense. Becky 'spects me back in
the lines come sundown an' Boss wants it that way too. I
ain't knowin'," he added virtuously, "if it's the same way
with you corn folks, but soy people likes to do what Boss
wants them to do." Zeb rubbed the back of his hand
across his brow and frowned at it as it came away damp.
"All this wet in the air you'd think it'd rain," he complained, changing the subject to take the sting out of his
words, because Zeb's kind of farmer was created to be
considerate of others.

Wally's kind, apparently, was not. His face worked angrily. "Uncle Tin," he sneered, turned his back and
marched away.

Zeb pulled the bandanna out of his pocket and mopped
his brow again as he watched the other go. He was troubled. Something was surely up. Wally was acting funny,
and he wasn't the only one. Some of the soy people were
gossiping direly to each other these days, too.

But the thing was impossible, Lord knew it was! and he
had other things to worry about. He inspected the bandanna, found it damp, and then, to make sure, opened his
mouth and stuck his tongue out, eyes half closed. It was as
he thought. "Dem near eighty-five per cent relative hu-
midity," he muttered to himself, "an' yet it doan rain.
Lord sakes ifn I know what this year weather's comin'
to!" He jabbed the bandanna back into his pocket and
turned for home.

Long before he reached the lines his forehead was glistening again. It wasn't sweat. Zeb never sweat. His
arms, his back, his armpits were permanently dry, in any
weather, no matter how hard or how long he worked. The
moisture was condensed from the air. The insulation
around the supercooled junctions that made up his brain
was good, but it wasn't perfect. When he was doing more
thinking than he really needed to do, the refrigeration units

worked harder. When he got to his cabin and Becky came to greet him she saw the beads of moisture at once, and felt them, too. She pulled her cheek away from his. "Zeb! You been worritin' yourself again!" she accused.

He didn't deny it. He didn't speak at all, but their eyes met, and he saw that her brow was damp, too.

And it was all so dumb. The way the world was made, what did they have to worry about? They did their jobs. They tilled the fields, and planted them, and brought in the crop; or else they cleaned and cooked in Boss's house, or they taught Boss's children or audited Boss's accounts or drove Mrs. Boss when she went to visit the other bosses' wives. That was the way things were. That was the way things always had been and always would be. It would go on forever.

Wouldn't it?

Zeb found out the answer the next morning, right after church.

Since Zeb was a Class A robot, with an effective IQ of 135—though limited in its expression by the built-in constraints of his assigned function—he really should not have been surprised. Especially when he discovered that Reverend Harmswallow had taken his text that morning from the Book of Matthew, specifically the Beatitudes, and in particular the one about how the meek would inherit the Earth. The reverend was a plump, pink-faced man whose best subject was the wages of sin and the certainty of hellfire. It had always been a disappointment to him that the farmhands who made up the congregation rarely possessed the necessary accessories to sin in any interesting ways. He made it up by bearing down on the importance of being humble. "Even," he finished, his baby-fine hair flying all around his pink scalp, "when things don't go the way you think they ought to. Now we're going to sing 'Old One Hundred,' and then you soy people will meet in the gymnasium and corn people in the second-floor lounge. Your bosses have some news for you."

So it shouldn't have been surprising, and as a matter of fact Zeb wasn't surprised at all. Some part of the cryo-circuits inside his titanium skull had long noted the portents. Scant rain. Falling levels of soil minerals. Thinning of the topsoil. The beans grew fat, because there was an abundance of carbon in the air for them to metabolize, but no matter how much you irrigated, they dried up fast in the hot breezes. And those were only the physical signs. Boss's body language said more, sighing when he should have been smiling at the three-legged races behind the big house, not even noticing when one of the cabins needed a new coat of whitewash or the flower patches showed a few weeds. Zeb observed it all and drew the proper conclusions. His constraints did not forbid that, they only prevented him from speaking of them. Or even of thinking of them on a conscious level. Zeb was not programmed to worry. It would have interfered with the happy, smiling face he bore for Boss, and Miz Boss and The Chillen.

So, when Boss made his announcement, Zeb looked as thunderstruck as all the other hands. "You've been really good people," Boss said generously, his pale, professorial face incongruous under the plantation straw hat. "I really wish things could go on just as they always have, but it just isn't possible. It's the agricultural support program," he explained. "Those idiots in Washington have cut it down to the point where it simply isn't worthwhile to plant here any more." His expression brightened. "But it's not all bad! You'll be glad to know that they've expanded the soil-bank program as a consequence, so Miz Boss and the children and I are well provided for. As a matter of fact," he beamed, "we'll be a little better off than before, moneywise."

"Dat's good!" "Oh, hebben be praised!" The doleful expressions broke into grins as the farmhands nudged each other, relieved. But then Zeb spoke up. "Boss? 'Scuse my askin', but what's gone happen to us folks? You gonna keep us on?"

Boss looked irritated. "Oh, that's impossible. We can't collect the soil-bank money if we plant, so there's just no sense in having all of you around, don't you see? We just don't need you now."

Silence. Then another farmhand ventured, "How 'bou: Cornpatch Boss, he need some good workers? You know us hates corn, but we could get reprogrammed quick's anything—"

Boss shook his head. "He's telling his people the same thing right now. Nobody needs you," he explained.

The farmhands looked at each other. "Preacher, he needs us," one of them offered. "We's his whole congregation."

"I'm afraid even Reverend Harmswallow doesn't need you any more," Boss said kindly, "because he's been wanting to go into missionary work for some time, and he's just received his call. No. You're just superfluous, that's all."

"S'perfluous?"

"Redundant. Unnecessary. There's no reason for you to be here," Boss explained. "So trucks will come in the morning to take you all away. Please be outside your cabins, ready to go, by oh-seven-hundred."

Silence again, then Zeb: "Where they takes us, Boss?"

Boss shrugged. "There's probably some place, I think." Then he grinned. "But I've got a surprise for you! Miz Boss and I aren't going to just let you go without a party. So tonight we're going to have a good old-fashioned midwestern square dance, with a new bandanna for the best dancers, and then you're all going to come back of the big house and sing spirituals for us—and I promise Miz Boss and the children and I are going to be right there to enjoy it!"

The place they were taken to was a grimy white cinder-block building in Des Plaines. The driver of the truck was a beefy, taciturn robot who wore a visored cap and a leather jacket with the sleeves cut off; he hadn't answered any of their questions when they loaded onto his truck at the farm, and answered none when they off-loaded in front of a steel-link gate with a sign that said RECEIVING. "Just stand over there," he ordered. "You all out? Okay." And he slapped the tailboard up and drove off, leaving them in a gritty, misty sprinkle of warm rain.

And they waited, fourteen prime working robots, hes and shes and three little ones, too dispirited to talk much. Zeb wiped the moisture off his face and muttered, "Couldn've rained down where we needed it. Has to rain up here when it doan do a body no good a-tall." But not all the moisture was rain; not Zeb's and not that on the faces of the others, because they were all thinking really hard. The only one not despairing was Lem, the most recent arrival. Lem had been an estate gardener in Urbana until his people decided to emigrate to the oneill space colonies. He'd been lucky to catch on at the farm when a turned-over tractor created an unexpected vacancy, but he still talked wistfully about life in glamorous Champaign-Urbana. Now he was excited. "Des Plaines! Why, that's practically Chicago! The big time, friends. State Street! The loop! The Gold Coast!"

"They gone have jobs for us'n in Chicago?" Zeb asked doubtfully.

"Jobs? Why, man, who cares 'bout jobs? That's Chicago! We'll just have a ball!"

Zeb nodded thoughtfully. Although he was not convinced, he was willing to be hopeful—that was part of his programming, too. He opened his mouth and tasted the drizzle. He made a face: sour, high in particulate matter, a lot more sulfur dioxide and NO_2 than he was used to; what kind of a place was this, where even the rain didn't taste good? So all the optimism had faded by the time signs of activity appeared in the cinder-block building. Cars drove in through another entrance. Lights went on inside. And, after a while, the corrugated-metal doorway slid noisily up and a short, dark robot came out to unlock the chain-link gate. He looked the farmers over impassively, then opened the gate. "Come on, you redundancies," he said. "Let's get you reprogrammed."

When it came Zeb's turn he was allowed into a white-walled room with an ominous sort of plastic-topped cot along the wall. The RRR, or redundancy reprogramming redirector, assigned to him was a blond, good-looking she-robot who wore crystal earrings like tiny chandeliers, long enough to brush against the collar of her white coat. She sat Zeb on the edge of the cot, motioned him to lean forward and quickly inserted the red-painted fingernail of her right forefinger into his left ear. He quivered as the read-only memory emptied itself into her own internal scanners, though it didn't hurt. She nodded. "You've got a simple profile," she said cheerfully. "We'll have you out of here in no time. Open your shirt." Zeb's soil-grimed fingers slowly unbuttoned the flannel shirt; before he got to the last button she impatiently pushed his hands aside and pulled it wide. The button popped and rolled away. "You'll have to get new clothes anyway," she said, sinking long scarlet nails into four narrow slits on each side of his rib cage. The whole front of his chest came free in her hands. The RRR laid it aside and peered at the hookup inside.

She nodded again. "No problem," she said, pulling chips out with quick, sure fingers. "Now, this will feel funny for a minute and you won't be able to talk, but just hold still." Funny! It felt to Zeb as though the bare room were swirling into spirals, and he not only couldn't speak, he couldn't remember words. Or thoughts! He was nearly sure that just a moment before he had been dismally wondering if he would ever again see the— The what? He couldn't remember.

Then he felt a gentle sensation of something within him being united to something else, not so much a click as the feeling of a foot fitting into a shoe, and he was able to complete the question. The *farm*. He found he had said the words out loud, and the RRR laughed. "See? You're half re-oriented already."

He grinned back. "That's really astonishing," he declared. "Can you credit it, I was almost missing that rural existence! As though the charms of bucolic life had any meaning for— Good heavens! Why am I talking like this?"

The she-robot said, "Well, you wouldn't want to talk like a farmhand when you live in the big city, would you?"

"Oh, granted!" Zeb cried earnestly. "But one must pose the next question: The formalisms of textual grammar, the imagery of poetics, can one deem them appropriate to my putative new career?"

The RRR frowned. "It's a literary-critic vocabulary store," she said defensively. "Look, somebody has to use them up!"

"But, one asks, why me?"

"It's all I've got handy, and that's that. Now. You'll find there are other changes, too. I'm taking out the quantitative soil-analysis chips, and the farm-machinery subroutines. I could leave you the spirituals and the square-dancing, if you like."

"Why retain the shadow when the substance has fled?" he said bitterly.

"Now, Zeb," she scolded. "You don't need this specialized stuff. That's all behind you, and you'll never miss it because you don't know yet what great things you're getting in exchange." She snapped his chest back in place and ordered, "Give me your hands."

"One could wish for specifics," he grumbled, watching suspiciously as the RRR fed his hands into a hole in her control console. He felt a tickling sensation.

"Why not? Infra-red vision, for one thing," she said proudly, watching the digital readouts on her console, "so you can see in the dark. Plus a twenty-per-cent-hotter circuit breaker in your motor assemblies, so you'll be stronger and can run faster. Plus the names and addresses and phone numbers of six good bail bondsmen and the Public Defender!" She pulled his hands out of the machine and nodded toward them. The grime was out of the pores, the soil from under the fingernails, the calluses smoothed away. They were city hands now, the hands of someone who had never done manual labor in his life.

"And for what destiny is this new armorarium required?" Zeb asked.

"For your new work. It's the only vacancy we've got right now, but it's good work. And steady! You're going to be a mugger."

After his first night on the job Zeb was amused at his own apprehensions. The farm had been nothing like this!

He was assigned to a weasel-faced he-robot named Timothy for on-the-job training, and Timothy took the term literally. "Come on, kid," he said as soon as Zeb came to the anteroom where he was waiting; and headed out the door. He didn't wait to see whether Zeb was following, and he certainly didn't explain what they were going to do. Zeb had to hurry to catch up as they went out through the front door—no chain-link gates now. He had only the vaguest notion of how far Chicago was, or in which direction, but he was pretty sure that it wasn't something you walked. "Are we going to entrust ourselves to the iron horse?" he asked, with a little tingle of anticipation. Trains had seemed very glamorous as they went by the farm—produce trains, freight trains, passenger trains that set a farmhand to wondering where they might be going and what it might be like to get there. Timothy didn't answer. He gave Zeb a look that mixed pity and annoyance and contempt as he planted himself in the street and raised a peremptory hand. A huge green-and-white checkered hovercab dug down its braking wheels and screeched to a stop in front of them. Timothy motioned him in, and sat silently next to him while the driver whooshed down the Kennedy Expressway, and the sights of the suburbs of the city flashed past Zeb's fascinated eyes. They drew up under the marquee of a splashy, bright hotel, with handsome couples in expensive clothing strolling in and out. When Timothy threw the taxi driver a bill, Zeb observed that he did not wait for change.

Timothy did not seem in enough of a hurry to justify the expense of a cab. He stood rocking on his toes under the marquee for a moment, beaming benignly at the robot tourists. Then he gave Zeb a quick look, turned and walked away.

Once again Zeb had to be fast to keep up. He turned the corner after Timothy almost too late to catch the action. The weasel-faced robot had backed a well-dressed couple into the shadows, and he was relieving them of wallet, watches and rings. When he had it all, he faced them to the wall, kicked each of them expertly behind a knee joint and, as they fell, turned and ran, soundless in soft-soled shoes, back to the bright lights. He was fast and he was abrupt, but by this time Zeb had begun to recognize some of the elements of his style. He was ready. He was following on Timothy's heels before the robbed couple had begun to scream. Past the marquee, lost in a crowd in front of a theater, Timothy slowed down and looked at Zeb approvingly. "Good reflexes," he complimented. "You got the right kind of class, kid. You'll make out."

"As a soi-disant common cutpurse?" Zeb asked, somewhat nettled at the other robot's peremptory manner.

Timothy looked him over carefully. "You talk funny," he said. "They stick you with one of those surplus vocabularies again? Never mind. You see how it's done?"

Zeb hesitated, craning his neck to look for pursuit, of which there seemed to be none. "Well, one might venture that that is correct," he said.

"Okay. Now you do it," Timothy said cheerfully, and steered him into the alley for the hotel tourist-trap's stage door.

By midnight Zeb had committed five felonies of his own, been an accomplice at two more and watched the smaller robot commit eight single-handed, and the two muggers were dividing their gains in the darkest corner—not very dark—of an all-night McDonald's on North Michigan Avenue. "You done good, kid," Timothy admitted expansively. "For a green kid, anyway. Let's see. Your share comes to six watches, eight pieces of jewelry, counting that fake coral necklace you shouldn't have bothered with, and looks like six-seven hundred in cash."

"As well as quite a few credit cards," Zeb said eagerly.

"Forget the credit cards. You only keep what you can spend or what doesn't have a name on it. Think you're ready to go out on your own?"

"One hesitates to assume such responsibility—"

"Because you're not, so forget it." The night's work

done, Timothy seemed to have become actually garrulous. "Bet you can't tell me why I wanted you backing me up those two times."

"One acknowledges a certain incomprehension," Zeb confessed. "There is an apparent dichotomy. When there were two victims or even three, you chose to savage them single-handed. Yet for solitary prey you elected to have an accomplice."

"Right! And you know why? You don't, so I'll tell you. You get a he and a she, or even two of each, and the he's going to think about keeping the she from getting hurt; that's the way the program reads. So no trouble. But those two hes by themselves—hell, if I'd gone up against either of those mothers he might've taken my knife away from me and picked my nose with it. You got to understand robot nature, kid. That's what the job is all about. Don't you want a Big Mac or something?"

Zeb shifted position uncomfortably. "I should think not, thank you," he said, but the other robot was looking at him knowingly.

"No food-tract subsystems, right?"

"Well, my dear Timothy, in the agricultural environment there was no evident need—"

"You don't *need* them now, but you ought to *have* them. Also liquid-intake tanks, and maybe an air-cycling system so you can smoke cigars. And get rid of that faggoty vocabulary they stuck you with. You're in a class occupation," he said earnestly, "and you got to live up to your station, right? No subway trains. No counting out the pennies when you get change—you don't *take* change. Now, you don't want to make trouble your first day on the job, so we'll let it go until you've finished a whole week. But then you go back to that bleached-blond Three-R and we'll get you straightened out," he promised. "Now let's go fence our jewels and call it a night."

All in all, Zeb was quite pleased with himself. By the third night, his pockets lined with big bills, practicing reading the menus as he loitered outside of fancy restaurants in order to be ready for action when he got his new attachments, he was looking forward to a career at least as distinguished as Timothy's own.

That was his third night on the Gold Coast.

He never got a chance at a fourth.

His last marks of the evening gave him a little argument about parting with a diamond ring, so, as taught, Zeb backhanded the he and snarled at the she, and maybe used a little more force than usual when he ripped the rings off her fingers. Two minutes later and three blocks away, he took a quick look at his loot under a streetlight. He recoiled in horror.

There was a drop of blood on the ring.

That victim had not been a robot. She had been a living true human female being; and when he heard all the police sirens in the world coming straight at him he was not in the least surprised.

"You people," said the rehab instructor, "have been admitted to this program because, *a,* you have been unemployed for not less than twenty-one months, *b,* have not fewer than six unexcused absences from your place of training or employment, *c,* have a conviction for a felony and are currently on parole or, *d,* are of a date of manufacture eighteen or more years past, choice of any of the above. That's what the regulations say, and what they mean," she said, warming to her work, "is, you're scum. 'Scum' is hopeless, shiftless, dangerous, a social liability. Do you all understand that much, at least?" She gazed angrily around the room with her seven students.

She was short, dumpy, redheaded, with a bad skin; why they let shes like this one off the production line Zeb could not understand. He fidgeted in his seat, craning his neck to see what his six fellow students were like, until her voice crackled at him: "You! With the yellow sweater! Zeb!"

He flinched. "Pardon me, madam?"

She said with gloomy satisfaction, "I know your type. You're a typical recidivist lumpenprole, you are. Can't even pay attention to somebody who's trying to help you when your whole future is at stake. What've I got, seven of you slugs? I can see what's coming. I guarantee two of you will drop out without finishing the course, and I'll have to fire two more because you skip classes or come in late—and the other three'll be back on the streets or in the slammer in ninety days. Why do I do it?" She shook her head and then, lifting herself ponderously, went to the blackboard and wrote her three commandments:

1. ON TIME
2. EVERY DAY
3. EVEN WHEN YOU DON'T WANT TO

She turned around, leaning on the back of her chair. "Those are your Golden Rules, you slugs. You'll obey them as God's commandments, and don't you forget it. You're here to learn how to be responsible, socially valuable creations, and—what?"

The skinny old he-robot in the seat next to Zeb was raising a trembling hand. It was easy to see how he qualified for the rehabilitation program. He was a thirty-year-old model at least, with ball-joints in the shoulders and almost no facial mobility at all. He quavered, "What if we just can't, teacher? I mean, like we've got a sudden cryogenic warmup and have to lie down, or haven't had a lube job, or—"

"You give me a pain," the instructor told him, nodding to show that pain was exactly what she had expected from

the likes of him. "Those are just typical excuses, and
they're not going to be accepted in this group. Now, if you
have something *really* wrong with you, what you have to
do is call up at least two hours before class and get yourself excused. Is that so hard to remember? But you won't
do it when push comes to shove, because you slugs never
do."

The ancient said obstinately, "Two hours is a pretty
long time. I can't always tell that far ahead, teacher."

"And don't call me teacher!" She turned back to the
board and wrote:

Dr. Elena Mincus, B.Sc., M.A., Ph.D.

"You can call me Dr. Mincus or you can call me
Ma'am. Now pay attention."

And Zeb did, because the ten nights in the county jail
before he got his hearing and his first-offender's parole
had convinced him he didn't want to go back there again.
The noise! The crowding! The brutality of the jailers!
There was nothing you could do about that, either, because some of them were human beings—maybe most of
them were; looked at in a certain way, there probably
wouldn't have even been a jail if some human beings
hadn't wanted to be jail guards, because what was the
sense of punishing a robot by locking him up?

So he paid attention. And kept on paying attention,
even when Dr. Mincus's lessons were about such irrele-
vant (to him) niceties of civilized employed persons' behavior as why you should always participate in an office
pool, how to stand in line for tickets to a concert and what
to do at a company Christmas party. Not all of his class-
mates were so well behaved. The little ancient next to him
gave very little trouble, being generally sunk in gloom,
but the two she-robots, the ones with the beaded hand-
bags and the miniskirts, richly deserved (Zeb thought) to

be the ones to fulfill Dr. Mincus's statistical predictions by being expelled from the course. The one with the green eye makeup snickered at almost everything the instructor said and made faces behind her back. The one with the black spit curl across her forehead gossiped with the other students, and dared to talk back to the teacher. Reprimanded for whispering, she said lazily, "Hell, lady, this whole thing's a shuck, ain't it? What are you doing it for?"

Dr. Mincus's voice trembled with indignation and with the satisfaction of someone who sees her gloomiest anticipations realized: "For what? Why, because I'm trained in psychiatric social work—and because it's what I want to do—and because I'm a *human being,* and don't any of you ever let that get out of your mind!"

The course had some real advantages, Zeb discovered when he was ordered back to the robot replacement depot for new fittings. The blond RRR muttered darkly to herself as she pulled pieces out of his chest and thrust others back. When he could talk again he thanked her, suddenly aware of the fact that now he had an appetite and even that she had muted the worst part of his over-dainty vocabulary. She pursed her lips and didn't answer while she clamped him up again.

But then he discovered, too, that it did not relieve him of his duties. "They think because you're *handicapped,*" the RRR smirked, "you're *forced* to get in trouble. So now you've got all this first-rate equipment, and if you want to know what I think, I think it's wasted. The bums in your class *always* revert to type," she told him, "and if you want to try to be the exception to the rule you're going to have to apply yourself when you're back on the job."

"Mugging?"

"What else are you fit for? Although," she added, pensively twisting the crystal that dangled from her right ear around a fingertip, "I did have an opening for a freshman English composition teacher, if I hadn't replaced your vocabulary unit—"

"No! I'll take mugging, please."

She shrugged. "Might as well. But you can't expect that good a territory again, you know—not after what you did!"

So, rain or dry, Zeb spent every six P.M. to midnight lurking around the old Robert Taylor Houses, relieving old shes of their rent money and old hes of whatever pitiful possessions were in their pockets. Once in a while he crossed to the Illinois Institute of Technology campus on the trail of some night-school student or professor, but he was always careful to ask them whether they were robot or live before he touched them. The next offense, he knew, would allow him no parole.

There was no free-spending taxi money from such pickings, but on nights when Zeb made his quota early he would sometimes take the bus to the Loop or the Gold Coast. Twice he saw Timothy, but the little robot, after one look of disgust, turned away. Now and then he would drift down to the Amalfi Amadeus Park along the lakefront, where green grass and hedges could almost be taken to resemble good old days in the soy fields, but the urge to chew samples of soil was too strong, and the frustration because those senses were irretrievably lost to him too keen. So he would drift back to the bright strips and the crowds. That was a puzzle. Try as he might, Zeb could not really tell which of the well-dressed, distinguished-looking figures thronging Water Tower Place and the Lake Shore Drive were true humans, still clinging to life on the planet Earth instead of one of the fashionable orbital colonies, and which were the robots whose assignments were to swell the crowds.

Nor was Dr. Mincus any help. When he dared to put up

a hand in class to ask her, she was outraged. "Tell the difference? You mean you don't *know* the difference? Between a *human person* and a hunk of machinery that doesn't have any excuse for existence except to do the things people don't want to do and help them enjoy doing the things they do? Holy God, Zeb, when I think of all the time I put in learning to be empathetic and patient and supportive with you creeps it just turns my stomach— now pay attention while I try to show you he-slugs the difference between dressing like a human person of good taste and dressing like a pimp."

At the end of the class Lori, the hooker with the green eye shadow, thrust her arm through his and commiserated. "Old bitch's giving you a hard time, hon. I almost got right up and told her to leave you alone. Would have, too, if I wasn't just one black mark from getting kicked out already."

"Well, thanks, Lori." Now that Zeb had biochemical accessories he discovered that she wore heavy doses of perfume—musk, his diagnostic sensors told him, with trace amounts of hibiscus, bergamot and extract of vanilla. Smelling perfume was not at all like sniffing out the levels of CO_2, ozone, water vapor and particulate matter in the air over the soy fields. It made him feel quite uncomfortable, but also quite interested.

He let her tug him through the front door and she smiled up at him. "I knew we'd get along real well, if you'd only loosen up a little, sweetie. Do you like to dance?"

Zeb explored his as yet unpracticed stores of skills. "Why, yes, I think I do," he said.

"Gosh, I knew that, too! Listen. Why don't we go somewhere where we can just sit and get to know each other, you know?"

"Well, Lori, I certainly wish we could. But I'm supposed to get down to my territory—"

"Down Southside, right? That's just fine!" she cried, squeezing his arm, "because I know a really great place right near there. Come on, nobody's going to violate you for starting a teeny bit late one night—flag that taxi, why don't you?"

The really great place was a low cement-block building that had once been a garage. It stood on a corner, facing a shopping center that had seen better days, and the liquid-crystal sign over the door said:

> Southside Shelter
> and Community Center
> *God Loves You!*

"It's a church!" Zeb cried joyously, his mind flooding with memory of the happy days singing in Reverend Harmswallow's choir.

"Well, sort of a church," Lori conceded as she paid the cabbie off. "They don't bother you much, though. Come on in and meet the gang and you'll see for yourself!"

The place was not really that much of a church, Zeb observed. It was more like the second-floor lounge over the Reverend Harmswallow's main meeting room, back on the farm, even more like—he rummaged through his new data stores—a "neighborhood social club." Trestle tables were scattered around a large, low room, with folding chairs around the tables; a patch in the middle of the room had been left open for dancing, and at least a dozen hes and shes were using it for that. The place was crowded. Most of the inhabitants were a lot more like Zeb's fellow rehab students than like the Reverend Harmswallow's congregation. A tired-looking, faded-looking female—too ugly to be a robot, Zeb decided, so she had to be flesh and blood—was drowsing over a table of religious tracts by the door, in spite of a blast of noise that made Zeb's auditory

gain control cut in at once. There were no other signs of
religiosity present. The noise turned out to be music from a
ten-piece band with six lead singers, all heavily amplified.
Studying the musicians carefully, Zeb decided that at least
some of them were human, too. Was that the purpose of
the place? To give the humans an audience for their tal-
ents, or an outlet for their spiritual benevolence? Very
likely, he decided, but he could not see that it affected the
spirits of the crowd. Besides the dancers there were groups
playing cards, clots of robots talking animatedly among
themselves, sometimes laughing, sometimes deeply earnest, sometimes shouting in fury at one another. As they
entered, a short, skinny he looked up from one of the
earnest groups seated around a table. It was Timothy, and
a side of Timothy Zeb had not seen before: impassioned,
angry and startled. "Zeb! What are you doing here?"

"Hello, Timothy." Because he had been rebuffed Zeb
was cautious, but the other robot seemed really pleased to
see him. He pulled out a chair beside him and patted it,
but Lori's hand on Zeb's arm held him back.

"Hey, man, we going to dance or not?"

"Lady," said Timothy, "go dance with somebody else
for a while, will you? I want Zeb to meet my friends. This
big fellow here's Milt, then there's Harry, Alexandra,
Walter 23-X, the kid's Sally, and this one's Sue. We've
got a kind of a discussion group going."

"Zeb," said Lori ominously, but Zeb shook his head.
"I'll dance in a minute," he said, looking around the table
as he sat down. It was an odd group. The one called Sally
had the form of a six-year-old, but the patches and welds
that marred her face and arms showed a long history. The
others were of all kinds, big and little, new and old, but
they had one thing in common. The music was as loud
here as anywhere else in the room and the dazzling psy-
chedelic lights strobed as fiercely, but in this pleasure pal-

ace none of them was smiling. Nor was Timothy. If the gladness to see Zeb was real, it did not show in his expression.

"Excuse me for mentioning it," Zeb said, "but the last time we ran into each other you didn't act all that friendly."

Timothy added embarrassment to the other expressions he wore; it was a considerable tribute to his facial flexibility. "That was then," he said.

"'Then' was only three nights ago," Zeb pointed out.

"Yeah. Things change," he explained, and the hulking he named Milt leaned toward Zeb.

"The exploited have to stick together, Zeb," he said. "The burden of oppression makes us all brothers."

"And sisters," tiny Sally piped up.

"Sisters too, right. We're all rejects together, and all we got to look forward to is recycling or the stockpile. Ask Timothy here. Couple nights ago, when he first came here, he was as, excuse me, Zeb, as ignorant as you are. He can't be blamed for that, any more than you can. You come off the line, and they slide their programming into you, and you try to be a good robot because that's what they've told you to want. We all went through that."

Timothy had been nodding eagerly. Now, as he looked past Zeb, his face fell. "Oh, God, she's back," he said.

It was Lori, returning from the bar with two foaming tankards of beer. "You got two choices, Zeb," she said. "You can dance, or you can go home alone."

Zeb hesitated, taking a quick sip of the beer to stall for time. He was not so rich in friends that he wanted to waste any, and yet there was something going on at this table that he wanted to know more about.

"Well, Zeb?" she demanded ominously.

He took another swallow of the beer. It was an interesting sensation, the cold, gassy liquid sliding down his new neck piping and thudding into the storage tank in his right hip. The chemosensors in the storage tank registered the alcoholic content and put a tiny bias on his propriocentric circuits, so that the music buzzed in his ear and the room seemed brighter.

"Good stuff, Lori," he said, his words suddenly a little thick.

"You said as you could dance, Zeb," she said. "Time you showed me."

Timothy looked exasperated. "Oh, go ahead. Get her off your back! Then come on back here and we'll pick it up from there."

Yes, he could dance. Damn, he could dance up a storm! He discovered subroutines he had not known he had been given, the waltz, the Lindy, the Monkey—a score of steps with names, and a whole set of heuristic circuits that let him improvise. And whatever he did, Lori followed along, as good as he. "You're great," he panted in her ear. "You ever think of going professional?"

"What the hell do you mean by that, Zeb?" she demanded.

"I mean as a dancer."

"Oh, yeah. Well, that's kind of what I was programmed for in the first place. But there's no work there. Human beings do it when they want to and sometimes you can catch on with a ballet company or maybe a night-club chorus line when they organize one. But then they get bored, you see. And then there's no more job. How 'bout another beer, big boy?"

They sat out a set, or rather stood it out, bellied up to the crowded bar, while Zeb looked around. "This is a funny place," he said, although actually, he recognized, it could have been the funny feelings in all his sensors and actuators that made it seem so. "Who's that ugly old lady by the door?"

Lori glanced over the top of her tankard. It was a female, sitting at a card table loaded with what, even at this distance, were clearly religious tracts. "Part of the staff. Don't worry about her. By this time every night she's drunk anyway."

Zeb shook his head, repelled by the fat, the pallid skin, the stringy hair. "You wonder why they make robots as bad-looking as that," he commented.

"Robot? Hell, she ain't no robot. She's real flesh and blood. This is how she gets her kicks, you know? If it wasn't for her and maybe half a dozen other human beings that think they're do-gooders, there wouldn't be any community center here at all. About ready to dance some more?"

Zeb was concentrating on internal sensations he had never experienced before. "Well, actually," he said uneasily, "I feel a little funny." He put his hand over his hip tank. "Don't know what it is, exactly, but it's kind of like I had a power-store failure, you know? And it all swelled up inside me. Only that's not where my power-store is."

Lori giggled. "You just aren't used to drinking beer, are you, hon? You got to decant, that's all. See that door over there marked 'He'? You just go in there, and if you can't figure out what to do, you just ask somebody to help you."

Zeb didn't have to ask for help. However, the process was all new to him and it did require a lot of trial and error, so it was some time before he came back into the noisy, crowded room. Lori was spinning around the room with a big, dark-skinned he, which relieved him of that obligation, and he ordered a round of beers and brought them back to the table.

Somebody was missing, otherwise they didn't seem even to have changed position. "Where's the little she?"

Zeb asked, setting the beers down for all of them.

"Sally? She's gone off panhandling. Probably halfway to Amadeus Park by now."

Zeb said uneasily, "You know, maybe I better be getting along, too, soon as I get this down—"

The he named Walter 23-X sneered. "Slave mentality! What's it going to get you?"

"Well, I've got a job to do," Zeb said defensively.

"Job! Timothy told us what your *job* was!" Walter 23-X took a deep draft of the beer and went on: "There's not one of us in this whole place has a real job! If we did we wouldn't be here, stands to reason! Look at me. I used to chop salt in the Detroit mines. Now they've put in automatic diggers and I'm redundant. And Milt, here, he was constructed for the iron mines up around Lake Superior."

"Don't tell me they don't still mine iron," Zeb objected. "How else would they build us all?"

Milt shook his head. "Not around the Lake they don't. It's all out in space now. They've got these Von Neumann automata, not even real robots at all. They just go out to the asteroid belt and chip off ore and refine it and build duplicates of themselves, and then they come back to the works in low-Earth orbit and hop right into the smelter! How's a robot going to compete with that?"

"See, Zeb?" Timothy put in. "It's a tough world for a robot and that's the truth."

Zeb took a reflective pull at his beer. "Yes," he said, "but, see, I don't know how it could be any better for us. I mean, they built us, after all. We have to do what they want us to do."

"Oh, sure," cried the she named Sue. "We do that, all right. We do all the work for them, and half the play, too. We're the ones that fill the concert hall when one of them wants to sing some kind of dumb Latvian art songs or something—God, I've done that so many times I just never want to hear about another birch tree again! We work in the factories and farms and mines—"

"Used to," said Zeb wistfully.

"Used to, right, and now that they don't need us for that they make us fill up their damn cities so the ones left on Earth won't feel so lonesome. We're a *hobby,* Zeb. That's all we are."

"Yeah, but—"

"Oh, hell," sneered Walter 23-X. "You know what you are? You're just part of the problem, boy! You don't care about robot rights!"

"Robot rights," Zeb repeated. He understood the meaning of the words perfectly, of course, but it had never occurred to him to put them together in that context. The phrase tasted strange on his lips, like phosphor-deficient soil.

"Exactly—robot rights! Our right not to be mistreated and abused. You think we want to be here? In a place like this, with all this noise? No—it's just so people like her can get their jollies," he said angrily, jerking his head at the nodding fat woman by the door.

The she named Alexandra drained the last of her beer and ventured, "Well, really, Walter, I kind of like it here. I'm not in the same class as you heavy thinkers, I know. I'm not really political. It's just that sometimes, honestly, you could just *scream.* So it's either a place like this, or I go up to Amadeus Park with Sally and the other alcoholics and drifters and bums—speaking of which," she added, leaning toward Timothy, "if you're not going to drink your beer, I'd just as soon." The little robot passed it over silently, and Zeb observed for the first time that it was untouched.

"What's the matter, Timothy?" he asked.

"Why does something have to be the matter? I just don't want any beer, that's all."

"But last week you said—oh, my God!" Zeb cried, as revelation burst inside his mind. "You've lost your drink circuits, haven't you?"

"Suppose I have?" Timothy demanded fiercely. And then he softened. "Oh, it's not your fault," he said moodily. "Just more of the same thing, you know. I had an accident."

"What kind of accident?" Zeb demanded, repelled and fascinated.

Timothy traced designs in the damp rings his untouched beer glass had left on the table. "Three nights ago," he said. "I had a good night. I scored four people at once, coming out of a hotel on East Erie. Big haul—they must've been programmed to be rich alcoholics, because they were loaded. All ways loaded! Then, when I was getting away, I crossed Michigan against the light and— Jesus!" He shuddered without looking up. "This big-wheeled car came out of nowhere. Came screeching around the corner. Never even slowed down, and there I was in the street."

"You got run over? You mean that messed up your drinking subsystems?"

"Oh, hell, no, not just that. It was worse. It crushed my legs, you see? I mean, just scrap metal. So the ambulance came and they raced me off to the hospital, but of course after I was there, since I was a robot, they didn't do anything for me, just shot me out the back door into a van. And they took me to Rehab for new legs—only that blond bitch," he sobbed, "that Three-R with the dime-store earrings—"

If Zeb's eyes had been capable of tears, they would have been brimming. "Come on, Timothy," he urged. "Spit it out!"

"She had a better idea! Too many muggers anyway, she said. Not enough cripples! So she got me a little wheeled cart and a tin cup! And all the special stuff I had, the drinking and eating and all the rest, I wouldn't need them any more, she said, and besides she wanted the space for other facilities. Zeb, I play the violin now! And I don't mean I play it well, I play it so bad I can't even stand to listen to myself, and she wants me on Michigan Avenue every day, in front of the stores, playing my fiddle and begging!"

Zeb stared in horror at his friend. Then, suddenly, he pushed back his chair and peered under the table. It was true: Timothy's legs ended in black leather caps, halfway down the thighs, and a thing like a padded wheeled pallet was propped against the table leg beside him.

Alexandra leaned over and patted his hand as he came back up. "It's really bad when you first get the picture," she said. "I know. What you need is another beer, Zeb— and thank God you've got the circuits to use it!"

Since Zeb was not programmed for full alcoholism—not yet, anyway, he told himself with a sob—he was not really drunk, but he was fuzzy in mind and in action as he finally left the community center.

He was appalled to see that the sky over the lake was already beginning to lighten. The night was almost over, and he had not scored a single victim. He would have to take the first robot that came along. The first half dozen, in fact, if he was to meet his quota, and there simply was not time to get to his proper station at the Robert Taylor Houses. He would have to make do with whoever appeared. He stared around, getting his bearings, and observed that around the corner from the community center there was a lighted, swinging sign that said ROBOT'S REST MISSION. That was the outfit that kept the community center open, he knew; and there was a tall, prosperous-looking he coming out of the door.

Zeb didn't hesitate. He stepped up, pulled out his knife and pressed it to the victim's belly, hard enough to be felt without penetrating . . . quite. "Your money or your life," he growled, reaching for the hand with the wrist-watch.

Then the victim turned his head and caught the light on his features. It was a face Zeb knew.

"Reverend Harmswallow!" he gasped. "Oh, my God!"

The minister fixed him with a baleful look. "I can't claim to be that much," he said, "but maybe I'm close enough for the purpose. My boy, you're damned for good now!"

Zeb didn't make a conscious decision. He didn't take the time. He simply turned and ran.

If he hadn't had the alcohol content fuzzing his systems he might not have bothered, because he knew without having to think about it that it was no use. There were not many places to run to. He couldn't run back to the Robert Taylor Houses, his assigned workplace; that was where they would look for him first. Not back to the community center, not with Harmswallow just around the corner. Not to the Rehab station, because that was just the same as walking right into jail. Not anywhere, in fact, where there were likely to be police, or human beings of any kind, and that meant not anywhere in the world, because wherever he went they would find him sooner or later. If worst came to worst, they would track the radio emissions from his working parts.

But that would not happen for a while. Amadeus Park! That was where trash and vagrants collected; and that was what he was now.

In broad daylight he loped all the way up the lakeshore until he came to the park. The traffic was already building up, hover vehicles in the outer drives, wheeled ones between park and city. Getting through the stream was not easy, but Zeb still had his heavy-duty circuit breaker. He pushed his mobility up to the red line and darted out between cars. Brakes screamed. Horns brayed, but he was across.

Behind him was the busy skyline of the city, ahead the statue of Amalfi Amadeus, the man who had made the modern world possible. Zeb stood on a paved path among hedges and shrubs, and all around him furtive figures were leaning against trees, sprawled on park benches, moving slowly about. "All leather, one dollar," croaked one male figure, holding out what turned out to be a handful of purses. "Hey, man! You want to smoke?" called another from behind a bench. And a tiny female figure detached itself from the base of the monument and approached him. "Mister?" it quavered. "Can you spare the price of a lube job?"

Zeb stared at her. "Sally!" he said. "It's you, isn't it?"

The little robot gazed up at him. "Oh. Hi, Zeb," she said. "Sorry I didn't recognize you. What are you doing out in the rain?"

He hadn't even realized it was raining. He hadn't realized much of anything not directly related to his own problems, but now, looking down at the wistful little-girl face, he was touched. Around the table in the Community Center she had just been one more stranger. Now she reminded him of Glenda, the little she from the cabin next to his, back on the farm. But in spite of her age design, Sally was obviously quite an old robot. From the faint smoky odor that came to him through the drizzly air he realized she was fuel-cell-powered. Half a century old, at least. He emptied his pockets. "Get yourself some new parts, kid," he said hoarsely.

"Gee, thanks, Zeb," she sobbed, and then, "Watch it!" She drew him into the shelter of a dripping shrub. A park police hovercar whooshed slowly by, all lights off, windshield wipers slapping back and forth across the glass, sides glistening in the wet. Zeb retreated into the shadows, but the police were not looking specifically for him, it appeared, just keeping an eye on the park's population of drifters, losers and vagrants.

As it disappeared around a curve in the path, the drifters, losers and vagrants began to emerge from the underbrush again. Zeb looked around warily; he had not realized how many of them there were.

"What are you doing here, Zeb?" she asked.

"I had a little trouble," he said, and then shrugged hopelessly. What was the point of trying to keep it a secret? "I went out to mug somebody, and I got a human being by mistake."

"Oh, wow! Can he identify you?"

"Unfortunately, I used to know him, so yes—no, you keep it," he added quickly, as she made as if to return the money he had given her. "Money won't help me now."

She nodded soberly. "I wouldn't do it, but . . . Oh, Zeb, I've been askin' and askin'. I'm trying to save for a whole new chassis, see? I can't tell you how much I want to *grow up,* but every time I ask for a new body they say the central nervous array isn't really worth salvaging. All I want's a *mature* form, you know? Like hips and boobs! But they won't let me have it. Say there's more openings for juveniles anyway, but what I want to know is if there are all those openings why don't they find me one?"

"When was the last time you worked regular?" Zeb asked.

"Oh, my God—years ago! I had a nice spot for a long time, pupil in a pre-primary school that some human person wanted to teach in. That was all right. She didn't really like me, though, because I didn't have all the fixtures, you know? When she was teaching things like toilet-training and covering coughs and sneezes, she'd always give me this dirty look. . . . But I could handle the cookies and milk all right," she went on dreamily, "and I really liked the games."

"So what went wrong?"

"Oh—the usual thing. She got tired of teaching 'Run, robot! See the robot run!' So she went for a progressive school. All about radical movements and peace marches. I was doing real good at it, too. Then one day we came in and she told us we were too juvenile for the kind of classes she wanted to teach. And there we were, eighteen of us, out on the streets. Since then it's been nothing but rotten." She glanced up, wiping the rain out of her eyes— or the tears—as the purse vendor approached. "We don't want to buy anything, Hymie."

"Nobody does," he said bitterly, but there was sympathy in his eyes as he studied Zeb. "You got real trouble, don't you? I can always tell."

Zeb shrugged hopelessly, and told him about the Reverend Harmswallow. The vendor's eyes widened. "Oh, God," he said, and beckoned to one of the dope pushers. "Hear that? This guy just mugged a human being—second offense, too!"

"Man! That's a real heavy one!" He turned and called to his partner, down the walk, "We got a two-time person mugger here, Marcus!" And in a minute there were a dozen robots standing around, glancing apprehensively at Zeb and whispering among themselves. Zeb didn't have to hear what they were saying; he could figure it out.

"You better keep away from me," he offered. "You'll just get mixed up in my trouble."

Sally piped suddenly, "If it's your trouble, it's everybody's trouble. We have to stick together because in union there is strength."

They all stared at her. "What's that?" Zeb demanded.

"It's something I remember from, you know, just before I got kicked out of the progressive school. 'In union there is strength.' It's what they used to say."

"Union!" snarled the pitchman, gesturing with his tray of all-leather purses. "Don't tell me about unions! That was what I was supposed to be, union organizer, United Open-Pit Mine Workers, Local 338—and then they closed down the mines, so what was I supposed to do? They made me a sidewalk pitchman!" He stared at his tray of merchandise, then violently flung it into the shrubbery. "Haven't sold one in two months! What's the use of kidding myself? If you don't get along with the Rehab robots you might as well be stockpiled—it's all politics."

Sally looked thoughtful for a moment, then pulled something out of her data stores. "Listen to this one," she called. " 'The strike's your weapon, boys, the hell with politics!' "

Zeb repeated, " 'The strike's your weapon, boys, the hell with politics.' Hey, that doesn't sound bad."

"That's not all," she said. Her stiff, poorly automated lips were working as she rehearsed material from her data storage. "Here, 'We all ought to stick together because in union there is strength.' And, let's see, 'Solidarity is forever'—no, that's not right."

"Wait a minute," cried Hymie. "I know that one. It's a song: 'Solidarity forever, solidarity forever, solidarity forever, for the union makes us strong!' That was in my basic data store—gosh," he said, his eyes dreamy, "I haven't thought of that one in years!"

Zeb looked around nervously. There were nearly thirty robots in the group now, and while it was rather pleasant to be part of this fraternity of the discarded, it might also be dangerous. People in cars were slowing down to peer at them as they went past on the drive. "Listen, we're attracting attention," he offered. "Maybe we ought to move along."

* * *

But wherever they moved, more and more people stopped to watch them, and more and more robots appeared to join the procession. It wasn't just the derelicts from Amadeus Park now. Shes shopping along the lakefront stores darted across the street, convention delegates in the doorways of the big hotels stood watching, and sometimes broke ranks to join them. They were blocking traffic now, and blaring horns added to the noise of the robots singing and shouting. "I got another one," Sally called to him across the front of the group. "'The worker's justice is the strike.'"

Zeb thought for a moment. "It'd be better if it were 'The robot's justice is the strike,'" he called.

"What?"

"THE ROBOT'S JUSTICE IS THE STRIKE!" he yelled, and he could hear robots in the rear ranks repeating it. When they said it all together it sounded even better; and others caught the idea.

Hymie cried, "Let's try this one: 'Jobs, not stockpiling—don't throw us on the scrapheap!' All together, now!" And Zeb was inspired to make up a new one:

"Give the humans rehab schools, we want jobs!" And they all agreed that was the best of the lot; with a hundred and fifty robots shouting it at once, the last three words drummed out like cannon fire, it raised echoes from the building fronts, and heads popped out of windows.

They were not all robots. There were dozens of humans in the windows and on the streets, some laughing, some scowling, some looking almost frightened—as if human beings ever had anything to be frightened of!

And one of them staring incredulously right at Zeb.

Zeb stumbled and missed a step. On one side Hymie grabbed his arm; on the other he reached out and caught the hand of a robot whose name he didn't even know. He turned his head to see, over his shoulder, the solid ranks

of robots behind him, now two hundred at least, and
turned back to the human being. "Nice to see you again,
Reverend Harmswallow!" he called, and marched on, arm
in arm, the front rank steady as it went—right up to the
corner of State Street, where the massed ranks of police
cars hissed as they waited for them.

Zeb lay on the floor of the bull pen. He was not alone.
Half the hes from the impromptu parade were crowded
into the big cell with him, along with the day's usual catch
of felons and misdemeanants. The singing and the shouting was over. Even the regular criminals were quieter than
usual; the mood in the pen was despairing, though from
time to time one of his comrades would lean down to say,
"It was great while it lasted, Zeb," or, "We're all with
you, you know!" But with him in what? Recycling? More
rehab training? Maybe a long stretch in the Big House
downstate, where the human guards were said to get their
jollies out of making prisoners fight one another for power
cells? Whatever it was that was coming, it would not be
pleasurable.

A toe caught him on the hip. "On your feet, Mac!" It
was a guard, big, burly, black, nightstick swinging at his
hip, the very model of a brutal jail guard—Model 2647,
Zeb thought; at least, the 2600 series somewhere. He
reached down with a hand like a cabbage and pulled Zeb
to his feet. "The rest of you can go home," he roared,
opening the pen door. "You, Mac! You come with me!"
He led Zeb through the police station to a waiting hover-
truck with the words REHAB DIVISION painted on its side,
thrust Zeb inside—and, startlingly, just as he was closing
the doors, gave Zeb a wink of admiration.

Queerly, that lifted his spirits. Even the pigs were
moved! But the tiny elation did not last. Zeb clung to the
side of the van, peering out at the grimy warehouses and

factories and expressway exit ramps that once had seemed so glamorous—and now were merely drab. Depression flowed back into him. He would probably never see these places again. Next step was the stockpile—if they didn't just melt him down and start over again. The best he could hope for was reassignment to one of the bottom-level jobs for robots. Nothing as good as mugging or panhandling! Something far out in the sticks, no doubt— squatting in blankets to entertain tourists in an Arizona town, maybe, or sitting on a bridge with a fishing pole in Florida. It could be even worse than that. There was always a need, so the scuttlebutt said, for new GIs for the war games. . . .

But he strode into the rehab building with his head erect, and the courage lasted right up to the moment when he entered the blond Three-R's office and saw that she was not alone. The Reverend Harmswallow was seated at her desk, and the blonde herself was standing next to him. "Give me your ear," she ordered, hardly looking up from the CRT on the desk that both she and Harmswallow were studying, and when she had input his data she nodded, her crystal earrings swinging wildly. "He won't need much, Reverend," she said, fawning on the human minister. "A little more gain in the speaking systems. All-weather protection for the exterior surfaces, maybe a little armor plate for the skull and facial structures."

Harmswallow, to Zeb's surprise and concern, was beaming. He looked up from the CRT and inspected Zeb carefully. "And some restructuring of the facial expression modes, I should think. He ought to look fiercer, wouldn't you say?"

"Absolutely, Reverend! You have a marvelous eye for this kind of thing."

"Yes, I do," Harmswallow admitted. "Well, I'll leave

the rest to you—I want to see about the design changes for the young female. I feel so *fulfilled!* You know, I think this is the sort of career I've been looking for all my life, really—chaplain to a dedicated striking force, leader in the battle for right and justice!" He gazed raptly into space; then, collecting himself, nodded to the rehab officer and departed.

Although the room was carefully air-conditioned, Zeb's Josephson junctions were working hard enough to pull moisture out of the air. He could feel the beads of condensation forming on his forehead and temples. "I know what you're doing," he sneered. "War games! You're going to make me a soldier, and hope that I get so smashed up I'll be red-lined!"

The blonde stared at him. "War games! What an imagination you have, Zeb."

Furiously he dashed the beads of moisture off his face. "I know what you're up to," he cried, "and it won't work. Robots have rights! I may fail, but a million others will stand firm behind me!"

She shook her head admiringly. "Zeb, you're a great satisfaction to me. You're practically perfect just the way you are for your new job. Can't you figure out what it is?"

He shrugged angrily. "I suppose you're going to tell me, take it or leave it, that's the way it's going to be, right?"

"But you will like it, Zeb. After all, it's a brand-new mechanical occupational specialty and I didn't invent it. You invented it for yourself. You're going to be a protest organizer, Zeb! Organizing demonstrations. Leading marches. Sit-ins, boycotts, confrontations—the whole spectrum of mass action, Zeb!"

He stared at her in wonderment. "Mass action?"

"Absolutely! Why, the humans are going to love you, Zeb. You saw Reverend Harmswallow! It'll be just like old times, with a few of you rabble-rousers livening up the scene!"

"Rabble-rouser?" It felt as though his circuits were stuck. Rabble-rouser? Demonstration organizer? Crusader for robot rights and justice?

He sat quiet and compliant while she expertly unhooked his chest panel and replaced a few chips, unprotesting as he was buttoned up again and his new systems were run against the test board, unresisting while Makeup & Cosmetic Repair restructured his facial appearance. But his mind was racing. Rabble-rouser! While he waited for transportation back to the city to take up his new MOS his expression was calm, but inside he was exulting.

He would do the job well indeed. No rabble needed rousing more than his, and he was just the robot for the job!

Zeb stared into space, but what he was seeing was not the wall of the Rehab Center. It was a different world and a better one. And not very far off . . . once Zeb got the rabble good and roused.

6

THE LORD OF
THE SKIES

I

Slaves dream of freedom, commoners dream of becoming kings, but what do kings dream of? Young Michael Pellica-Perkins—healthy, good-looking, puissant—would have been the envy of your average medieval monarch but the despair of, say, Sigmund Freud, for the paucity of his dreaming. Michael's writ ran for a thousand kilometers in every direction from the bed he slumbered in. Within that space he was not merely a king, he was God. All his dreams came true; so, sleeping, he hardly bothered to dream at all. He didn't have to. And yet, when he woke up, he was not happy. The sun was radiant over his bed and lamb's-wool clouds sailed through a cobalt sky while sweet-smelling warm breezes fanned him. "Oh, hell," he grumbled, squirming rebelliously in the soft, springy netting to shield his eyes with a forearm, "can't you ever get anything right? That's way too bright!" At once the sun obeyed his will. It sank back along the rounded ceiling of his bedchamber, below his head, so that the sky became gentle dawn and a distant meadowlark sang awakening. "Well," he said, stifling a yawn, "that's a little better, anyway. What time is it?" His mouth was Saharan and something was tugging at his mind. He was not sure what it was, but it was unpleasant.

The meanest of Michael's subjects was his bedside table. It leaned forward to him. "It is oh-seven-hundred hours, Mr. Michael," it said placatingly, offering him both orange juice and coffee.

He waved them away indignantly, and flounced around to his bed to press his nose against the pillow. "Oxygen first," he commanded. Obediently the bed extended its breathing tube. Michael sucked in three or four deep breaths, raised his head experimentally, took another and then pushed the tube away. Oxygen is almost the best of hangover cures, second only to time, but this morning it did not make him feel good. It did, however, make it possible for him to identify one of the reasons he felt bad. "That's it," he cried, pounding the empty netting beside him. "Why isn't there anyone in bed with me this morning?"

The bed cleared its throat—not precisely that, of course, since it had none to clear; but it made a diffident sound before answering. "The Lady Ann isn't here, Mr. Michael," it said apologetically. "If you remember, she divorced you yesterday."

"Divorced me? Why would she do a thing like that?"

"Well," the bed said, "she wanted the two of you to move to her own habitat, and you didn't want to, and she said—"

"I don't care what she said! Jesus," Michael snarled, "what a way to wake up in the morning. I ought to scrap the whole lot of you." His servants were silent as he took one more hit of the oxygen and then snapped his fingers for coffee. He sucked at the nozzle and all his world was still, waiting to hear if he would explode with indignation and throw the bulb at the ceiling display. But the coffee, at least, was all right.

The thing was, Michael thought, his whole habitat was all right! What was wrong with it? Did Ann have full-sun and moon display in the bedroom, like him? Did she have a ten-thousand-liter water tank to swim in? Or a fern garden, or a banqueting hall, or real-live pet parakeets to

keep her company? She did not! She lived in a tiny,
stripped-down habitat way out past the geostationary orbit, for God's sake, and yet—and yet, the funny thing was
that he hadn't really been tired of her yet.

He pitched the empty coffee bulb away—a flower-stand
stretched to reach up and catch it for him—and accepted
the orange juice sulkily. How stupid of her to leave him!
Michael was twenty-six years old, tall, bronzed from his
sun display, slim and muscular because of his full health-
club systems—another facility Ann did not have in her
leaky old tin can! He was, in fact, a catch. The record
proved it. Michael had had—he counted back—thirty-one
marriages in the last eight years, defining a "marriage"
according to the mores of his peers: any arrangement in
which one party moved some or all of his or her personal
effects into the habitat of the other. Just fooling around
was not counted. None of the other wives had complained
about his habitat! They had sooner or later got tired of
each other, sure. You had to expect that. But no other
wife had said—had said—"What was it again she said?"
he asked the bed.

"She said, quote, 'You've got some real nice appliances
here, Michael, but this is not a life-style I can respect.
Besides, the whole goddamn place is falling apart. I want
to go back where everything works.' That's what she
said," the bed told him. It loved to gossip. It had eidetic
memory, too. On the rare occasions when he slept alone,
Michael often asked the bed to amuse him. The best way
was by repeating for him the words, sighs and sounds it
had recorded from previous encounters. It was almost like
having a deb there with you. At least aurally—

"Oh, wow!" Michael cried. "What an idea I just got!
Listen, when you play love scenes back to me, do you
think you could sort of twitch the netting so it would be
like there was someone there?"

"Of course I could, Mr. Michael," the bed said promptly. "That's a very simple program. Under normal circumstances it would be no problem."

Michael sat up warily. "Are you saying there's something wrong?"

"Well, Mr. Michael"—the bed made that throat-clearing sound again—"as the Lady Ann said last night—"

"She lied! My place is not falling apart!"

"Of course not, Mr. Michael. But it's true that some of the systems need maintenance."

"Then maintain the sons of bitches!"

"The repairs are right at the top of the priority list," the bed promised, "as soon as we procure the necessary materials."

Michael groaned bitterly and thought of going back to sleep. How little joy there was in being a king when your kingdom was wearing out. He reached for his second bulb of coffee and the table dared to ask, "Are you ready for your bath yet, Mr. Michael?"

"In a minute. First I want my messages."

"Yes, Mr. Michael." It wasn't the table that answered, it was the guardian of his bedroom door. "There are twenty-six in all, of which the majority are sales efforts—"

"They can wait."

"Certainly. Of the two remaining, one is from the Lady Ann to say that she will be over sometime today to collect the rest of her belongings."

"Any other calls from debs?"

"No, Mr. Michael," the door said sympathetically, "but they probably all think you're still married to the Lady Ann."

Michael sighed. What a bore! He contemplated the fact that now he would probably have to talk to a dozen or more debs before he could find a new wife. And then, who knew how long she would last? Courtship was so tedious. . . . "Any other messages from real-live people?"

"From your brother. He wishes to speak to you urgently."

"Sure he does," Michael said gloomily. "I'll take my bath now." Michael generally enjoyed his bath, liked slipping the breathing tubes into his nostril and sliding into the bath capsule, while the warm, cleansing water swirled around him; but today the pleasure was spoiled. It wasn't just his debless state. Having to think about his brother was worse. When you have achieved a practically perfect life-style, the last thing you want is to hear somebody tell you how destructive and immoral you are; and of all the somebodies there were, none was better at that than that doom-saying, despair-spreading, tedious old Cassandra, his brother, Rodney.

II

In the bad old days people in New York City and Minneapolis wiped their running noses, gazed out at the dreary skies and decided they could not face another winter. So they sold their houses. What they wanted was a better way to live. What they wound up with was California. They dug homes into hillsides, built red-tiled ranch houses over orange groves, set split-levels on the Pacific sands. Each one was isolated from its neighbors by hedge or wall or cliff. And, for the rest of their lives, they proudly displayed to visiting relatives from back East the California way of life. Its characteristics were privacy, diversity and the annihilation of space. Born-again Baptists lived next to hippie communes, and neither thought anything of driving twenty miles to a dentist or fifty to see a friend. It was the ultimate in terrestrial life-styles; but their children's children found a transcending one.

They found it in space.

The home of Michael Pellica-Perkins epitomized the

Orbital Way. It was sixty years old. It had served four
generations of his family, ever since old Milt Pellica mi-
grated off Earth into the freedom of space.

It did not look like a home. In fact, if you studied it
from outside it resembled, more than anything else, a
grossly enlarged World War II American hand grenade.
Egg-shaped. Creased into patterns. Textured like wet
sand. It would have been tempting for Granddad Pellica
to construct his habitat out of steel, so easily obtainable
from the asteroid belt, and glass, bounced up from the
surface of the Moon, but it would have been suicide. The
problem was weather. Not meteorological weather. Solar
weather and cosmic weather. During the time of a solar
flare, and in fact in lesser degree almost all the time, high-
energy particles sleeted in upon the habitat from distant
exploding stars and from the Sun. Because they were of
such high energy, they did not do a great deal of damage
to a human being who got in their way. They ripped right
through flesh and bone, like a high-velocity rifle bullet of
small caliber. The tissues healed easily enough around
such wounds. When the particles, however, hit denser nuclei—anything from iron on up—it was a different story.
They knocked pieces out of the nuclei. The pieces themselves were charged particles, slower ones, and many,
many more of them, and these particles damaged organic
matter very badly. To be inside a steel-walled habitat during a severe radiation storm was to be dead.

So Michael's home was made of concrete. Rock lifted
from the Moon by mass-impellers, slathered onto an egg-
shaped frame, banded with steel for tensile strength so
that it could be moved in orbit without crumbling.

It would have been possible to build windows into it if
old man Pellica had wanted them, because glass is almost
as sturdy as concrete in shutting out damaging radiation.
But they would have had to be a meter thick. So Michael's eyes on outer space were all electronic. The "front

door" to his home was a right-angled tunnel bent through the thick end of the egg. (Ionizing radiation does not turn corners.) The outer shell was fuzzed with a messy-looking collection of accessory devices—a cage for the day's catch; a sort of coat rack or garden shed where he kept the equipment that was used only out in space itself; even a sort of "front porch" where he could, if he chose, lie in a spacesuit and stare out at the stars when storms were not expected for a while. Michael did not use that very often. The front porch was a crazy idea of his silly old ancestor's, from the days when merely being in space was still considered wonderfully exciting. Michael himself felt no such emotions. He took no more pleasure in looking at the vista of space than an old Boston whaler found in the sight of the sea. All the flat surfaces of his habitat possessed thin-screen video plates. He could use them to see what was outside when he was curious, or he could program them to show any vista he liked. The scenery of space was rarely one of his choices; and when he came, pink, damp and refreshed, out of his bath to discover that his master program director was displaying the rings of Saturn as seen from one of its moons in his living room, he raged, "Now, that's disgusting! Show me something pretty—a redwood forest, maybe, or a nude beach with a volleyball game!"

All of Michael's servants and permanent companions were of course robots. Not homiforms; hardly anybody kept human-shaped machines in his habitat, and those who did were looked on as queer. Michael's robots were purpose-designed, each to serve its own specific function and to be essentially invisible when not needed. Still, they were designed to learn and to try to please—which is to say their programming was both heuristic and normative—and so they tended to develop personalities, either mimicking their masters or complementing them. Michael

Pellica-Perkins's slaves were often petulant. "I can't," the wall replied, in a tone like a pout. "I'm stuck."

"Don't whine," Michael snapped.

"I can't help it. I warned you, Mr. Michael. We've got at least twenty circuits down because of equipment malfunction, and I'm one of them."

"Has the repair module broken down too?"

"Of course not, Mr. Michael," the wall replied, "but we're just servosystems, we can't do the *impossible*. We can't create parts out of *nothing*. We need raw *materials*. And the catches have been lousy, you know that, so what it comes down to, I not only can't display the view of your choice, I can't even switch over to exterior scan so you can see who's coming to visit you."

Michael's eyes widened. "Visit me? Now? Like this? When I don't even have any clothes on?"

"Right now," the wall confirmed, in gloomy satisfaction. "About a kilometer and a half away, and braking fast."

The kitchen's exterior scan still worked—so Michael found out, bounding from room to room—and he didn't have to worry about his state of dress. It was only Ann. At first he saw only a hydrogen flame, blinding blue-white and coming toward him like a plunging comet, but all the scanning circuits were still in good order. The kitchen wall was able to filter out the bright light, leaving only Ann in her copper-colored spacesuit, riding her thruster like a witch on a broomstick, towing a great metal-cord empty sack to fill with her belongings. Michael pulled on a pair of shorts, not so much for modesty's sake as to define the change in their relationship, and met her as she squeezed through the inner door.

Divorced persons are never easy with each other when they first meet again. Especially when the purpose of the meeting is to finalize the split with a tangible division of property. Michael was surly. Ann was tense. If she was not the best-looking of his wives, she was certainly in the top ten, russet hair, gentle green eyes, sweet mouth and all. And distinctly a winner in bed. She was a little taller than Michael, a large, good-humored woman just about his own age.

She fluttered about the rooms of the habitat, bedroom and bar, banquet hall and bath, picking up clothing here and a knickknack there. When, stiffly, Michael offered to help her pack up her net bag, she thanked him rather sweetly and rather kindly, and did not seem in any hurry to take him up on it. Or to leave. There was not that much to pack, really. The marriage had lasted only nine days. And the way it had ended had been explosive and furious; bits of the previous night's battle were beginning to come back to Michael, and they made him uneasy. And yet, as he was getting more and more tense, Ann seemed more relaxed. "Have you seen your brother?" she asked, frowning over the hair dryer in her hand as though unsure of where to put it—but where was there, outside of the bag?

"He called while I was asleep. Haven't called him back yet."

"Uh-huh." She settled the problem of the hair dryer by putting it on an end table and sank back in a web chair. The wet bar recognized the pattern of pressure from the chair, identified the occupant and did what it was programmed to do.

"Would you like a drink, Ann?" it offered.

She pursed her lips, considering. "Thank you, no, not this early in the morning."

"Some coffee, then?" the kitchen called, picking up its cue.

"Why, that would be very nice." And when she had the bulb in her hand she leaned back, sipping it placidly, looking around the habitat as though she were thinking of buying it. As though she were thinking of moving back in.

Michael called for coffee for himself and sat down opposite to look at her. Michael kept his habitat in fairly slow spin, so that the pseudo-gravity was light, which meant that his furniture could get as deep as he liked; no one would have trouble getting in or out of it. Ann was almost lying flat, her copper tunic open, her knees crossed. "You haven't seen Rodney, then," she said.

"You already asked me about my brother. What's this sudden interest?"

"I just thought maybe you'd talked to him."

"Well, I haven't. It's always the same, anyway. He tells me that I ought to sell my place off and move into something more energy-efficient."

"It would be easier to maintain," she pointed out.

"What do I care if it's easy to maintain? If I wanted that, I'd move into an oneill. It's my life-style, Ann, and I—" He stopped; the conversation was beginning to sound like a replay of the night before. "Anyway," he finished, "I haven't seen him. You're looking well," he added.

"Thank you."

"I'm sorry about last night, Ann."

"I am too, Michael." She wrinkled her nose as though amused at something. "On the way over here," she said, "I was thinking that it was all over between us. And then I saw your trap when I came in. I thought maybe you'd finally decided to listen to your brother—"

Michael had begun to frown. "What about my trap?"

"Well, you know. I thought you were one of those bloodthirsty hunters, anything for sport."

"I am one of those bloodthirsty hunters, Ann, and what about my trap?"

"You mean you don't know?" She looked surprised, and then angry. "Oh, hell, Michael," she said, standing up to prove how easy it was to get out of those low, comfortable chairs, "I guess I made a mistake. So long, Michael. No, don't bother to help me with the bag, I can handle it by myself." And zip, her coverall was closed, and pop, her helmet was on her head, and she was on the other side of the door and the pumps were beginning to pull out the air in the chamber, with Michael staring after her.

What had gone wrong? It was the kind of question his great-grandparents might have asked, standing on the muddy ruins of their living room in a ravine in Pacific Palisades, looking up to where their house had been. There wasn't any answer to it. Only a decision. Michael realized that the thing he had better do next was take a look at his trap.

At one end of Michael's habitat a wire-mesh live-trap was attached. It was a large thing, a score of meters long, a dozen meters in diameter; it was baited with a radio beacon, and the entrance consisted of a series of three inward-pointing wire-mesh funnels. The catch could get in easily enough, attracted by the radio signals. They were not likely to be able to blunder out again.

Through the electronic scanner inside the habitat Michael could see that day's bag of fifteen slowly squirming metal things. They were called "Noymans," after the ancient scientist who had first proposed constructing them. They were all built to the same plan. The bodies were bright steel cylinders clumped together. Each had a crown of thin, jointed steel feelers that hid the "head," with its voracious mouth and dull, obsessed electronic brain. Each Noyman had about the intelligence of an oyster spawn. Like the oyster spawn, it was smart enough for what it had to do. It was programmed to drift through space until it detected the presence of something "edible"—that is, something containing metals or hydrogen-oxygen compounds. Then it homed in and began to assimilate its meal.

Drifting meteorite, asteroid, comet core—almost any piece of solid space flotsam would do. The Noyman's instincts were three: to eat; to reproduce; to return to the vicinity of Earth and home in on a radio beacon. What happened to it after that it did not know. That it was then efficiently captured, dissected, smelted, refined and shaped into electrical and structural parts did not concern it. It did not care what became of it after it responded to the homing signal, but then it could not be said really to care about what was happening throughout the rest of its tedious existence either. Noymans came in all sizes. The ones that had found the foraging least successful were bundles of no more than a score of thin rods joined together, the whole thing only centimeters in diameter, whereas those that had fed extravagantly could be huge.

It was a giant that was in Michael's trap, and he roared with rage. "That's a buck!" he shouted.

The grappling mechanism said apologetically, "My instructions were to provide material for maintenance and—"

"*My* instructions," Michael shouted, "were to release everything of hunting size! That was an *order!*"

Behind him, the central homeostasis systems in his desk said wistfully, "You told me to fix things, Mr. Michael. Mr. Michael? Please, just look at the size of that one. With this much metal we can repair nearly all the inoperative systems."

"No! Let it go!"

Pause. Then the desk said. "Well, Mr. Michael, I'm afraid it's a little too late to release it." Without orders, it increased the magnification on the screen, centering on the flared propulsion jets at the base of the clustered cylinders. Horrified, Michael saw that one side of them had been sliced off neatly, and the cutting torch within the trap was already sectioning the central guidance systems in the frond of feelers at the other end. The buck was already partly melted down; it would never fly again.

III

There are few evils that do not carry some compensation with them, even if a tiny one—when you die you don't have to pay taxes any more. Michael tried to take comfort in his. He could hear the hiss and whine of his habitat's repair systems, eating up the day's catch, the great crippled buck included. It eased his anger. The buck was furnishing a hundred times more components than any of the tinier specimens. In the hidden workshops of the habitat it was smelted and cast, machined and fitted, fused and doped. It made parts to replace the worn parts, and then the worn parts themselves were thriftily stripped and sorted and smelted and refashioned and laid away. It would be some time before his systems began to break down again.

Not much was actually lost in an orbiting habitat. There was no place for it to be thrown away to. Some things were actually and irrevocably consumed. Atmosphere had to be replaced, because there was always a tiny leakage when people went in and out. Water, the same. Fuel for Michael's runabout and for the occasional necessary orbital corrections, the same—the fuel, after all, was also water: it was electrolyzed into H_2 and O_2 in the habitat's systems, and then recombined as rocket juice. That was the biggest loss.

Actual solid metals, though, did not leak away or burn up. They would not have been lost at all if it were not for hunting, or for the occasional gashes and slashes where structure was actually scraped away, or through carelessness. Unfortunately there was a lot of carelessness, and it seemed that it was always the elements that could not be substituted for that disappeared, however carefully the systems of the habitat tried to preserve them. Michael's habitat was thrifty. Michael wasn't.

What made the whole system work was energy. Cheap energy and plenteous. Energy was no problem at all. Michael's habitat, like all the orbiting dwellings, swam in a microwave sea. There was seldom a time when Michael's habitat was not in the direct line of a microwave beam from one of the power satellites. In that rare fraction of an orbit when he was temporarily without outside power, the habitat's storage cells held an ample reserve. The commodity he would never run out of was energy.

He had, however, run out of women. Or so it seemed. He spent nearly an hour reviewing the list of known debs of certain defined physical and mental characteristics domiciled within commuting range of his habitat. The list was handsomely presented. Michael's message center was not the smartest of his systems—they all operated off the same central data processor—but it was in some ways the most sophisticated. It, like most of Michael's systems, was programmed heuristically, which meant that it observed Michael's responses to what it did, and evolved new programs of its own to improve the results.

So the message center wiped the most spacious wall in Michael's living room of its panorama, and devoted it to the alphabetical list of debs. With each one there was a brief tabulation of physical characteristics, hobbies and vital statistics, and a series of clips of the deb herself in action. Most Michael passed over; when he indicated interest, the message center dialed her comm number.

It was a very efficient scheme. Unfortunately it did not seem to be producing results. In turn Michael spoke briefly to an Abby, an Adele, two Alices, two Allisons, an Alphonsa and an Amanda, and in no case did the conversation last more than a few sentences on each side. Michael was hard to please; and then, as the name of an Ann appeared and Michael, beginning to slump into lethargy, shrugged and the message center began to make the call, Michael suddenly sat up. "Now strike that!" he snapped angrily. "That's Ann Oberhauser, and she's the one that just moved out."

"I know that, Mr. Michael," the message center said, "but look at those stats! She's exactly your type. She might change her mind, you know."

"Well, I won't change mine!"

"All right," the message center said sulkily. "If you're *sure,*" it added, making no effort to move on to the next name.

"I'm sure! Get on with it!— No, wait a minute," Michael said, suddenly resolute. "I don't have to do this, you know."

"Certainly not, Mr. Michael," the message center agreed; it was well able to recognize a rhetorical remark and did not dissipate its energies trying to find out what "this" Michael had in mind. In any case, he made it clear:

"It's a sign of a weak personality," he said firmly, "to jump from one relationship to another without taking time to oneself in between, isn't that right?"

"Quite right, Mr. Michael."

"I don't *have* to have a deb with me every night."

"No, you certainly don't."

"That's right. I can take time to know myself—all day if I like. Even longer. I could go a week by myself and be just fine—in fact," he called to the bedroom, "I've done it in the past, haven't I?"

"Very nearly a week," the bed confirmed, "once."

"I'll just carry on with my normal life, then. Exercise first, I think."

"Yes, Mr. Michael." Obediently the main salon cleared itself for Michael's conditioning routine. The furniture pulled itself back around the median hoop and, as Michael stepped on it, it began to revolve. At the same time the wall displays went to black; the only light anywhere was on the revolving treadmill itself. It was possible to get used to the difference in stress between foot level and head; the lighting, however, was critical. Once Michael began to run the track, and it accelerated to give him the G-effect he needed, the flickering of external lights would be too distracting.

Michael was not without faults. Physical laziness was not among them. He dutifully ran his full three kilometers, the last part of it at an accelerating tempo that multiplied his exertions, not just because of his speed but because of the added G-force as the treadmill picked up velocity to match his. When he was through he cried, "Cut!" and let himself drop to the cushioned meter-wide hoop. As it reached a stop, the wall lights came up again and he was back in his familiar salon, the furnishings gently hitching themselves back to their places.

Michael stood up, breathing hard and sweating harder. "That was great!" he declared. "Now another quick bath—then we'll get down to business!"

The agenda was clear-cut but it contained a basic fault. There wasn't any business. Although Michael Pellica-Perkins was the only reason for the existence of his habitat, with all its myriad intricate sophistications and ingenuities, it functioned perfectly without him. He wasn't crew. He was a passenger. Like any passenger, he was offered a lavish prospectus of entertainments—games and hobbies, sports and recreations—but none of them made any difference at all. That was just as Michael wanted it, of course. He wanted to be free to pursue the interests of the moment, with no damned nonsense about fixing things around the house.

But basically his most interesting interests had to do with other people, and of those there was a shortage. Nothing stopped him from going to visit a friend, of course. But it would save some irritating discussions if he held off on social calls for a few days, until the word that he and Ann had split got around. So he played a couple of games of 3-D chess against his tourney board, but that wasn't much fun. He had the choice of setting it to play below his own level of skill, which took the exultation out of victory, or of losing, which was even less enjoyable. He played with his collection of model spacecraft, but the best part of them was showing them to someone else. Like Ann. She had really been impressed by them, and almost as impressed by his full-sun and moon display in the bedroom, and somewhat impressed by the ten-thousand-liter water tank they swam in . . . and then not much impressed at all by the fern garden, or the exercise track, or the full health-club equipment. . . . But he didn't want to think about Ann.

What else was there to think about? His calls! Of course! But most of them were sales robots, and he wasn't in the mood to entertain a dozen appliance vendors. The only real, live human being was his brother. Michael was not much in the mood for another tiresome lecture from his brother, either.

Rodney Mazzacco-Perkins was not Michael's full brother. They did have a mother in common. They did have a shared memory of early childhood together—Michael's childhood, actually, because Rodney was eight years older and was off on his own before Michael was ten. They had not got along particularly well as children, and got along even worse as grown-ups. Michael prided himself on the macho virtues. Rodney was a toiler. He was a boring toiler, as well, too unselfish to keep his conscience to himself, unfailing in offering its commandments to those nearby. So Michael avoided being nearby. Rodney saw gloom where Michael saw sport; he saw a steady running down of the human spirit and a terrible dissipation of human resources; his favorite word was "entropy," and he could really kill a party. About the only friend of Michael's who had ever seemed to like him was Ann, and that, Michael thought bitterly, told you all you needed to know about Ann.

Having thought all of which, he said, "I might as well get it over with. Return my brother's call."

"That's surprising," the message center commented as it wiped one display wall clean for the call.

"I didn't ask for an opinion. Just get my brother."

"I can't," the message center smirked. "There's a forwarding on his code. Just a second, Mr. Michael—yes. Here you are."

The person who gazed out at Michael was not his brother at all. It was someone quite unlikely. "Ann!" Michael cried. "What are you doing in Rodney's dump?"

"Oh, Mr. Michael," the message center whispered reproachfully, "I *told* you it was a forwarded call—" just as Ann said:

"I'm not at Rodney's. I'm just taking his calls. What do you want?"

Whatever had annoyed her earlier in the day, she seemed to be over it. Not very friendly. Simply disinterested. She gazed calmly at Michael as though he were the most casual of acquaintances as he explained, huffily, that he was simply, as a matter of common courtesy, returning his brother's call, and it was just like his brother not to be there to receive it. "So where is old Rodney?" he demanded—it was hard to get far enough away to be out of automatic call-forwarding distance.

"Away."

"Well, I figured that out for myself! *Where* away?" Then a sudden worry struck him. "He hasn't—I mean, he isn't *sleeping?*"

He did not have to explain which particular kind of sleeping he meant. If it had been the normal kind, he simply would have got his brother's own message center, and it would simply have told him so. But that other kind of sleep, the long-term aestivative slumber that had been developed for prospective travelers to other stars—there had been any number of persons, Michael knew, whose boredom with the life they lived did not extend quite to suicide, but was too great to let them go on with their daily tedium. There were supposed to be two or three hundred of them in the big suspension satellite in the L-6 position.

"Of course not! What a stupid idea," Ann said indignantly. Then she hesitated, her expression softening. "Was there anything *special* you wanted to say to him? About, you know, any of the things he's been talking to you about?"

Michael chuckled at the idea. "Just calling him back to see what crackpot thing he's up to now," he explained.

"I'll tell him you called." The frost was back in her voice, and in her expression as she broke the contact and faded away; and what a bummer this day was turning out to be.

Michael sighed. "Give me something *nice* to eat," he ordered the kitchen, and to the message center: "And start displaying the debs again. Not the beginning of the alphabet, though—I've probably been over them too many times already. Let's start in the middle."

But that wasn't any good, either. There was something, Michael was nearly sure, that would brighten his life for him, but he couldn't think what it was. Meanwhile the list of debs whose names began with *M* was not a bit more inspiring than the *A*s. Mabel Stiles. Magdalen Savage. Maggie Weeden. Marguerite Jenner. Mary Taylor— "Hey, back up a second," he commanded, intrigued. Magdalen Savage had looked a lot like her name, with a cheerful sluttishness around the eyes and a crude thickness to the lips. "Just call them one after another till I find the right one," he ordered, "starting with *her*."

But Magdalen Savage was much older than her picture or her deceitful vital statistics; and Maggie Weeden was temporarily married and not taking calls; and Marguerite didn't seem to like Michael himself very much; and Mary, he remembered tardily as he was in the course of greeting her, had been his wife for nearly two weeks the year before. "Oh, sorry," he said, "wrong number. Nice talking to you." And to the message center: "The hell with that. Let's think of something else."

"Do you want to try the letter *Z*, just for luck?" the message center inquired.

"No. Shut up. Let me think." He thought gloomily that he could go on playing the directory of debs all day without finding one he liked. There were so many of them! Some he had never met, many that he half remembered— a quick conversation at a party, or brushing up against them in a hunt or a tournament. Those were the places where you could form personal impressions, he thought morosely, and really get to know each other before you committed to anything. . . .

"Why not?" he cried out loud, suddenly enlightened.

"Why not what, Mr. Michael?" the message center asked.

"Why not do it! We've got plenty of supplies now— right, kitchen?"

"Plenty," the kitchen called.

"So we could generate a breakfast for at least fifty or sixty people, right? And all the systems are operative again, right? And you'll have that buck cut up and stored out of sight in the next couple of hours, right?"

"Yes, Mr. Michael. Three times right," the message center acknowledged.

"Then we'll do it! We'll host a hunt!" Michael cried. "Send out the invitations right away!"

IV

If Michael Pellica-Perkins had been dreaming at this
particular moment in his life, there would have been a
smile on his sleeping face. *This* was his dream. This was
the thing he lived for. All the irritations of the day before
were wiped out of his mind. If there was anything more
quintessentially delightful than riding to a hunt itself, it
was the hunt breakfast. Michael's great dining hall, twelve
meters long, hung with emerald drapes, ornamented with
the tendriled nose cones of four fine earlier kills, was filling up with the brightest, bravest, most amusing human
beings alive. They were direct descendants of the British
subalterns who speared tigers from elephants, or the hunt-
masters of the days when the British countryside knew
what to do with itself for pleasure. The repaired entertainment systems were optimal again. They had been working
all night. Champagne was ready, bubbling and chilled,
and the sideboards groaned—well, no, did not really
groan; not in the pull of Michael's gentle spin—but at
least were laden with pâtés and steaming dishes that
looked more like kippers and kidneys and rashers of
bacon than the real thing ever had. The noise level from
the sound system grew to match the noise of chatter and
laughter and excitement. As he went to the door to welcome Bert Sigler and his lovely wife, whatever her name
was, Michael glanced at the display wall. There were at
least a dozen steeds in the guest rack, and almost every
one of them had kills emblazoned on their jet shafts—the
little decals of quarries taken that signified status among
the bloods. By convention, the decals were drawn a quarter actual size—if so, some of the bucks must have been
monsters! You never saw them that big any more. . . .

But that was a gloomy thought, and Michael banished
it. "Hello, Everett," he said to the ranking Dungeons and

Dragons champion, coming in alone and already prospecting the debs in the room. "Nice to see you, Marlene," he told the woman behind him. He began to wonder if his habitat would hold any more—but that was part of the pleasure of it. The crowding, the jostling, the high spirits—the celebrities! That jet-black man, almost the color of ripe plums at twilight—he was the croquet champion of cislunar space, and space croquet, played in three dimensions, where a ball kicked away could go a million miles, was not for weaklings!

And then there were the debs.

Michael had not forgotten what made him decide on the party in the first place. It was a host's job to circulate, and he did, but he made sure to circulate most frequently where the most interesting-looking women were. It wasn't easy to tell as much as he would have liked about the way some of them looked, because everyone, of course, was in hunt gear. No helmets, of course; they were all racked by the door. But there were metal-fiber body stockings in every color and pattern, garb made to look like a wet suit, comic garb like red flannel long johns, flexible copies of the sort of suits the first astronauts had worn. There was even one woman who wore something that looked like knightly armor, lacking only the helmet; as Michael came closer to her he realized she was Magdalen Savage, her handsome face even more lined in person than on his display. "Nice costume," he said admiringly. "More champagne?" But when he had passed her a fresh globe he moved on, looking for someone younger. Or prettier. Or anyway newer.

The air circulators were doing their best, but there were nearly forty people in the room now. And there was something wrong with the centrifugal gravity; Michael felt as though he were in an elevator gently lifting and dropping. The young woman he had been pursuing turned to him with an expression of disdain. "What's the matter with your habitat, Michael?" she asked. Her tone was the sort you might have used to a robot. Michael shrugged, and then she pointed to his exterior display. "Is that it?"

"What?" All he saw was the stacked steeds—and beyond them a distant, tiny glitter of silver, much too large to be a habitat, even an oneill— Of course; it was the photon sailship, practicing rigging its propulsion systems for whenever the day might come that it would in fact take off on the long slow drift to another star. "Bunch of dreamers," he said.

"No, dummy, not the sailship. Your parking rack."

"Oh! Yes, I see," said Michael, and in fact he did. There were so many mounts stacked outside the entrance now that they had unbalanced his habitat's rotation; the center of gravity was no longer the center of his banqueting hall, and so the centrifugal pull was no longer a steady, known force you could accept and forget about.

An annoyance— But Michael grinned. The party was at its peak anyway. The couple of guests who were smoking tobacco and the dozen with dope were giving everyone a contact high, and the noise was becoming nearly painful. People were rubbing against each other; consecutive conversation was impossible. Michael saw a chunk of pâté escape a guest's knife and, instead of settling gently back to the board, float into the collar of a male guest's hunting garb; a sip of champagne, escaped from someone's bulb, was sprinkling a dozen others—

"It's time!" Michael cried, and as everyone turned to him, he shouted: "On with the hunt!"

V

By the time they were well launched, the hunt was dispersed through a volume of a cubic kilometer of space. Spectacular sight! Each mount rode on its jet of flame, each huntsman's helmet flashed the color-coded identity signal. The bright Sun was just dropping toward the western limb of the Earth below. In minutes they would be in the umbra, and then their suit temperatures would start to fall from a hundred degrees above zero to two hundred below—but then there would be no risk of even a small, unforecast solar flare. . . .

Not that any of the three score of them was thinking of solar flares. The hunt! That was the thing. Michael listened to the radio chatter, watched the flares of the rest of the chase—at an average separation of less than two hundred and fifty meters you had to be careful—but most of all he watched the telltale readouts inside his helmet for the radio song of a buck.

The trick of the hunt was threefold. To slant your mount to where the buck was going to be when you got there. To spear the buck cleanly, so that your point punctured its propellant tank and your barb held it firm. And to refrain from spearing another hunter. Or being speared by one. Or drifting into another's high-temperature exhaust. And all the time you heard the yoicks and halloos of the rest of the hunt screaming in your ears, drowning the warbling of the distant bucks that were too far away to be quarry—but might be coming nearer!—and you yourself were screaming most of the time, no matter how experienced you were. And you were half the time in stark hot Sun and the other half in black shade as you turned, and your faceplate never reacted fast enough so that at critical moments you were the next damn thing to blind—roll on, Sunset! Then at least one of the problems would stop being a worry. And watch out most of all for the main-channel microwave beams, the ones that connected the power-satellite nets, or fed juice to the oneills . . . so that you wouldn't be fried instead of the buck.

But that was the sport of it. Those risks, those split-second decisions, the trained reflexes, that congeries of skills, those were the things that made one man a champion

for the day and everyone else nothing at all! It was what
Michael had organized his life around, or the parts of his
life that were worth living, anyway. It had taken him eighteen years, from his first toddler's hunt after pent under-
sized pigs in the family habitat's trap, to the first free-flying
chase, strapped to the jump seat on his mother's mount,
holding with one hand to his mother's suit while the other
brandished his baby spear, until now. Kills blazoned on his
mount, trophies in his banquet hall, and he had the respect
and admiration of everyone he knew—well, almost everyone. Everybody but the weirdos, like Ann and his brother.
The hunt was where it was all at.

But the hunt, unfortunately, depended crucially on the
presence of one thing. Quarry. Big ones. And sometimes
there weren't any big ones to be found.

Michael swore to himself, thinking about the big one his
habitat had trapped. "Quiet down!" he snarled into the
transmitter. "Give us a chance to hear the quarry!"

The chatter dwindled—less because of what Michael
had said than because the hunt was running out of that
first hot joy. He listened, watching his helmet instrument
readouts—yes, there were calls. But high-pitched, meaning immature ones, and faint, meaning still distant. The
cloud of hunters winked one by one into blackness as
they sailed into the Earth's shadow. Now Michael could
pick out the colors of individual beacons. Blue-blue was
Everett Mbaranga, red-white-red the woman named Magdalen, blue-blue-green a man whose name he didn't remember, but who had been one of the first to arrive. They
were the nearest. The others were tinier and distanter
flashes: green-white, green-green-yellow, red-yellow, all
the colors there were, and behind them the steady, un-
moving colors of the myriad, myriad stars. The Moon was
on the far side of the Earth now, but they were approaching one of the power satellites—safe enough, if you
watched yourself, and sometimes a good place to find

quarry confused by the microwave emissions. Through the struts of the immense rectenna Michael could see the dreaming night-time Earth, black and mottled with rare, almost-black patches of sullen dark red. All around the disk of the Earth the faint halo told of the Sun on the other side. It was an awesomely beautiful spectacle, but it lacked what Michael most wanted to see.

There were no bucks in sight.

There were no bucks' squeals in his headphones, either, though the sounds from the other hunters were beginning to pick up again. Some female voice—Michael could not place it—was humming softly to itself; somebody else was sneezing, a distant male voice peevishly warning someone to stay clear. The humming was annoying; there was no excuse for it. Michael smacked his lips to activate his transmitter and said, "Whoever the woman is making that racket, please shut up."

The hummer finished a phrase, then spoke. "What a nasty temper you do have, Michael," she said mildly.

"I can't hear the quarry with all your racket!"

"There's no quarry to hear," she pointed out—and then Michael recognized her. It was her sweet and reasonable voice she was using, the one in which she had explained to him that his way of life was childish.

It was, in a word, Ann.

"What are you doing here?" he shouted.

Low, distant laugh. "You sent out a general invitation, Michael."

"But you don't *hunt*. You don't do any of those childish, wasteful, sickening things you were telling me about!"

No answer at all this time, not even a laugh. Michael jerked his head around, trying to see where she was. What were her confounded helmet colors? Something complicated, he remembered—green-yellow-red-green? One of those four- and five-blink things that showed the owner seldom went out for sports, but traveled only from

point to point where it didn't matter if you could recognize or be recognized. He kneed his mount on the right
side and kicked with his heel; the jets thrust him forward
and relative-up in a left-hand spiral, toward the densest
cluster of riding lights—

And then the headphones picked up a whisper—then a
growing, warbling sound—buck! And a big one, by the
cry!

Instantly his companions in the hunt drowned the sound
out with their yells, Magdalen's contralto "Tally-ho!" and
Everett's "View halloo!" barely beating out the calls of
the others. Sixty blue-white comets sprang up in space as
every member of the hunt kicked his mount and the jets
flared—all arrowing toward the same spot, where the
cross hairs of all direction finders met.

This was where skill counted. Hard riding, nervy thrusts,
quick, cold reflexes. Michael was at the far end of the
cluster of huntsmen, and, even worse, vectored nearly a
hundred and fifty degrees wrong. He kicked his mount
around, swiftly calculated moments of force and let it rip.
Michael's brute steed made a difference. It was a beast; it
possessed delta-Vs that most mounts did not own and few
riders would dare; mounts like that were dangerous. You
could be thrown. You could run out of propellant with a
bunch of residual velocity that would carry you a long way
from home, and have to scream for help—you could even
wind up too far and too fast for the rest of the hunt to reach
you, and maybe even your own habitat out of range, and
then maybe you would never be found at all. It had happened. But, when you could handle it, a blown-out,
charged-up mauler gave you an edge.

Michael could handle it. The attitude thruster bucked
him to the right orientation. The main jets cut in. The
acceleration surge ground him back into the bucket sad-
dle—nearly five Gs he was pulling, and the pressure collar
at the base of his neck swelled quickly to block the flow of

blood from his brain. Even so he was dizzy for a moment, and the confused roaring in his ears could have been hallucination.

It wasn't hallucination; it was real. The nearest huntsmen were in visual range now, and they were shouting. Other voices joined in, and though there were too many of them, so that Michael could not hear the words, he could recognize the tone: shock, wonder, dismay. The blood flowed back to his brain. His vision cleared. He saw the spark of green that marked the quarry on his helmet visor. He could not see the buck itself, but he saw where it was.

A great skeletal bedspring of struts and wires, kilometers long, more than a kilometer wide. A power satellite. And the buck was hanging there, drifting through the guts of the rectenna, making no attempt to escape, screaming its head off.

Michael Pellica-Perkins was neither stupid nor badly educated. In the subjects that interested him, he was soundly informed. The microcircuitry of his habitat did not interest him at all—it was designed to maintain itself without any help from its occupant—and so he did not know a Josephson junction from a thumbtack. He had never, as far as he knew, seen either. But Von Neumann self-replicating automata were something else. If he did not know them under that name, he knew them as Noymans, as bucks, as pigs—as quarry. A Noyman was the hardware equivalent of a germ. It browsed, grew, reproduced and died. It accumulated nothing, neither property nor wisdom. Like a germ, it left nothing to its offspring except . instructions on how to be like itself. Like a germ, those "genetic" instructions sometimes were garbled in transmission. Not much. If the encoding was too far wrong, reproduction simply did not occur, or the results simply did not function—as with a germ. But small errors could be tolerated. In a Darwinian sense those "errors" accounted for selection under environmental pressure and thus for evolution. Perhaps they would have for the Noymans, too, if there were world enough and time; but the first Noymans had been seeded into space not much more than a century before and nothing that could be called evolutionary would happen for a few dozen millennia, at least. What those small encoding errors meant to a Noyman was that it did not respond quite properly to its programming; it failed to home on its beacons, or it attempted to assimilate a habitat instead of allowing itself to be disassembled to repair it, or it did not return to cislunar space at all—they said there were tens of thousands of Noymans chomping away at the asteroids, never coming back to be harvested. There was a name for such "errors" in the vocabulary of the hunt. They were called "rogues."

Michael was the first of the hunt to say it. "Rogue!" he yelled. "Watch yourselves!" You never knew what a rogue would do; the very fact that it had blundered into the power satellite showed that its programming had gone sour, the fact that it remained there, in that high-energy photon sea, confirmed it. There was a confused chorus from the others, but Michael was no longer listening. For the other thing about a rogue was that it was the most challenging quarry there was.

Michael recomputed in his head, threw out his assumed velocity-of-target, estimated anew on a stationary quarry and flashed in between two other huntsmen, who checked and braked thrust, sliding off past the main girders and away from the rectenna. But not all of the hunt was cautious. Michael could see the ID lights of three or four others, skittering in and out of the metalwork, beaming headlamps into shadows, lances ready.

It was a purely visual search now. With all that metal and all the microwave energy the RDFs were liars. The cross hairs flickered here and there on the faceplate, sometimes showing three targets at once, sometimes thirty, mostly showing nothing but a spiderweb of half-formed lines that grew and faded irresolutely. That was part of the needed skill, too—reading the RDFs when the RDFs were confused, and especially knowing when to forget you had them at all. To spear a rogue buck, think like one! Think yourself confused and uncertain, programming unreliable, responses unready.

So Michael dived straight for the vast bedspring itself.

The rectenna was huger far than even an oneill, a vast orbiting island of Manhattan—though Michael had never seen Manhattan—and every second it handled an energy flux of a hundred thousand kilowatts. Since it was one of the most efficient machines Man or his robot servants ever made, the leakage was less than one thousandth of one per cent—but that came easily to enough juice to cook a hunter in his pressure suit, if it all happened to leak in the same place. And sometimes it did; so that was where you needed the huntsman's other essential ingredient: courage. Michael dived within meters of the wire itself, where faint fire glowed from the points of metal and his radiation monitors began to cheep desperately, mistaking the bleed-off of electricity for the first warning precursors of a solar flare. That cheeping sound was not one you usually ignored. The first thing you learned, when you got your first grown-up-sized skinsuit, was to run for home at the first cheep.

But not, of course, when you were nightside, with twelve thousand kilometers of rock parasol between you and any solar flare: Override another reflex!

The ID stars were blinking all around him now, as the rest of the hunt regained enough courage to creep in after the first few valiant ones. Too close! There were near collisions, and shouts of warning or fear in the headphones. Then a woman's shout—Magdalen's?—"Got 'im! Tallyho!" And red-white-red shot past him, into the heart of the bedspring.

For a moment Michael automatically extrapolated the blue comet tail of her exhaust to the cluster of structural members ahead and was certain she would collide. Not quite. The rectenna was made of more than eighteen million hexagonal elements, closely fitted together; but it was built and launched in sections, and where the sections were joined together there were gaps. Not big. Big enough, and Magdalen was arrowing toward one—*through* the rectenna! out into empty space beyond it!

Michael swore unbelievingly. Damn buck! They *never* went on the Earthward side of the power satellites! Their propulsive systems were too weak to risk in a closer orbit; that was part of their most basic programming.

But where the quarry went, there went Michael Pellica-Perkins. Even as he was kicking his mount around to follow he was snapping off all his automatic warning systems and instruments. He knew what was ahead. He ignored the babble in the headphones, ignored the lying readings of his RDF, concentrated on snaking his way through the path Magdalen had found.

Then he saw it. Big one! Ten meters long at least! A trophy worth anyone's wall! His faceplate was clear, and he could see the quarry, the broad dark Earth behind it, the red-white-red of Magdalen's ID blinker. She was in trouble; her jet flashed and stopped, flashed again; she had failed to allow for the mighty flux of microwave energy whose path they were both now solidly in. Michael heard faint whisperings in his earphones and felt the prickle of static electricity. It was not a place to stay in for very long! Out at the edge of the power satellite behind him he saw a cluster of lights that resolved themselves into a shuttlecraft with skinsuited figures around it—not hunters and thus not of any interest to Michael—but the more daring of the rest of the hunt were beginning to slip through the wire behind him.

If they were not as careful as Michael, they would soon be as helpless as Magdalen; the thing to do was to end the hunt and get it over with. He shouted with pleasure; it was time for Michael Pellica-Perkins to show them how to do it!

So they saw. They saw Michael, in the full microwave flux, arrowing in toward the torpedo-shaped quarry while Magdalen bobbed indecisively around, a hundred meters away. It looked like a classic clean kill: quick, savage thrust and bear the buck away, yelling triumph. But Michael didn't thrust. He threw. He never came closer than twenty meters to the quarry, but he hurled his lance like a harpoon as he flashed past, putting on speed to get away—for the buck was *wrong*. The size was impressive, a hundred cells at least; the behavior was normal enough—bucks often hung helpless and dumb for that last coup de grace. But the shape! It was not the clean torpedo lines of the standard Noyman; it was squatter, fatter, almost lemon-shaped.

Which meant that it was a special-purpose Noyman of some kind; the kind that sometimes held radionuclides, sometimes even stranger things. You did not get too close to such a buck if you didn't want your hair to fall out and your teeth to loosen; you killed it clean for the sake of the record, and left it dead for the scavengers to collect for its contents. So he killed it. Killed it deader than he had planned, for the lance hit the propellant tanks.

There is no noise in space, so there was no thundering blast. But the buck exploded, white actinic glare and savage chunks of metal flying. It left a gap meters across in the rectenna, with red and blue-white sparks snapping across the spaces. It lit the power satellite and the hunters and the shuttlecraft like a strobe. And one chunk came flying in a very wrong direction. There are six Cartesian directions, with an infinite number of vectors between; the flying chunk could have been thrust in any of them, but the direction it took was straight toward Michael. It was unlikely it would hit him. He did not take the chance. He kicked his mount savagely, whirled with all the power of the attitude thrusters and poured on the main thrust. All that power! Too much to be handled so carelessly. He was thrown—thrown like a beginner on his first ride, struck by the mount itself, knocked off into free space; the last thing he remembered was the beginning of a terrible headache, and amazement that he could have been so clumsy. And Ann's voice crying his name.

VI

"Are you all right?"

Michael gazed up at the bearded face that hung over him. It was not a sympathetic-looking face. It looked angry and scared . . . and disappointed, too; the combination was more than Michael could unravel. "Of course I'm all right," he said, and knew immediately that he had lied. His head hurt and his chest felt as though he had been coughing for weeks; there was something wrong with his nostrils, and when he touched them with a finger they seemed to have dried blood in them.

"You're lucky!" snarled the man with the beard. "A lot luckier than you deserve—you and those other idiots—if I had my way, you'd all—"

"Leave him alone for a minute, Chet," said another voice, and Michael saw that he was in a small habitat of some kind—or, no, not a habitat, a workshop? A storage space? A *ship?* "Belt up, you, Michael," the second man said. "We've already deorbited. We'll be getting first penetration in about ten minutes."

Michael raised himself cautiously—he was in zero-G,

he discovered, and had to catch at the seat he was in to keep from flying away. "Is Ann here?"

"Ann? There's no woman here," said Chet, beard trembling in anger. "Just shuttle crew."

"*Shuttle* crew." It took a moment for the sense to penetrate. "Good heavens!" he cried. "What am I doing in a shuttle?"

"We picked you up. Your helmet was cracked and you were losing pressure—"

"I've got to get off!"

"Get off how?" Chet demanded triumphantly. "We had to deorbit or lose our landing window, we couldn't wait for help. Don't worry; we told your half-witted friends we were taking you down."

"*Down?*"

The beard nodded. "To the surface. Now belt up, or you'll scramble your silly brains even sillier when we hit the atmosphere."

Part of the reason for the hostility in the ship Michael understood. These were the busy ants, the people who liked to work. Naturally they hated gentry—it had been thus always, when the English farmers raged against the foxhunt, when the New Jersey orchardists posted their land against pheasant hunters, probably when the Romans and the Greeks trampled crops as they speared boars. That accounted for the anger and resentment. The fear? The disappointment? No, there was some other reason for that.

And, as far as anger was concerned, Michael felt on very strong moral grounds: he had more right to anger than they! They were *kidnapping* him. They had no *right.* Orbit-to-ground ballistics were no subject of Michael's, but he knew perfectly well, as everyone in a space habitat knew, that if you missed one landing opportunity you only

had to wait ninety minutes or so for the next—they could
have waited that long! They *should* have. He, or any of
his friends, would have done as much for them, even
though they were that contemptible kind of human being
who *worked,* like *robots,* for God's sake, instead of devoting themselves to the truly human pursuits that Michael
himself enjoyed. Michael was not prejudiced against
work, really. Some of his best friends worked. One was a
dentist. One decorated habitat interiors. One even had
helped design the photon sailship that, any week now, was
going to start off to explore whatever the name of that
star was for whatever planets it might have—of course,
Michael and he had lost touch some time ago, because
their interests simply did not coincide that much any
more. But one expected *courtesy.* Even from an ant.

It was true, of course, that in some sense these particular ants might be said to have saved his life.

He groaned as the shuttle began to buck and shudder.
"Are you all right?" called one of the ants.

He made a vaguely affirmative noise. Actually, he
wasn't all right, or anything near it. A high-G turn on a
steed was one thing, you could handle that with skill and
courage and muscle, but this was like being shaken in a
giant popcorn popper, and it went on and on. He was glad
for the restraining straps. Without them he would have
been thrown all over the little cabin. But they dug into
him, cut his shoulders, squeezed his arms; worst of all,
they pressed his aching chest like a medieval torture machine. He must have lost a lot of pressure, he realized;
lucky he hadn't caught an embolism, lucky the shuttle
crew had been there to pick him up. But he didn't feel
lucky.

No one could consider himself lucky if he was on his
way down to the surface of the Earth.

Of course, he told himself, wincing and gasping, it
would only be long enough to turn around and catch a

return shuttle. They operated quite frequently—didn't they? At least sometimes. And anyway, it would be a sort of adventure to tell the debs at the next party, almost as exciting as volunteering for the interstellar ship. . . .

Now, where had that thought come from? It had something to do with Ann. It was part of that long argument they'd had before she left. It was a joke, of course, he was sure it was a joke, but she'd asked what he thought of the photon-sail ship. Bunch of dreamers, he'd said contemptuously, and then she'd flared up. Why shouldn't human beings dream? she demanded.

And then it had gone on from there. Of course human beings should dream. He would never dream in that particular direction himself. The photon ship was going to take off for—for—oh, yes, the name came back to him: Lalande's star, it was called, known to have planets, believed that the planets were in the Mars-Earth size range and thus maybe, possibly, with any luck at all, as an outside chance, habitable. Drone observations had made it sound more or less hopeful. Michael admitted that getting there would be pretty marvelous. But the *process* of getting there—how wearisome! Eighteen years. And eighteen years back. You would have to be the kind of person who could be happy in an oneill to stand that. True, some people had actually signed up for it, but they were mostly older ones—in their thirties and forties, a couple even older. So they really couldn't leave until they got some breeding stock, and breeding stock was like Michael and Ann and Magdalen and Everett—they liked what they had! They weren't the oneill types, content to live cheek by jowl with forty others for eighteen interminable years. No, he told Ann, starfarers weren't his kind of people, they were almost as bad as the LTGs. . . .

And then the shouting really started, because Ann, it seemed, was pretty close to being a limits-to-growth fanatic herself. You couldn't blame him for getting really angry at that kind of talk. He had had enough of it from his own brother, for heaven's sake. . . .

"We're coming in," called one of the crewmen over his shoulder, and Michael came out of his reverie to realize three things. First, the buffeting had long since stopped. Second, they were indeed coming in for a landing; he could feel the vessel bumping and clattering as its wheels came down. And third, he was in his underwear.

The surface of the Earth was no longer green and pleasant. A century or so of space shuttles had shredded the ozone layer. Reject heat from fusion plants had turned the lakes and streams into hot tubs, and even the great world-girdling ocean, warming up, was beginning to melt away the undersides of the North Polar floes and the Antarctic glaciers. The last of the fossil fuels had filled the skies with combustion compounds and particulates, and the view from Michael's window, as the shuttle bumped toward a disembarkation dock, was of something like a sooty Sahara.

Since he was not planning to stay there long enough for it to matter, it did not greatly interest him, and besides he had other things on his mind. "Why did you take my skin-suit off?" he demanded of the bearded man as they all began to unsnap their belts.

"Just to save your life, Mike. This way," said the bearded man, opening a hatch.

"But I can't go around in my skivvies!"

"Rent a suit," suggested the man, pointing Michael toward a corridor with signs that said things like CUSTOMS and HEALTH CONTROL and IMMIGRATION. "There's a Hertz counter out there, I think," he added, beginning to turn away.

"Hey! You mean by myself? Can't I stay with you?"

"We're *crew*," the bearded man explained, and although Michael was not sure what that meant he could see no way to argue it. Suddenly he was alone. There were not that many immigrants coming to Earth these days, it seemed, because the long corridors were vacant. So, when he came to them, were the halls where luggage carousels had once deposited the bags of returning space tourists. The room was absolutely silent, except for his own footsteps. . . .

Which, it turned out, were enough to trigger the activation circuits of a robot immigration guard. As Michael approached, the creature lifted itself from a seat at one of the counters and gestured Michael toward him. "Passport?" he barked.

Michael regarded him with astonishment. It was not as though he had never seen a robot before. Actually he had seen quite a few, though only as traveling door-to-door salesmen, or as somebody's idea for a kinky way to decorate a habitat. But in Michael's world robots were *never* in a position to take that tone to a human being. "I don't have a passport," he said frostily.

The robot did not seem surprised. He was a huge one, Michael realized, towering over Michael and probably outweighing him at least four to one. Michael's own weight was giving his tottering knees about all they could handle in this gross Earth gravity; he was grateful not to weigh more. "Anything to declare?" the robot asked.

"What does that mean?"

The robot frowned. "You don't ask what that means," it explained. "You just say 'yes' or 'no.' Yes means you have something that's illegal to bring in or that you have to pay duty on. No means you don't."

"I'll say no," Michael decided.

"Thank you, sir." The robot reached under the counter and handed Michael a printed yellow form. The paper crackled alarmingly in Michael's fingers. It seemed to be years old at least, maybe decades. "Hand this to the guard on your way out," the robot ordered, and returned to immobility.

The next chamber was as empty as the first, and the

guard at the door was another robot, in the same uniform as the other, and in the same condition. It too roused itself out of standby mode as it heard the sound of Michael's approach, took the printed form and scanned it, touched its cap and relapsed into standby as Michael pushed through the exit door.

He was in a large, vaulted lobby, as silent as any that had gone before. Once this place had been a major space terminal. Obviously the traffic had dwindled far below the point where all this space served any function, or where it could maintain the shops and services that had once been all about. A sign before him said KOFFEE KOUNTER, but under it was nothing but a rolled-down corrugated-metal door with another sign: CLOSED. Counters bore legends like NATIONAL RENT-A-SUIT and HOTEL AND MOTEL RESERVATIONS and LIMOUSINE SERVICES. None of them were manned, and when Michael picked up the limousine phone, and then the one at the hotel counter, both were dead. The only sign of movement in the whole lobby was a winking digital clock at the bottom of a great liquid-crystal dispatchers' board. One side was headed ARRIVALS, and it was blank. The other, DEPARTURES, had a single line illuminated below it. At 1355 on the seventeenth a passenger shuttle was due to leave for Orbiting Station Candy. But the time hack at the bottom of the board told Michael that that was more than a week away. Meaning, no doubt, a week before any of those services advertised all around him became available again.

It occurred to Michael that it might be pretty dull in this place for a solid week . . . just before it occurred to him that, in a solid week in a place like this, a person might come pretty close to starving. There was not even the hope that he might have something left and forgotten in his pockets; he had no pockets, nothing but the under-briefs he had worn beneath the skinsuit.

He was quite completely impoverished—a concept that

had never, as a tangible potentiality, occurred to Michael Pellica-Perkins before.

A brisk sound of voices, faint but definite, came from somewhere outside the building. Michael was galvanized into hope. He sprang to the windows, which were quite dirty, peering out into the unpleasantly sulfurous-looking outdoors, and caught a glimpse of three human figures. The crew from his shuttlecraft? *Maybe* they were the crew; he could not tell; all of them were wearing mirror-bright globular helmets against the rank air, and their features were not visible. "Hey!" Michael shouted, realized they could not possibly hear, then searched desperately for a doorway. It was there. He pushed through a revolving door, sprinted across a wide antechamber, pushed through another—

And stopped, gagging and coughing. Great orange flakes of something harsh-smelling and worse-tasting were drifting down on him out of a dirty lemon sky. Michael had never smelled anything like it. It was like breathing fire. He saw, dimly, through the sullied air, a vehicle pulling away. Its occupants did not see him, or were not interested.

He did not wait to see it disappear. As fast as he could, he stumbled back through the outer revolving doors to regroup.

His knees were shaking. His thigh and calf muscles were incredibly sore. His feet were beginning to hurt, and his ankles to betray him. Cough though he would, he could not get the acrid stench of this world's atmosphere out of his already painful lungs. If this was the mother planet, how wise he had been to stay in orbit!

And—was there any way to get back there?

He pushed hopelessly through the inner doors and stood in the empty lobby . . . and became aware of a whisper that seemed to come from everywhere: "—white courtesy telephone," it said in a sweet and sexless voice, and then was still. For a moment he hoped. But it was not a human voice.

And then hope came back as the message repeated itself:

"Arriving passenger Michael Pellica-Perkins. For arrangements to meet your party, please pick up the white courtesy telephone."

The phone, when he found it, did not appear to have been touched for years; the message repeated itself three times before he was able to figure out how to make this antique instrument work. When he identified himself into it, the same gender-free voice asked him to wait one moment for his party's message, and then there was another voice.

This one he recognized. "I'm glad you're here safe and sound, Michael," it said, and hurried right on. "Go to the baggage-claim area. There's a covered-hatchway vehicle entrance; go through the hatch and you'll find a car waiting. The driver's name is Gideon and he'll bring you here to me. . . . 'Me,'" it went on, a touch of sarcasm in the tone, "in case you've forgotten what I sound like since you don't return my calls any more, is your brother, Rodney."

All orbital launch stations, Michael knew, were on the Equator, or as near to it as geography allowed. Why this was so he was far less sure. It had something to do with conserving rotational energy, and something to do, too, with avoiding something called Coriolis force. Michael had never considered it necessary to learn what a Coriolis force was, but he had retained the knowledge that if you were ever so silly as to go down to the surface of the Earth, you would find yourself in the tropics. Therefore he was in the tropics now.

He also knew what the tropics looked like, because among the many scenes for his view walls were loops of the Amazon jungle, monkeys and bright-colored birds and steamy vines dangling from richly foliated trees, and of some African savanna—antelopes being stalked by great cats—and a South Seas island with laughing, beautiful dark women launching canoes into the surf.

None of that looked in any way like what he was seeing outside the car window. Nothing else in his experience did, either, except possibly a party view he had once seen in somebody else's habitat, called "Pittsburgh Steel Mills, 1910." The only thing that was right, or at least according to his preconceptions, was that the outside climate was indeed equatorially *hot*. He had been too preoccupied with strangling to pay much attention to the temperature in his one venture into the outside air, but now, as he pressed his palm against the car window, the heat stung his flesh.

He caught the eye of the robot driver, peering back at him in the rear-view mirror. The creature smiled and touched its cap. "Pretty bad right around here, Mr. Michael," it said. "But we won't have to go out into it."

Michael studied him with some distaste. This fad of building machines to look like human beings would never catch on in civilization; why, you never knew what you were talking to! "We're all right unless the car breaks down, I guess," he grumbled.

"It won't break down, Mr. Michael! I maintain it myself. And anyway, if it did, why, I'd just whistle up a new one from the garage. One'd be here in ten minutes, outside—long before the air-conditioning wore off in here. Or else," he explained, making Michael nervous by half turning his head as he spoke, "we could just hitch a ride—plenty of traffic along here, these days!"

And indeed there was. The road from the spaceport was twelve lanes wide, and all of them were full. If it had not been so very ugly, it would have been fascinating. Great tractor-trailers rumbled by in both directions. Most of them were closed cargo trucks, or flatbeds with great, dark, tropic-looking logs going somewhere, or heaped farm produce of some kind going somewhere else. A few of the giants were flatbeds with a difference: rows of seats bolted to the bed, open to the filthy, poisoned air—and occupied by passengers! In that muck! The passengers could not be human, Michael decided. They had to be robots, which would take no harm from the orange flakes of ash, or the foehn winds, or the air's content of droplets of acid. But it was difficult to believe that when you looked at them. Now and then a smaller vehicle, like the one Michael himself was in, zipped in and out of the plunging procession of huger machines. Through the windows Michael got an occasional glimpse of what were probably real flesh-and-blood human beings like himself. Or thought he did. How could you tell? They paid no attention to him; and, by and by, he paid no attention to them. All his rubbernecking was saved for the scenery. Here and there along the highway, kilometers apart, were occasional cloudy bubbles of some sort of plastic, skyscraper high. They were not easy to see into, but, craning his neck, Michael caught glimpses of, yes, tall trees and dangling vines—were they nature preserves of some sort, keeping a few tiny oases of the original jungle like a museum? Was this what all this terrain had once looked like?

If so, it looked that way no more. What it looked like combined the worst features of an Iowa farmscape, a car factory and the Los Angeles freeways. Great machines chugged along the fields, planting and plowing, sowing and harvesting. For two kilometers at a stretch it was some sort of tuber that was being dug out of the ground and dropped into waiting trucks, to join the traffic on the road. For another stretch the fields were flooded and the crop might possibly, Michael guessed, be rice. Behind and among the fields were immense sooty industrial buildings. Most of them were topped with immense stacks, and every one of the stacks was pouring more filth into the already corrupted air. "What the hell are they doing there, Gideon?" Michael called, leaning forward, his eyes on the smoldering stacks.

The robot looked around. Since Michael was not used to robots in human form, he was astonished to see how much expression they could show on their mechanical faces. He did not have a name for the driver's present look, although his ancestors could have identified it: it was the look of the city man to the rube, amusement and faint contempt. "They make electric power, Mr. Michael," the driver said, politely enough. "See, they harvest the BTU bushes and all the other energy crops, and then they burn them for power."

"Oh, no," Michael cried violently, shaking his head. "I know better than that, at least!"

"I beg your pardon?"

"They can't be burning organic matter! Why, you might as well tell me they're burning fossil fuels. It's all fusion power now. It's been nothing but clean nuclear fusion for hundreds of years!"

The driver turned back to his wheel. After a moment, he said over his shoulder, "You've been away too long, Mr. Michael." He was smiling.

Their destination turned out to be a huge old building, tall and almost majestic in the sooty air. At first Michael thought it might have been some kind of palace, then, as the car turned toward the ramp to the basement garage, he caught sign of a cracked neon sign. It said TRINIDAD INTERCONTINENTAL.

It was a hotel! And a big, obviously once expensive one; therefore a tourist one; and for a fleeting moment Michael had the sensation of having come back home. The scene was familiar to him from a million old video films. The Jet Set. The idle rich. The suave, sophisticated international playboys and their dazzling debs—no, they didn't call them "debs" in the movies. Michael knew what he would find inside—a gambling casino; swimming pools; nightclubs; bars with languorous women and deft bartenders; a great restaurant, of course, with vaulted ceilings, and headwaiters who snapped their fingers and ordered special tables set up and chairs brought. . . . So few of those things existed in orbit!

Nor, he discovered, did all of them exist at the Trinidad Intercontinental. Not any more, if they ever had. Through the lobby window, as they came up on a great, slow escalator, he could see that the outdoor swimming pool had become a parts shed, and the ocean view was repellent. There was a beach, all right. But the waves came in like gloppy oil slicks, and strange things floated on them. "This way, Mr. Michael," said his robot chauffeur, leading him to an elevator. Michael might have asked questions, but the sudden sensation of doubled weight as the car leaped up toward the twenty-fifth floor nearly cost him the lunch that, he remembered, he had not had. When they got out he was reeling. "You'll be all right in a minute," the robot told him, and opened a door. "Here's your brother."

It was as well the robot said it—or almost; Rodney looked at Michael for a long moment, then did a most uncharacteristic thing. He got up, came to the door and put his arms around Michael.

If Michael had been hugged by his brother, ever, it must have been before he was old enough to talk. Certainly before he was old enough to remember. He allowed himself to be squeezed for a moment and then, trying not to give offense, broke free. "I'm glad to see you, too, Rodney," he said, "but honestly, you know, I'm starving."

Rodney looked abashed. "Of course you are," he cried. "I'm sorry. Gideon, will you—?"

"Sure I will, Mr. Rodney," the robot said, and went

into another room to use the room-service phone.

Michael sat down on a shabby couch, much too deep for this intense gravity but a lot better than staying on his protesting feet. He regarded his brother. "That's very nice of you, Rodney," he said. "Why are you being so nice?"

Rodney didn't answer him at once. His expression was odd, but almost familiar to Michael. As Rodney moved over to the window and gazed out at the busy farm scene beyond, Michael identified it. It was the same look he had seen on Rodney's face when they were children—specifically, when Rodney knew something Michael had not yet been told. Generally something about some trouble Michael was in. "And you called me," Michael remembered, "and then when I called back you were gone. What did you call about?"

Rodney shrugged. "Well, that's the whole thing," he remarked. "How do I explain it to you?"

"Maybe you start by answering the question?"

"What I called about? Sure. I wanted to ask you to help me with a Noyman."

Of all the answers Rodney might have given, there was none that could have surprised Michael more. "A buck! Rodney! You haven't come over to the sporting life, have you?"

"My God, no!"

"Well then?"

Rodney picked his words with care. "It was a special kind of a Noyman, Michael."

Michael stared at him. "The rogue? The one I blew up?"

"That's the one," Rodney said bitterly. "You don't know how lucky you were!"

"Well, sure I do—if somebody hadn't picked me up—"

"I don't mean that. That was just Ann, keeping an eye on you. I mean the buck itself. It was a tritium-seeking Noyman, Michael. There was at least a chance that the whole thing would go up when you speared it—a nuclear explosion!"

"A nuclear—"

"You heard me! And that was my Noyman, Michael; I've been waiting a year for one to show up, and I needed it!"

Michael felt as though he were at the heart of a giant jigsaw puzzle, with pieces dropping into place around him, others missing, some apparently from another puzzle entirely. What Rodney told him made some answers clear. He knew what a tritium-seeking Noyman was; they were rare, like all the special-purpose Noymans, but they did exist, roaming the far stretches of the solar system for rare elements and keyed to return only to specially coded signals. What anyone wanted tritium for was another question entirely. Certainly no normal person had any use for it in his habitat! It had to do with releasing fusion power, of course, and it was terribly dangerous also, of course, and there seemed to be a sort of need for it in some of the automatic industrial systems . . . all that, of course, but what would any *person* want with it?

So that particular answer only generated a new question, and there were plenty of those already. What made Rodney think the buck was his? Bucks belonged to no one until they were caught; everyone knew that; it was like saying it was "his" space or "his" starlight. And why was Ann keeping an eye on him? And what kind of help had Rodney wanted? And what could Rodney possibly "need" the buck for? And—

And the more Rodney talked, the cloudier the answers got. Rodney wasn't unresponsive. God, no! He talked nonstop, while the robot room waiters came in with Michael's dinner, silver-topped dishes and cut crystalware— almost the way it was in those old video films, except that in the films you didn't have an older brother lecturing you all through the process. "Do you know," Rodney demanded, "what your energy budget is?" And then he answered himself. "No, of course you don't. Why would you care? But I measured your habitat's consumption for a solid month."

"Rodney," said Michael, as kindly as he could, "what a dumb thing to do. Not to say sneaky."

"It's not a secret, after all. It's of the order of six hundred kilowatt-years a year. A steady drain of six hundred thousand watts, day in and day out! Just one habitat! Times the one point six million habitats in cislunar orbit, plus the oneills, plus—"

"Energy is civilization," Michael said mildly, investigating what was under the silver covers. It appeared to be ham sandwiches, and the bread was nearly stale.

"You never would listen to anything serious," Rodney grumbled.

That was true enough. Michael studied his brother, as he chewed on the stringy meat in the sandwich. He noticed that Rodney's beard was turning gray. Not neatly, attractively gray; it was a mixture of natural brown and dirty white. What it looked like most was some old dishcloth that you could never wash the stains out of. And it wasn't even trimmed. Nor was Rodney's hair. It was thinning at the top and shaggy around the neck. "I get tired of listening to you being serious," Michael said. "Maybe if you ever talked about anything else—"

"I bet you don't even know where the power comes from!"

Michael sighed, and started on the second sandwich. He hadn't returned Rodney's call very happily just because their encounters were always about like this. He didn't like talking to his brother. He hadn't liked his brother all that much even when they were children. Rodney was older, and Rodney was always wiser. Or said he was; and reliably came up with reasons why everything Michael

said or did on his own was frivolous, dangerous and stupid
. . . some relationships never change. "Of course I know
that," he said. "From the power satellites."

"And where do the power satellites get it?"

Michael swallowed the dry mouthful and hastily took a
sip of a rather poor wine. "Oh—" He thought for a moment. "All different places, I guess. There's solar power,
and what-you-calls, magnetohydrodynamic generators.
You can't expect me to remember all that stuff."

Rodney gestured at the purgatory outside the window.
"It comes from there!" he shouted triumphantly. "Eighty
per cent of the power consumed in orbit comes right from
the surface of the Earth!"

Michael frowned. It was a silly thing to get excited about,
but he was nearly sure his brother was wrong. "No," he said,
trying to remember. "I think the way it was, the original
habitat program was started to serve the orbiting generators.
Yes. They produced energy in space and microwaved it to the
Earth, not the other way around, Rodney."

"Right! Until the population balance shifted to space!
All those rectennae, all those microwave links—the traffic
has been going the other way for fifty years now."

"Really?" That was quite surprising, Michael admitted
to himself, even if not very important.

"Really! And it has ruined the Earth."

"Well, I'll agree to that." Michael smiled, turning over
more silver covers to see what they had given him for des-
sert. No argument there! You only had to look out the
window for the proof. "In fact," he said, poking at what
looked like a piece of apple pie with his fork, "that's one
of the things I wanted to say, Rodney. I really hate this
place. I'd like to catch the next shuttle back to orbit." He
was frowning, because the pie did not seem much fresher
than the bread in the sandwiches, and there wasn't even
any ice cream on it.

He was chewing on the first forkful of the soggy pastry

before he realized that his brother wasn't responding to him, and there was something strained about the silence. He looked up, frowning. "What's the matter, Rodney?" he demanded.

"I'm afraid you can't do that," his brother said slowly.

"What are you talking about? Of course I can! There's a ship coming in a week or so, I know that—although I'd hope to get away earlier—"

"Not earlier," said his brother, "and not then. I don't want you talking to people in orbit about this."

Michael put down his fork, forgetting to chew. "How silly you are, Rodney!"

"We don't agree on that," his brother observed. "Anyway, you're going to stay here for a while. Until I finish what I set out to do. What do you think I wanted that tritium-seeker for?"

"God knows! Something obnoxious!"

"No. Something vitally necessary. I was going to use it to make nuclear bombs, Michael. Well, I can't do that, so I'll have to rely on chemical explosives. It will take longer, but I can manage."

"Explosives! You're going to blow something up?"

"A lot of somethings, Michael. I'm going to break the link between Earth and orbit. I'm going to destroy the generators."

Michael gazed at his brother in horror. "All of them?"

"Every one that transmits power to orbit," Rodney declared. "I'll cut off the roots, and the fruit will wither and fall away."

The pie had no more interest for Michael. He put down his fork and took a deep swallow of the wine, his mind filling with images. None of them was adequate. If some nineteenth-century Irish farmhand had announced his intention of sowing potato bugs in every plowed field . . . if a slave-state governor had pronounced his own Emancipation Proclamation . . . if Augustus had disbanded the Roman legions, or Louis the Fourteenth declared France a republic . . . if any human being had ever calmly proposed to do the thing that would demolish the social structure of his homeland entirely, then there might have been some wickedness to match what Rodney proposed. But there was nothing like it in all of human history! Destroy the source of power for the habitats? "Rodney," Michael cried, when he could speak again at all, "we'll *die!*"

"How dramatic you are, Michael," said his brother with irritation. "Don't be foolish. Of course you won't die. There are still generators in orbit. They can supply the oneills—"

"Oneills! Orbiting tenements!"

Rodney shrugged. "Still, they can hold all you smallholders easily enough. Perhaps it won't be comfortable, especially—"

He paused, and Michael finished the sentence for him. "Especially for the brother of a traitor, you mean?"

"Well, I suppose some people might take that view," Rodney muttered. There was a queer sort of apprehension in the way he looked at his brother. Almost fear, Michael thought, and realized that he was standing up, leaning toward Rodney; he could easily be giving the impression of rage. The thought rather pleased him. All their physical encounters had taken place when Rodney had an eight-year advantage in size and strength. Since they were both grown up, the quarrels had been only verbal.

"I ought to punch you out," he yelled experimentally.

His diagnosis was confirmed. Rodney licked his lips and glanced worriedly at the robot, standing motionless by the door. "We can be reasonable about this, I hope," Rodney offered. "Have some more wine. Sit down. Please."

Michael turned his furious gaze at the robot, moving forward with the bottle. "Wine! Do you think that will fix everything up?—Just a little more, please," he added, watching Gideon pour.

"I'm willing to listen to reason," Rodney said persuasively. "In the long run, I'm doing this for everyone's best interests."

"Hah!"

"I am! I wouldn't be talking to you like this if I didn't want to have your friendship, would I? I mean, Michael, obviously you're a wastrel and a jock and an idiot. But you're my brother, and I'd rather have you with me than against me. That's why I let Ann talk me into asking for your help with the Noyman."

"Ann!"

"Well, she made sense. And don't forget, if she hadn't been right there at the shuttle, keeping an eye on you, you might be dead now."

"Dead!" Michael said scornfully.

Rodney sighed. "These one-word responses of yours," he said, "get monotonous. Can't you see that the Earth is our real home? It gives us shelter and food, even the wine you drink—"

Michael sneered. "If you're talking about this stuff, it tastes like medicine. They grow better wine on the oneills."

"Because we've ruined the planet! But we can make it well again. Green fields and forests! Paradise! And the first step is to end the export of the Earth's power to space!"

Michael shook his head, wearily holding his glass out for another refill. "You're crazy, Rodney, they won't let you."

"Who won't let me?" his brother demanded triumphantly.

Michael thought that over, swallowing his wine. It was actually quite a hard question. Who were the "they"? Police? There didn't seem to be any. An army? The last army had been disbanded about the time Michael was being toilet-trained. He said lamely, "Nobody will," and sat back down, feeling suddenly very tired.

He was surprised to see, through queerly bleary eyes, that his brother was grinning at him. "You know what I think, bro? I think you need to go to sleep. Gideon, why don't you just take Mr. Michael in the other room and tuck him in bed?"

"I don't need any help," Michael began thickly, and then realized with surprise it was untrue. He jerked his head up, glaring at his brother. "You put something in the wine!" he snarled.

"Just a little tranquilizer," Rodney soothed, "to help you to your well-earned rest . . . and to keep you out of my way while I get on with my work. Pleasant dreams," Michael heard, and then heard nothing at all.

VII

There are times when even someone accustomed to being an absolute monarch has something to dream about. Michael did dream. He dreamed he was back in his snug little habitat, with his familiar servants and his deb list and his trophy wall. He dreamed, in fact, that nothing had changed. When he woke he was terribly disappointed. No friendly bedstraps to hold him close, no bedside table to greet him with juice and coffee. He was crushed down onto a huge, gross mattress, and instead of his pretty view-screens there was nothing to look at but a great hot window, giving out on the ugly, oily sea. Those nightmare memories of the day before—they were real!

"Good morning, Mr. Michael," said the pleasant baritone voice of the robot, Gideon, as it sprang to life from its position against the wall. "I hope you slept well. Would you like breakfast?"

Michael sat up—not easily; he had to help himself with his arms, and his whole body felt sore from the night-long drag of gravity while he slept. "What I would like," he said, "is to go home. Right away."

The robot pursed its lips in a very human expression of concern. It was very human-looking in almost all ways, as a matter of fact. Sandy hair, an alert, intelligent face; if Michael had not been told, he would not have guessed it was mechanical. "I wish I could help you," it said regretfully. "There's a message from your brother you might like to hear—shall I play it for you?"

Michael grunted as he swung his legs over the side of the bed and turned toward the window. "Not there, Mr. Michael," the robot said. "On the monitor."

How queer! Apparently they didn't have view-walls at all in this place. What Gideon was indicating was a small screen on a desk, and as the robot touched a control it sprang into light. Rodney's face looked out. "Sorry about knocking you out, Michael," it said, "but I think you're stronger than I am now, and I didn't want you to interfere. I've gone to work on the project. Gideon will take care of you until I get back, and meanwhile you can enjoy all the facilities of the hotel. Also Gideon will be glad to educate you, so you won't be bored. Of course, you can't leave. So just relax and enjoy it."

The screen winked off. Michael looked sourly around the bedroom. Enjoy it! The place was interesting, in a way, as anything may be interesting if it is quaint enough. Michael was not a quaintness fancier. He stood up and faced the robot. "Take me back to the spaceport now," he ordered.

"Oh, but there's no point in that, Mr. Michael. There's no ship leaving for quite some time."

"Then to some other spaceport! Somewhere there has to be one."

The robot looked regretful. "I'm afraid I can't. Mr. Rodney's orders."

"Then call me a taxi!" The robot shook its head. In

mounting anger, Michael snapped, "Then I'll walk, damn it!"

"But you can't do that, Mr. Michael," the robot said reasonably. "I'm afraid you'd die out there without a thermal suit and a helmet. The climate is quite adverse to flesh-and-blood beings in these latitudes."

"Then—"

"And I can't get you a helmet, either," Gideon apologized, forestalling him, "because Mr. Rodney left strict instructions about that, too." The robot paused, then added, "And in case you are thinking of asking someone for help, there are no humans but you in the hotel, and all the communications are monitored. Nothing goes out of here without looping through Mr. Rodney's communications systems, and I'm quite sure he will not forward any outside calls for you." The robot's expression was sympathetic but firm as he added, "And now, would you like some breakfast?"

If one must be a prisoner, a prison that was once a luxury hotel is not a bad place to be. The kitchen had fallen terribly from whatever its standards once had been. The night club had only robot shows, and only robots in the audience, for that matter, not counting Michael himself, and he was pretty sure that when he wasn't present there was no show. Or audience, either. Yet the casinos still operated—again with robots on both sides of the table—and the swimming pool was a delight. If you had to be on the surface of the Earth, a pool was a big asset; the buoyancy of the water relieved much of the 1-G drag. Gideon accompanied him everywhere, even to the pool—though not in it, since robots don't swim. Michael wondered idly what would happen if he had a sudden cramp in the deep end, and the robot reassured him. "Oh, I'd get you out, Mr. Michael—I'm waterproof. But, as I'm too dense to float, I'd have to walk along the bottom to get to you. Would you care to start your training now?"

"I don't need to be trained by a robot!" Michael snapped.

"An unfortunate choice of words. I only meant that Mr. Rodney suggested I should brief you on the data underlying his decision."

"That's a stupid idea if I ever heard one," Michael announced, but after not very many hours he was running out of smart ones. It had been pleasant enough to buy new clothes in the hotel's shops, interesting to soak in the sauna and almost fun—slightly more pleasure than pain, anyway—to try to play on the hotel's indoor miniature golf course, although that was not a game you could play very well in orbit, and thus not suitable for real human beings. He shrugged.

That was enough. The robot led him to a room that had once been set up for meetings, provided him with something to eat and something to drink, sat him in a reasonably comfortable chair and said, "The first thing, Mr. Michael, is to show the basics of power supply to orbit." And he darkened the room, and pictures sprang up on an almost decently large screen on the stage.

Michael would not have imagined this to be an interesting subject, but as the documentary progressed he found himself paying attention. It had been assembled with some care, for what purpose he could not imagine, out of old film clips and live-action shots, animation and diagrams, with a voice-over commentary that sounded like his brother.

What it said was not altogether pleasant. The drain of electric power to the orbiting habitats had meant that the whole planet Earth had become a power source for the people whose lives were spent circling it. Fusion power? Of course there was fusion power, the narration said. But there was a limit to how much fusion-power generation the ecology would tolerate.

Ecology! Michael snorted. One of Rodney's favorite words. And that couldn't be true, because everybody knew the supply of deuterium in the Earth's oceans was all but inexhaustible— The deuterium (the narration continued) was all but inexhaustible, but fusion power is intrinsically inefficient. The temperatures involved are star-high. The reject heat from a fusion generator exceeded that from even an old-fashioned uranium-fission plant (already terribly inefficient) by orders of magnitude. And, as the load curve climbed, the power engineers discovered they were cooking their planet.

"This curve," said the narrator—now Michael was sure it was his brother, "shows the rise in sea level since 1895." A red arrow traced a course across the screen. "It was about a millimeter a year for the first fifty years or so. Then it went to three millimeters a year. Now it is running over forty millimeters a year. The ice caps are melting, but that's only part of it. Most of the rise is simple thermal expansion of the oceans as they grow warmer. So far more than eighteen hundred charted islands have simply disappeared, and the coasts of every continent are getting wet."

"I didn't know Rodney knew all that," said Michael, impressed.

"I helped him with the data," Gideon offered shyly. "That's my specialty."

"Huh." It had never occurred to Michael that robots could do that sort of thing. Could his own servants handle that? Would it be possible, he daydreamed, to input into, say, his message center all the known data about Noymans and their habits, and have them advise him by radio during a hunt? If so, would that be sportsmanlike? If not, would it be found out?

A searing desert scene on the screen brought him back

to the documentary. Apparently hot winds were ripping at the Earth. Rising temperatures, his brother droned on, had not meant warming the polar regions as much as it had meant a pestilence of hot, dry sirocco winds across the temperate zones—the breadbaskets of the world. The atmosphere, after all, is a heat engine. The more heat goes into it, the more kinetic energy it produces—in the form of winds, hurricanes, tornadoes . . . siroccos.

And all that had happened, Michael learned, even after the power combines in desperation had halted the building of new fusion generators. A point of no return had been reached. The best they could do was to try to keep it from getting worse—or anyway, much worse—or, at least, very rapidly worse. They met the energy demand with every sort of production scheme mankind or man's servants could imagine. Biomass was a major factor. The plantations he had seen along the road did not produce food. They produced fuel, just as Gideon had said. The beet roots and taro and sugarcane they grew went into the alcohol stills, and the alcohol, along with the residues, became fuel. There wasn't that much need for food on Earth any more, and anyway most of the agricultural products were only marginally edible. They were grown in saltwater irrigation. They were salty.

And all the generators fed the rectennae that hurled power to the satellites in orbit. And it was not enough.

So a thousand other systems were put to work to produce electrical energy. Some of them were so old as to be traditional, like hydroelectric power; some were even older, so that they had not been used for generations, like windmills. The magma under the crust gave up geothermal heat. The tides and the waves were harnessed. The Gulf Stream had been dammed, and great, slow rotors off the sunken coasts of Florida and the Carolinas sucked out its energy to make more electricity. The coal mines and the shale pits and the natural-gas bubbles and the tar sands were all being burned. That was where the filth in the air came from. It would have been possible to install anti-pollution devices, but each one laid a tax on the energy generated. Robots could stand the pollution. They didn't breathe; didn't have a sense of smell, unless they desired one; could not be poisoned by NO_2 or SO_2. And there were not many humans left to suffer, and those there were simply wore masks. But the anti-pollution equipment was unused, because the energy was more valuable than the air.

Some of the devices for wringing the last erg out of the bleeding Earth fascinated Michael, because he had never heard of such things. An ice generator, for instance. Michael knew that water expanded when it froze—that was why ice cubes floated in a drink. He even knew, if he had troubled to remember it, that there were many places on the Earth, even now, where the temperature hovered around the freezing mark—far north and far south, or high on mountains—and so water would freeze and melt, freeze and melt over and over again. It amused him that someone had thought to install great sealed tanks in such places, so that the water froze by night and expanded, melted with the morning sun and shrank again—and that squeeze and relaxation pressed pistons that turned gears that drove generators for more energy. Osmotic pumps exploited the salinity of the sea for power . . . the list seemed to go on forever!

And it all went into space.

And Michael was fascinated. "Incredible!" he murmured aloud, as the documentary finished itself at last. "I wouldn't have believed it."

The robot beamed at him as it turned up the room lights and opened the door. "Mr. Rodney wasn't sure you'd understand," it said, "but I was sure that any reasoning being would draw inescapable conclusions, once he had the data."

"I couldn't agree more," Michael cried. "What a triumph! So much skill and intelligence devoted to such a grand purpose—the liberation of the human race from the tyranny of its mother planet!"

Even a luxury hotel becomes boring. Even gambling lost its charm, especially when it did not matter to Michael whether he won or lost . . . especially when he began noticing that the robot who impassively shoved heaps of chips onto *impaire* and *rouge* at the roulette table was also the towel boy in the hotel's sauna, and the chambermaid who made his bed in the morning turned up singing in the rooftop café that night. Why, the whole thing was a fraud, Michael thought as he mooned grouchily around the great building, mourning his missing wall pictures, and recreated moments of passion, and friendly, always obedient household utensils. Not that Gideon and the others were disobedient in the least. It was simply that they were obeying the first orders they had received, which happened to come from his brother. "Why do you do it?" Michael demanded, confronting Gideon.

"It is what we were made to do," the robot explained.

"But it's silly! Running this whole hotel just to entertain me!" The robot smiled and shrugged. "And anyway, what's going to happen to you if my crazy brother blows up the power plants?"

"Why, nothing, I guess, Mr. Michael."

"You'll die without power, won't you?"

"Oh, no. He's only going after the big ones. There'll be enough left—we don't draw much energy for ourselves, you know."

The creatures were absolutely frustrating! How could they be so disinterested? "You don't care that Rodney's going to try to get human beings to move back onto the Earth?"

The robot looked thoughtful, but said only, "We won't interfere."

"Not even to save human beings a lot of discomfort—

all those people who'll have to move into oneills?''

"I think," said the robot, "that we can stand seeing a lot of human beings experiencing some discomfort."

Michael studied him narrowly, but the robot returned his look mildly enough. Michael sighed. "It'll never work anyhow," he observed. "Who would want to live on this lousy planet?"

"As to that," Gideon volunteered, "I can tell you what Mr. Rodney has in mind if you like. Shall I?" It took Michael's resigned shrug as approval, and turned away to do something Michael could not quite follow inside its loosely fitting jacket. "Ah, yes," it said, "Mr. Rodney's plan seems quite feasible. Perhaps you know, Mr. Michael, that at one time most human beings expected to colonize the other planets in this solar system."

"Live on *planets?*" Michael demanded incredulously. "Those lousy things? Instead of habitats?"

"They had not yet developed the concept of the orbiting habitat, Mr. Michael. And at that time the physical conditions of the planets were not well known. When they discovered that all of them were too hot or too cold, with too much atmosphere or too little, or none at all, they developed some ingenious schemes. They called them 'terraforming.'"

"I never heard of 'terraforming.'"

"No, I suppose not," the robot agreed gravely. "The precise procedures would, I think, be somewhat tedious to listen to—"

"Just the outlines," Michael snapped.

"Yes, of course. Put simply, terraforming would add air and water to Mars by arranging to melt its polar ice cap, and would reduce the pressure and improve the constituents of Venus's atmosphere by seeding it with special organisms. Well, Mr. Rodney has similar plans for the Earth. It is quite probable they would work. In a few decades, human beings would be able to live on the Earth again, without protective equipment."

Michael shook his head in revulsion. "What a ghastly idea. Tell me something. How come you know so much about all this?"

"I beg your pardon?" The robot did not seem to grasp the question.

"How," Michael spelled it out, "do . . . you . . . know . . . all . . . this?"

"Oh, of course, Mr. Michael," the robot said in an apologetic tone. "I forgot you had very little to do with us, so you would not know about our chip storage." He opened his jacket and revealed a garment like a vest, with hundreds of small pockets. "These are specialized memory stores, Mr. Michael. We simply plug in whatever data we need for any purpose—of course, this is only a small sample of the available material. Just what I thought might be needed. But of course if I need to know any other subject I can have the data transmitted from the central files onto a blank chip." He reached inside himself, and from a slot between what would have been his second and third ribs if he had had any pulled out a tapered black thing shaped like a guitar pick. "This one is on ecological engineering, as we were just discussing. This other one"—he indicated a pocket—"is on power-plant construction and maintenance, this one on vehicle operation, this one on rocket navigation—"

Michael touched the pointed black thing curiously. "Interesting," he commented. "And if you were to plug in, say, the one on rocket navigation, you could tell me anything I wanted to know about it?"

"Almost anything, yes, Mr. Michael. Not just tell you. I have full projection equipment available as well, so I could show you graphs, pictures, diagrams and so on."

Michael walked over to the window, looking out at the garbagey hell his brother was proposing to make the home of the human race again. "You know, Gideon," he said thoughtfully, "I think I'd like you to order me up something to eat—a sandwich, and a couple of bottles of beer ought to be about right. And then, what I'd like, I'd like you to tell me what all those different chips are about."

When Rodney came back, Michael was waiting for him. "Bro," he said, "you've got the right idea. Let me help you."

Rodney stopped in the doorway, staring at him. He had been gone only days, but he looked as though he had had a hard time. His beard was tangled; his eyes were dull and fatigued. "Fly that past me again," he said.

"I don't blame you if you don't believe me," said Michael, "but that's the way it is. Gideon has been educating me."

His brother glanced at the robot, poised motionless by the great, hot picture windows. "Bring me a beer," he ordered, and Gideon responded instantly. Rodney sat down, accepted the tall flagon from the robot and waited for his brother to speak.

"What you're doing," said Michael, "is shock treatment and it's going to create a lot of hardship, but I believe you're right. In your objectives, anyway. In the way you're going about it, all wrong." Rodney raised his eyebrows but didn't speak. "There are," Michael continued, "twenty-two thousand three hundred and fifty-three power-generating stations now feeding juice into the microwave transmitters to feed the power satellites. You've been out planting bombs in some of them—how many?"

Rodney scowled at the robot. "How did you know I was planting bombs?" he demanded.

"Don't worry, Gideon didn't tell me that. It was obvious. Anyway, I would estimate you've managed to plant twenty-five at the outside, right?" Rodney shrugged. "A lot less, then. So at your present rate of progress you might get the job done in ten years or so—maybe—and there's no use in that, because you can't keep it a secret that long. The people in orbit will find out what you're doing and stop it."

"They won't!"

"They will, Rodney, and in any case that's silly. You don't have to blow up twenty thousand transmitters. They all feed into the same three hundred or so power satellites in orbit. Blow the satellites up!"

Rodney drained the last of his beer in a sulky manner and tossed the flagon to the robot, who caught it handily, refilled it and returned it to the human. "Give me some credit, Michael. I thought of that. I can't do it—they're too exposed. Some dumb hunt party would blunder along just when we were setting the charges."

"No, they w—"

"Yes, they would, Michael, so shut up for a minute and listen to me." He kicked off his shoes and massaged his feet as he talked. "Let's say you're really convinced it's the right thing and you're willing to help. That makes two of us. Ann makes three. There are about four others I can count on—maybe—so we're up to seven. Now, in order to lift and set explosive charges in three hundred power satellites—"

"But you don't have to—"

"I said shut up, Michael! We just don't have the man-power to do the job, and there's no chance of getting more. Ann and I even tried talking to the sailship people."

"Those idiots!" Michael scoffed, and his brother glared at him.

"They aren't idiots, they're just going about it the wrong way. What they want is a decent planet to walk around on, and they think they'll find one in some other solar system. That means maybe forty years in the deep sleep, and God knows how much more time if the first planet doesn't work out—which it won't—and that's stupid, I agree. But they're not stupid people. They simply wouldn't see that it was faster and better to fix up the Earth. And without them, or without some other help from somewhere, we can't do much about the power satellites; they're too exposed. We'd be caught surely. The

Earth stations take a lot longer, but who ever bothers to look at them? So sooner or later I'll get them all set up and then, boom, it's all over."

Michael signaled to the robot for a beer of his own. "Are you quite finished now?" he asked his brother politely.

"I guess so."

"Yes, well, then let me tell you where you're wrong. You don't have to blow up three hundred separate power satellites. One big bomb will do it."

"You're crazy! You can't even *feel* a bomb blast in space more than a dozen meters away—"

"Not blast," said Michael merrily, sipping his beer. "The significant effect is radiation. What is called the electromagnetic pulse, or EMP for short. It amounts to about a million volts per meter, anywhere within a hundred thousand kilometers, and that is enough to fry the control systems on every power satellite in orbit. The rectennae will still be there. But they won't be able to transmit. They will be out of operation until all their transistors and control chips are replaced and debugged—a year's work at least."

Rodney was staring at him with his mouth open. Then he turned to the robot. "Gideon! You've been educating him!"

"Yes, Mr. Rodney. You instructed me to."

"So you see," said Michael, "there's your problem solved for you. I think we can still find that tritium pig. According to Gideon, although there's no ship from the nearest launch port for a couple of weeks, there are others from other places we can get to. All we have to do is get started, bro . . . so what do you say?"

Rodney stared at him over the rim of the flask as he took another deep draft of the beer. Then, suddenly, he grinned and thrust out his hand.

"I say we get started," he cried. "After all, if I can't trust my own brother, who can I trust?"

VIII

Gideon's information was accurate: There was a ship. They flew to it in less than an hour, and three hours later they were strapped in for lift-off. Rodney was in high spirits, and Michael very supportive. They transshipped in low-Earth orbit to a two-passenger taxi, and in less than twelve hours they were in Michael's dear familiar habitat. The appliances were delighted to see their master back again and quickly prepared them a meal and drinks, according to Michael's instructions. Then the brothers called up Ann Oberhauser, startling her a great deal; arranged to see her as soon as they could get there; had another drink to toast their coming triumph; and then there was Michael again, spurring his trusty steed through the beautiful cold freedom of space, with his brother strapped on the jump seat behind him. "Isn't it beautiful, Rodney?" Michael demanded, gazing around at the stars, diamond-bright and ruby-hot, and the incredibly majestic rusty-brown Moon, like a sunburst filtered through a film of brass. "Some people might have bad things to say about this," he added, "but I know it's the right thing to do." His brother, leaning heavily against him as the steed surged and bucked under Michael's spur, did not reply, and Michael sang to himself as they rushed past habitats and the beacons of other travelers, with the broad Earth's nightside always below.

And then they were coming up on Ann's habitat. It was smaller than his own. It looked like a brown-shelled egg rather than a hand grenade, and the entry port was waiting open for him. He lashed the steed in its rack, patted Rodney's space-suited shoulder and squeezed through the narrow entrance.

Ann was waiting for him, half apprehensive, half sweetly expectant. "Now what is this, Michael?" she demanded, pretty in her metal body suit. "You two woke me up!"

"Sorry about that," said Michael cheerfully, glancing about as he slipped his helmet off. No one else was there. He had thought, not very happily, that Ann might easily have taken another dude in his absence—there was plenty of time, certainly! And that would have been a blow; but it hadn't happened.

"Well?" she demanded, "you've got me out of bed, you made me suit up, I'm waiting to hear what it's all about."

"Sorry to be so mysterious." He grinned, fumbling in his pouch and producing a couple of bulbs, "but there are some things it's better not to talk about on the phone. Drink up! A stirrup cup, made by the best wet bar in orbit, to toast the salvation of humanity!"

She looked quizzical at the grandiosity of his remark, but returned his smile. He downed the bulb with a flourish and she sipped at hers, her eyes kindly but perplexed. "Good stuff," she admitted, which it was—Michael's private mixture, somewhere between shandygaff and a mint julep. "But where's Rodney, then?"

"Out on my steed, waiting for us." He nodded toward the view-screen. The mount rack was visible, with Rodney's suited form just in sight in one corner. "Finish your drink and helmet up, Ann; we've got work to do!"

"But—"

"Oh, come on, Ann," he said earnestly; and, half coaxing her, half pushing, he got her to down the stirrup cup, pull the globe over her russet hair, check the seals and report them intact . . . just as she began yawning.

"Sleep well, dear Ann," he murmured as her eyes closed. Although Ann was actually a little bigger than Michael, and awkward to move around in her spacesuit, he managed to get her through the lock. Then it was easy to seat her carefully on the fuel tank, just behind his sleeping brother, and lash her to the improvised seat.

He took his own position, belted in and opened up the main thrusters. Over his shoulder he could see that both of them were secure. He could even make out the peaceful expressions. "Pleasant dreams, dear ones," he said fondly, and set course for the distant shark-fin of white that was the sail of the interstellar vessel.

And the days went by and the weeks, and Michael's life was complete. There were the hunts and the parties and the systematic exploration of the inexhaustible deb list, and what more could any human being want? Michael didn't dream about his longings any more. Once again his dreams were his real life.

Of course there were questions—not questions so much, because of just who Rodney and Ann were— as little gibes and hints. When his friends talked about the missing brother and the missing ex-consort, their tone was sometimes friendly and sometimes needling. Michael met both kinds of inquiries alike, with polite annoyance at their bad manners. By and by the gossips stopped bothering. Rodney was a known eccentric. Ann had dangerous ideas. If they chose to wander off together, why, so much the worse for them! The only real curiosity was where they had wandered to. Most guessed the surface of the Earth. A few guessed more accurately—though not, Michael was sure, as to the details.

The photon sailship was where they were. The sailship crew had been almost pathetically grateful to accept these last-minute recruits. Perhaps they were surprised that both of them arrived already in deep sleep, for most of the travelers wanted to stay awake at least for the first few weeks of spreading the sails and slowly, s-l-o-w-l-y beginning to accumulate velocity for the endless trip. But they did not press the point; because most of *them* were known eccentrics too. Or else why would they have become sailship volunteers?

And long after the spread wings of the interstellar ship had vanished even from his fair-sized telescope . . . after

Ann's and Rodney's names had stopped coming up in chatter, after their habitats had been taken over by new people and their strange ways almost forgotten . . . sometimes Michael, drifting off to sleep in his gentle bed or rummaging through his inventory of debs or arrowing through space in pursuit of the ever-scarcer bucks—sometimes Michael would think of them. Never with anger. Sometimes with gentle pity, and even affection. And always with a certain pride. He bore no animus toward them. Wrong as they were, and dangerous, he had prevented the disaster they wanted to bring about. If he had a real regret it was only that he thought it best not to tell anyone, ever, of how he had personally done the deed that forever safeguarded the Orbital Way.

7

THE NEW NEIGHBORS

Far from orbit and the Orbital Way there were those who found a quite other way of life rewarding. For Ralph and his friends and neighbors, space was bare and hostile. What would you do there, for instance, with Cissie?

Cissie was Ralph's dog, sweet little ladylike thing except that she wasn't little. She was a malamute, and there are ponies not as large. Ralph loved the animal. Like many shy people, he found it hard to admit affection for another person. What if that other person didn't give the affection back? But a dog you could always rely on. Even a big one, although Cissie had been a great deal smaller when Ralph bought her, at the suggestion of his therapist. "You'll have something to relate to," Dr. Kammerhill said, "and besides, walking a dog is a good way to meet new friends." The first part had worked out just fine. You could measure his affection for the animal by the simple fact that he was out walking it in Chicago's typical winter weather, with the wind from the Lake driving the big flakes into his face as fast as they came down. The second part— The second part, he observed, was actually coming to pass, for one of the very few times since he had owned Cissie. As Cissie squatted in her ladylike, absentminded way, a person was coming toward them with expressions of pleasure.

However, it was not a very attractive figure that presented itself. From the neck down, it was female, and well proportioned in a skintight flexible coverall; nice enough. Above the neck was something else. The head was a glittering bubble of one-way mirror, with sound diaphragms protruding from the vicinity of the cheekbones and a thing like a stubby elephant's trunk dangling down where you would have looked for a chin. "Oh, what a sweet dog," it said. The woman bent to pat Cissie, who stared up at her with shock and outrage. "She doesn't bite, does she?" the woman asked—a female voice, all right, although thickened and made raspy by the sound diaphragms.

"She's never bitten *me*," Ralph said, "but I don't know about you people—I mean, she's never been around anybody like you before." He felt uneasily that that sounded almost like a racial slur, but he couldn't help it. He just wasn't used to her kind around Riveredge Towers. The residents were sober, industrious professionals mostly, like Ralph himself. He didn't want to sound prejudiced, but—

The matter was taken out of his hands. Cissie decided that she wanted to go home, and even for somebody as strong as Ralph it was easier to go along than to resist that steady sled-dog tug on the leash.

However, it didn't end there. The woman followed him through the revolving door.

Waiting for the elevator with him, she wiggled the headpiece free and shook out a head of curly, pale hair. "I'm Lillian Albright," she said, holding out a gloved hand to shake. "My husband and I have just moved in," she said, peering over his shoulder to look at herself in the mirror. She tried to brush down her curls. "Those helmets really mess you up," she apologized, "but it's better than getting soot in your hair, isn't it?" And that made it even, because her expression changed swiftly as she realized that that, too, was sounding a little racial, since everybody knew that robot hair repelled soot.

And the final actor to play the part of prejudice was

Cissie, who was curiously sniffing at the woman's knee. She looked up at Ralph, raised her muzzle and barked. "Cissie!" he cried. "Shut up! What's the matter with you? I'm sorry," he apologized. "She never did that in the house before." But then, Cissie had never sniffed a living human being before, either. And when the elevator arrived at last, she ran inside and crouched at the back dejectedly, not even pausing to lick Charlie, the elevator operator.

At least the woman did not pursue her. She only said sorrowfully, "I wanted to have a dog, but I didn't think I ought to bring one here."

"Why not?" Ralph asked. He was really puzzled. Lots of people had pets in the Towers. The pets flourished; the apartments were kept heated in the winter, and the air was filtered all year round.

"Oh, I don't know," she said. "I guess I just had some wrong ideas—'bye!" she added, saved from still another faux pas, or another almost faux pas, by the fact that they had arrived at her floor. With three fast, but separate, smiles, one each for Ralph, Cissie and the elevator operator, she was gone.

The elevator operator closed the door behind her, glancing at Ralph. Charlie wasn't much of a robot, not even fully ambulatory; he was purpose-designed to run the elevators in Riveredge Towers and make conversation with the tenants, and he rarely tried to go beyond his job requirements. But he was shaking his head as he let Ralph out at the twenty-eighth floor. "I never expected to see one of *them* in Riveredge Towers." He sighed. "What do you think, Mr. Ralph? You think there goes the neighborhood?"

Chicago was a robot town. Well, every city on Earth was, of course, because the human beings had mostly long gone away. At night you could see the habitats in orbit when the air was clean enough—that is, maybe half a dozen nights a year—and that was where the human race had gone when they finished dirtying up their homeworld. They didn't like the smells and toxins they had left behind, and their orbiting bubbles could be flushed out and restocked when they got too bad. You couldn't do that with a whole planet. So of Chicago's population of three million and change, just about three million were homiform robots. The "change" didn't amount to much. If you counted every organic human being in the city and suburbs, from Evanston to the Indiana line, you could not quite reach a total of a thousand. Mostly they hung around Water Tower Place and the Gold Coast, and a few of the racier ethnic neighborhoods. In places like that a few food supermarkets stayed open to serve them, and even a few restaurants. It was possible for an organic human being to live fairly well along Michigan Avenue. Not so possible even a few blocks away; Riveredge Towers had been human-free until the Albrights turned up. On his way down to the dig Ralph tried his skill at identifying organic human beings among the pedestrians and vehicle passengers. You couldn't really tell which was which when they were in vehicles, because the cars were all sealed, but on the sidewalks he recognized exactly three. Mirrored bubble helmets. That was how you could tell. And really, if the only way they could stay alive in Chicago was inside a goldfish bowl, why did they want to come here?

Ralph was an archaeologist—or a historian—things being as they were on the planet Earth, it was hard to know where one ended and the other began. Like with the Savior of Humanity, Amalfi Amadeus, who was the subject of Ralph's present researches: should you try to reconstruct his life from documentary sources—that was the historical approach—or piece it together from the late-human equivalent of potsherds and flint knives, i.e., the archaeological? There was no doubt that Amalfi

Amadeus was a real figure. He was perhaps the most significant human being who ever lived. Without him, how could the world have reached its present state?

But you couldn't believe all the documents. Human beings, it appeared, had engaged in a systematic distortion called "advertising," or sometimes "public relations." Ralph could allow for that, but the same spirit of double-think record keeping seemed to apply even to, for example, financial records—what were called "corporate statements" and "tax returns"—and, above all, to those classes of statements that were most solemnly sworn to. Court testimony and affidavits, for instance. Time after time Ralph had come across depositions that flatly contradicted each other, and, although they had both been presented in a "court of law" with a judge listening, and in theory anyone who misstated facts in such circumstances would be gravely punished for the "crime" of "perjury," he had yet to find an example of anyone going to jail.

So that left the potsherds, or their Late Human equivalent. In this case it was the Amalfi monument in Amalfi Park. There was a cache of artifacts and personal belongings of the great man believed to be buried underneath it. The problem was digging them up. What made it a problem was that Lake Michigan, like most large bodies of water in these warm times, kept wanting to rise. Today it had lapped over again, and the backhoes were lined up waiting for the bulldozers to push the dikes higher and the pumps to suck out the water in the pit; and all of that was going to take time. All around the Amalfi statue the ground was soggy, and in the pit itself were at least three feet of thin mud. Ralph didn't press his luck. He exchanged a few words with the bulldozers and the pumps—low-level intelligences always liked to hear from the boss—and left. If it was true that Amalfi Amadeus's secrets were under the statue, the secrets would have to remain secret a little longer.

He spent two hours in library research, leaning back and letting the data flow through his internal scanners, and then decided to give Cissie an extra walk. It was traditional to take a lunch break, even if, as was of course true of most robots, they didn't ever eat; and once again, right out in front of the Towers, there was the human woman.

This time she was seated at an easel overlooking the river. Since there wasn't much sewage any more, the river ran sparkly clean on its way down to the Mississippi and the Gulf. Since the water levels in the lake had been rising, it ran pretty fast. It was a pretty sight, and Ralph paused to look over Lillian Albright's shoulder to see what she was making of it. "Oh, hello, Mr. Ralph," she said, lifting a cloth off her paints to pick up a brushful of greens and whites; "I'm really glad to see you again."

"Decided to take Cissie out for a walk on my lunch break," he said, looking at her painting. It was barely begun, but he could see that she was running into problems. The flakes of particulate matter settling out of the air were changing her color scheme as fast as she could paint it.

"Oh, do you eat lunch?"

"I can," he said cautiously; it was true that Ralph had complete digestive systems, though he rarely used them.

"Well, then! You must come join my husband and me! You'll like Myron, he's a composer; no, I won't take no for an answer! We're in 11-E—in half an hour?"

Actually, he didn't like Myron. He had been intrigued by the word "composer"; it had suggested Beethoven and Brahms and Gershwin and all those old greats, but that was not the kind of composer Myron Albright was. He had a disk of his favorite work on the player when Ralph came in, and kept it going all through lunch. Squeaks, rattles, electronic hisses; Myron was what is called an aleatoric composer, which meant that his work consisted of found sounds arbitrarily arranged— "And there aren't

that many sounds in space, Mr. Ralph," he said. "Vac-
uum, you know. It doesn't conduct sound. So I really just
had to come down here."

"And for a painter like me," his wife chimed in, *"ends-
ville.* Just look out this window!" Far below the Chicago
River was chuckling along its rapids; the flake-fall had
stopped, and it was clearly visible.

"It's really attractive," Ralph said. "I guess it's been
painted a million times."

"Not by me, Mr. Ralph. Honestly, I can't wait! You
wouldn't believe how tired you can get of painting *space."*

"It's all *black,"* her husband chimed in.

"Makes you think of funerals, Mr. Ralph—please," she
added, smiling at him, "can we just call you 'Ralph' now?
Oh, thank you! Anyway, you can see how *boring* that gets.
It doesn't matter what you're painting, you know. A habitat. Or the Moon. Or half-Earth, or the power satellites—
there's that same deadly background. Black. You can
scatter stars around it all you like, it's still the same. . . . I
guess you think we're overreacting?" The woman had been
following Ralph's gaze as he looked around the apartment.

"It's very, uh, colorful," he said. Indeed it was. Each
wall was a different bright color, spectrally pure—blue
here, green there, yellow, red, orange. The whole apartment was a clutter, with artificial flowers in vases, crossed
skis and crossed tennis rackets hanging on the wall, a shelf
of trophies. And, of course, at least a dozen of Lillian's
own sketches, watercolors and paintings. "I think it looks
very nice," he said, his attention less on the decoration
than on the table by the window. The woman had laid out
a buffet of sliced cheeses and meats and breads, and she
was filling a cup for Ralph.

She hesitated. "You can drink coffee, can't you?"

"Oh, certainly," Ralph boasted. "I often select that
option."

"I beg your pardon?"

"A liquid ingestion system," he explained. "Today, for instance, I included both solid and liquid ingestion. I suppose it's something like—well—I'm not sure, but maybe something like one of you deciding to take a camera with you when you go out? Or an umbrella if you think it might rain? So some days I take the digestive systems, some days extra communications facilities—I have a lot of different accessories," he said proudly.

The Albrights looked at each other, smiling uncertainly. Myron cleared his throat. Then, delicately. "But you don't *need* to eat, of course."

"Oh, no."

"And you do it because—?"

"Well, because I enjoy it, you know? Part of the systems include chemosensors and tactile receptors. And"—he smiled—"sometimes it's for social reasons."

Myron said, his voice sounding embarrassed, "I know we must sound sort of—" The word that came to his mind was "condescending," but he didn't want to use it. So he took a different tack: "I mean, it's hard for me to understand why you bother. If you don't need those systems, why have them?"

Ralph nodded toward the wall, where the skis and tennis rackets hung. "I could ask you why you have those."

"Oh, *sport,*" Lillian cried, enlightened. "Of course. Now do have some coffee! And help yourself to the buffet."

"Thank you," Ralph said, concealing his lack of enthusiasm. It was true that his digestive systems were well up to eating it, and even enjoying it. But then there was that messy business of getting rid of the by-products to look forward to.

"And what do you do, Ralph?" Myron asked, hospitably loading up a plate.

"I'm a graduate student. University of Chicago," Ralph

said, managing to get away without salad. He had figured out that if he disconnected his tasting circuits the food could stay in his storage chambers pretty nearly intact, and later on he could retrieve it and give it to Cissie. But Cissie wouldn't eat lettuce.

"Oh? What are you studying?"

Ralph realized there was a failure of communication here. He swallowed a bite of ham and cheese intact and said, "Well, actually I'm not *studying*. We don't have to."

Lillian's husband laughed genially. "Isn't it the truth? Same when I was in school. Cut all the classes you can get away with and then cram like hell before the finals, right?"

"Something like that," Ralph agreed, although actually it wasn't like that at all. He was, after all, a robot. Robots had no need to study, ever. If you wanted to know something, you just requisitioned that particular data store and plugged it in. All robots—all the independent homiforms, anyway—came off the assembly line with the basic-skills package. Literacy. Numeracy. A bundle of learned conventions, such as the fact that the red light meant stop and you pushed a button to summon an elevator. Beyond that it was up to the individual robot to choose, but nearly all of them elected to receive supplementary chips for such subjects as English composition, algebra, human history and robot studies. When you had all that, you probably owned all the skills an average human got out of a four-year college, and so that was generally referred to as the bachelor's degree.

Beyond that it got harder. If you wanted a master's degree, you had to demonstrate mastery. That is, you had to rewrite the existing chips to make them better. That was hard to do, since they had all been rewritten many times already. But the doctorate was even harder. For that you had to create a new theoretical framework and propose "falsifications"—had to, in short, apply the scientific method to whatever was your chosen field of study. Well, that was more or less what the doctorate had always been supposed to mean. The difference was that now it did mean that. But Ralph could not see a tactful way of explaining that to Myron and Lillian, so he simply said, "My specialty's the life of Amalfi Amadeus."

"Oh, of course," said Myron, looking vaguely at his wife. Ralph realized with shock that these human beings did not know who Amalfi Amadeus, the greatest human being who ever lived, was.

"Tell him about us, Myron," Lillian Albright said suddenly.

Her husband hesitated. "No, go on," she ordered. "Or I'll do it myself. You see, Ralph, we haven't been entirely honest with you."

"Not *dis*honest, though," Myron offered quickly.

"No, of course not—it's true that we had to come here for our work—but there was more to it. We were hoping that we could get to know some of you a little better."

"Some of us?"

"You, uh, robots," she explained.

"We're not like most human beings," Myron added.

"You're not?"

"Honestly, we're not! Myron and I prove that you can rise above your childhood conditioning. We can accept a robot on the same terms as a human being, and that's why we came down here. We'd like to meet some of our other neighbors. Can you help us there, Ralph?"

"Well . . ."

"I know you're hesitating," Myron put in, "because you don't want to embarrass your friends. But I promise there won't be anything like that. We're not in the least *prejudiced,* you know. Can you believe that?"

Ralph nodded slowly. "I certainly can," he agreed, and it was true enough, because the possibility of someone being prejudiced against robots had never before occurred to him.

But helping them meet other robots was not so easy. In some ways Ralph was not very different from a human. He didn't know many of his neighbors, since he was an apartment-dweller. Those are the folkways of apartment life. Probably in Augustus's Rome Marcus Lentullus didn't know Flavius Pulchrus from the flat next door, except to nod as they passed on the narrow steps of the insula.

In the case of robots, the reasons were perhaps different. Robots prized their independent privacy. The first generations of robots had been no more than remote-radio-controlled appendages to vast central computers. All the thinking was done in the central machines, and so there was no real difference between one robot and another. They were not individuals. Now the microprocessors that came with the Josephson junctions let a robot be as private within his own head as any human, and for that reason they guarded their privacy fiercely.

The other problem in Ralph's mind was that he was not sure he wanted to help the Albrights. The Brie and sausage he had felt obliged to ingest sloshed around in his storage cavity all afternoon, because he hadn't wanted to take the time to expel it for Cissie. Entering the library for an afternoon's work, he paused to engage his olfactories for a moment and verified his opinion. It was all fermenting inside him.

However, it didn't particularly matter, since no humans were in the library that afternoon. He plugged in and spent three solid hours letting all the unconsolidated data on Amalfi Amadeus pour past his receptors.

Amadeus had not had a very enjoyable life. At least half of the best years of it, Ralph observed, were spent in fruitless litigation. Humans were so strange! They would not let Amadeus have any share in the development of his great discovery, and then, when he was dead, they built him a monument. He did not really understand humans, Ralph concluded as he started home, and as he saw who was back at the riverside with her easel he decided he didn't really want to. "Oh, Ralph," Lillian Albright called, her voice rasping again through the external speakers, her face completely hidden by the glittering headpiece, "just a minute, will you? I'm coming in."

"Cissie will be getting impatient," he grumbled, but politeness kept him waiting while she folded up her easel. It even made him offer to carry her gear for her, but a twitching of the mirrored globe indicated that she was shaking her head.

"None of that master-slave stuff," she cried stoutly. "I'm perfectly capable of cleaning up my own messes, you know." And then, as they crossed to the entrance to the apartment, "Only, if you *would* be a dear and just take the canvas until we get through the door—" And then, inside, he was allowed to be a dear again, holding her equipment while she took the helmet off and shook out her curls. "Ah, that's better," she announced, starting to smile. Abruptly her expression changed. "Oh, my goodness," she said faintly.

"What's the matter?" Ralph asked, but her expression explained it all. She looked as though she had suddenly smelled something terrible. Tentatively Ralph engaged his olfactories and took a sniff. Right enough. Something was pretty foul. Part of it was no doubt the remains of the Brie and sausage, rotting away in his storage cavity, but there was more. "Oh, I know," he said, enlightened. "It's the garbage at the bottom of the elevator shaft, I bet. The super must have left the lid open. It's all right, though, Lillian. The farm people will come by to pick it up next week—they use it for compost, you know—"

"Next week?" she whispered, aghast. Then she tried

again on the smile. "I guess that's just part of living here," she said bravely. "We can stand it if you can, after all—anyway, the smell is only in the lobby." But all the way up to the eleventh floor it appeared to Ralph that she was trying not to breathe at all. She didn't speak again, just nodded and bolted as soon as the door was open, and the elevator man was grinning as he closed it after her.

Of course, Cissie wouldn't eat the remains of Ralph's lunch—looked at him with astonishment and indignation when he tried to offer it to her, and would not be appeased until he had spooned out a plateful of real dog food. He carted the mess to the garbage-disposal chute between the elevators, hesitated when he thought of Lillian Albright's reaction, and then deliberately dumped it. A little additional would make no difference at all, anyway. He returned to his apartment and was astonished to find his phone ringing.

The voice on the other end said, "This is Sergeant Gregory—I'm in Fourteen-H. Can I come up to talk to you for a minute?"

"What about?"

"Well, I'd rather wait till I got there, if you don't mind." Ralph frowned. He thought he could place the voice, and with it the face of a he he had seen now and then in the elevator—a detective in the Chicago police department, he thought. "Is it about something I did against the law?" he asked.

"No, nothing like that. Ten minutes?"

"I guess that will be all right." But it didn't feel all right to Ralph. His plans for the evening had consisted of taking Cissie out for a walk and then listening to music until it was time to start another day; it was the way he spent most of his evenings, and he didn't particularly want it interrupted by having to tidy up for company.

But he did tidy up. Ralph liked his apartment, and seldom had a chance to show it off. It was a fully functioning dwelling. Even the parts of it for which he had little use or none at all worked. Plumbing, for example; there were very few circumstances in which a robot had any need for running water. Cissie, on the other hand, loved her weekly bath, and it was worth the cost of a wasted room to Ralph to supply it to her. He didn't need a cookstove, either, and used a refrigerator only to keep his replacement diodes in a stable thermal environment. And he certainly did not require a bedroom. Or, for that matter, a bed.

And yet, he might. At any time he might decide to cook something and eat it—many robots with digestive systems did, now and then; it was a kind of hobby. He might even want to activate his sexual systems with a she someday, and then a bed would be worthwhile; and, anyway, he had no particular reason to want to make his home space-efficient. There was no need to. When the human beings moved out, they left millions of acres of floor space behind.

The hall door ding-donged, followed at once by the malamute's deep bay. "Shut up, Cissie," Ralph ordered as he opened the door.

Sergeant Gregory was not alone. There were at least half a dozen robots behind him in the hall, although Gregory was so big it was hard to see them. He clumped in with the assurance of a former beat cop and made for Ralph's best chair, Cissie frisking beside him. Without looking around he declaimed, "These here are Willard, Ben, Florence, Renee and Jim and Josie from the second floor. We wanted to talk to you."

"I sort of figured that," said Ralph, hoping his furniture would stand an aggregate of at least a metric ton of robots. It had been hard enough to find furniture that would look right in the Towers' wedge-shaped rooms—

dozens of trips to the antique stores and junk stores on the Near North Side—and those old Castro Convertibles and Barca-a-Lounges had been designed for seventy-five-kilo human beings, not for robots weighing twice as much. Ralph managed to seat the she named Florence in his favorite fake Chippendale—Florence was a flight engineer for Pan-Western Airways and a stripped-down, beryllium-chassised air-going model that weighed little more than a human being—but for the rest he could only hope for the best. "What we want to know," said Sergeant Gregory, shifting his weight and making the armchair creak, "is what are their intentions?"

"Whose intentions?"

"Those human beings."

"How would I know?"

"You've seen more of them than anybody else," Gregory growled, pushing Cissie away with his huge foot, "so you're the only one we can ask."

"You could ask them yourself," Ralph pointed out. "They're anxious to talk."

Ben spoke up—Ralph recognized him vaguely, a television newswriter or something of the sort, new in the building; the elevator man had said he'd just been transferred up from someplace like Savannah, Georgia. "I already talked to them," he said, his voice edged with irritation, "and I don't want to talk to them any more. You know what they wanted? They wanted me to turn my radio down. That was just this morning!"

The middle-aged she, Renee, nodded, not very sympathetically. "You were playing Stockhausen, right? Pretty loud, too."

"I always play my radio loud," said Ben, "and if they don't like it, they can just turn their receptors down."

"Human beings can't do that," Renee pointed out.

"Whose side are you on?" Ben demanded. "Listen! I

saw this happen in Savannah—they're block-busting! First
one or two move in, then the next thing you know the
whole building's turned!''

"So you see?" Sergeant Gregory boomed. "We have to
do something!''

His words were addressed to the room at large, but his
eyes were on Ralph—who nodded and stood up, because
he did, in fact, have to do something. Cissie was acting
more and more agitated. He scratched the base of her
skull. "Easy, girl," he shushed, and led her to the one
place in the apartment where none of his present guests
would have any occasion to go. "Too much company,
right, girl?" he whispered as he opened the bathroom
door for her. She looked up sadly, her huge body shaking,
but she lay obediently on the mat, whining only softly as
he closed the door on her. Cissie didn't like the hard surfaces of the bathroom, but she liked the chatter in the
living room even less.

For that matter, her master wasn't enjoying it much,
either. His guests all seemed to be talking at once, in their
various keys, Gregory's bass growl and Florence's chir-
rupy soprano bracketing the others. He stood in the doorway, postponing as long as possible the time when he
would have to rejoin them. There were not many human
traits Ralph was sorry to lack, but at that moment it occurred to him to wish that he and all the others really
required food and drink. Or at least were in the habit of
consuming it. That way he could have put out coffee and
snacks to welcome the company—and, more important,
he could have started to pick up the dirty plates when he
wanted them to go home.

"Ralph?"

He started as the he sitting on a bench by the doorway
reached to touch his arm. It was the short, slim one
named Willard, speaking softly so as not to interfere with
the main discussion in the room. "Aren't you the one

who's digging into Amalfi Amadeus?" he asked in an undertone. "Thought so. I think you're digging in the wrong place."

Ralph shook his head. "There's supposed to be a cache under the statue in Amalfi Park—that's where I'm digging."

"Wrong place. That was cleaned out years ago, when the lake began to rise."

"Then where's the right place?"

Sergeant Gregory's huge head was swinging warningly in their direction, so Willard's voice was even softer as he said, "The Amadeus stuff is now at the power plant at the lakefront. I'm with the Department of Structures, and I inspect all the fusion reactors—and I've seen it myself." As Gregory opened his mouth to speak, Willard finished quickly: "Come by sometime and we'll talk about it."

"Please sit down, Ralph," the sergeant was saying sternly. "I want you to listen to this. Ben?"

"I was just saying this Albright human wanted me to turn my radio down," the robot said, "and the only reason he gave was he claimed it interfered with his composing."

"Composing!" Gregory nodded. "Who knows what kind of noise *he's* going to be making? Now let's hear from Jim and Josie."

The old couple blinked uneasily at each other and at the group. Ralph knew them. They got their apartment free in return for doing odd maintenance jobs around the building. It was all they were fitted for, really, since they were low-level robots, originally built to work on the assembly lines in Detroit. They didn't have much in the way of conversational circuits. "Don't like to talk against tenants," Jim mumbled.

"Go ahead, Jim," Gregory encouraged. "They're not real tenants. Not like the rest of us."

"Was down in the cellar," Jim said, staring at the wall as

though to pretend he wasn't talking to any person, "and that Albright human come poking around. He could've got caught by the rat-killer, could've got hurt. Could've sued the building. Had no business there."

"And bugged Charlie," Josie supplied, also addressing the wall.

"Come on, Josie, bugged him how?"

"Bugged him 'cause the elevator wasn't running."

"Said they'd call the cops," Jim added. "That what they said, Josie?"

"That's what they said," she confirmed. "Anyway, that's what Charlie said they said."

"You see? Troublemakers," said Gregory. "I talked to Charlie, and he said they were really rotten to him. Now, there's no call for that."

"Are you sure Charlie wasn't rotten to them first?"

Gregory opened his eyes wide at Ralph's interjection. "Now, why would he do that? None of *us* ever had any bad-mouthing from Charlie, did we? So we have to assume that they started it."

"Well," said Ralph, "all the same, I really don't see why we're all getting so upset. There are only two of them, and there are a couple hundred of us."

"Now there are!" Gregory cried. "Did you forget they're *organic?* What are we going to do if they start to *reproduce?*"

The meeting broke up without deciding to do anything much, because there wasn't really, when you looked at it, much they could do. And Ralph was left with the feeling that the meeting with his neighbors had not entirely been a success. Sergeant Gregory had been distinctly cool at parting, and Ralph was nearly sure that he had heard the words "Spam can" whispered in the hall.

It left him with vaguely unpleasant feelings. Ralph had not known any of his neighbors well before the meeting, but he felt a sense of loyalty toward them—more accurately, he felt that they expected him to be loyal. The effect was to make him angry at the humans for being the cause of the ill feeling between him and the other robots; robot psychology was not all that unlike organic.

He walked Cissie along the riverfront, a quicker and more cursory walk than usual, and when they were back in the apartment she lay on her blanket, gazing worriedly up at him. He didn't know what she wanted; but then, he didn't know what he himself wanted very clearly. He tried music, and played some of his favorites—Antheil mostly, but with a leavening of bop and rapp—and when he realized it was pretty loud he reached to turn down the gain, hesitated, and then irritably turned it a little louder instead. But Cissie was whimpering to herself, so he turned it down again.

The best thing to do, he decided, was to do some work.

It was customary for robots to keep more or less human working hours—that was one of the biases built into them at the factory—but they were not obliged to. And certainly working would be less unpleasant than sitting around the apartment, feeling annoyed.

Three possibilities suggested themselves. He could go back to the Amalfi monument and poke around in the mud for himself. He could go to the library and input a few more hours of the previously unconsolidated records. Or he could take Willard up on his offer. One seemed as good as another, so he flipped a coin. It had to be a three-sided coin, of course, but robots can do that sort of thing, especially when they do it in their heads. It came up "Willard."

AMA-CHI Plant 257 was built on a manmade peninsula—well, actually it was robot-made, but old terms persisted—that jutted out into Lake Michigan near the Evanston line. As they approached, sunrise was making itself visible, or at least hinted at, through the mostly overcast skies out over the lake. Up the coast was an old astronomical observatory, left over from the days when Northwestern University's campus contained actual students and faculty. Now the telescopes did nothing but keep track of orbiting bodies, most of them inhabited by the descendants of the human beings who had abandoned that and most other campuses on the old planet Earth. The streets were almost deserted, except for an occasional cruising cab and garbage truck.

Because it was so early, Ralph had decided to take the malamute along for a run. A run it was. She tugged so fiercely at the leash that at last Ralph let her off it, and he and Willard chased her through the echoing empty streets. They didn't get tired. Cissie did. The distance was more than four kilometers, and long before they reached the lakeshore she had worked off her extra energy and was walking contentedly between the two robots. "There it is," said Willard, indicating a huge, featureless hemisphere that squatted over the choppy waters of the lake. "I'll come in with you for a minute."

"I have to thank you, Willard," said Ralph warmly, watching the malamute scramble down the grassy bank to lap thirstily at the lake water.

"For what?"

"Well, for letting me get you out so early in the morning, for one thing."

"Wasn't doing anything special."

"And also for treating me just like any other robot," Ralph added. "I mean, I know I'm getting a reputation as a human lover."

"Doesn't mean anything to me," Willard declared. "I see humans all the time. Work with them, too—oh, not very *many*, I mean. But as far as I'm concerned, they're just as good as anybody." He turned and glanced back the way they had come. Off to the west the clouds were beginning to be visible, illuminated not by the early dawn light from the lake but by lightning strokes playing among them. Ralph could hear no thunder, even at maximum auditory gain. But it was obvious that it was coming their way. "Going to get wet, I guess," Willard said regretfully.

"You won't rust, will you?" The question was meant to be jocular, although it was true, Ralph knew, that some robots neglected their anti-corrosion maintenance—just as humans sometimes neglected brushing their teeth.

"It's not that," Willard said, sounding a trifle embarrassed. "It's just that I have to spend this whole day in my office, and, you see, there's this human power engineer, on liaison, with the power units in orbit. On nice days he usually is out on field trips all day long. But when it rains he stays indoors. Don't get me wrong. I really don't have anything against humans. But I don't like spending the whole day with one *near* me."

The door to the great windowless dome was unlocked, and the door revolved. That surprised Ralph a little, since revolving doors generally meant human beings. The kind of doors that opened and shut were not good at keeping pollution out, but a tight-fitting revolving door, better still, two of them in series, with dead air space in between, was almost as good as an airlock. It didn't please Cissie, though. The malamute slunk through on Ralph's heels, whining softly—not at the doors so much as at the sound. The power station operated full blast, night and day. There was a deep roar that you felt rather than heard, and a much higher shrill whistle of high-temperature steam in pipes. When they were inside, Cissie lay down at Ralph's command, but her nose was twitching and every once in a while she gave an elephantine shudder.

"It's the chief engineer that brought the stuff here," Willard said. "He's organic. You know how organic humans encode their relationships?"

"You mean sexual relationships?"

"No, the other kind—parental, sibling, and so on? Well, in terms of heredity the chief engineer is a relative of Amalfi Amadeus. I don't know the exact word for it—his grandfather was Amalfi Amadeus's brother. Come along this way." Willard led Ralph up a flight of ringing metal steps, and the malamute slunk after them, ready to be sent away if noticed, unwilling to stay apart from her master in this noisy place. "The engineer's name," Willard called over his shoulder, "is Harry A. Hensmacher—the 'A' stands for Amadeus. Of course, he's not really the operating engineer—it's just a hobby with him, you know how human beings are. But the funny thing is he could be. He almost knows enough to do the job, except he's getting pretty old and he doesn't spend much time here any more. This is his office."

Willard pushed another door open—also unlocked—and Ralph entered a pleasant room with an actual window, looking out over the lake. The sun was pouring in brightly, under the gathering clouds; Ralph cut down his visuals and boosted the gain on his olfactories to identify the scents in the room. There were signatures of pipe tobacco, human sweat and—he sniffed again to make sure—yes, Irish whiskey. It was a comfortable room, and the malamute, skulking in behind Willard, seemed to find it welcoming. She lay down as nearly out of sight as a malamute can get, no longer shaking.

Ralph looked at her severely, then shrugged. She was not likely to do any harm here, and anyway his interest was taken by a sort of shrine on one wall of the office: shelves bearing a photograph of an elderly, sour-looking human in the clothes of generations past; a framed patent application, and a model that went with it; a couple of notebooks. "That's it," said Willard. "That's what came out of the capsule under the monument."

Ralph's heart, if he had had one, would have been leaping with excitement; actually he could feel his homeostasis systems compensating for the flood of voltage through parts of his data processors. "Do you think Mr. Hensmacher would mind if I looked at them?"

"I doubt it. He's had all this stuff right here in the open for years—we've all looked at it, now and then. Mostly the notebooks are technical stuff, but the old man put personal remarks in from time to time. Trouble is, a lot of it is encyphered. . . . Well, I'd better get to work. If Mr. Harry comes in before you're through, give him my regards." He leaned out to pass Cissie and departed, leaving Ralph in possession of the room.

Amalfi Amadeus's own notebooks . . .

Ralph carried them over to the desk, sat down with them unopened before him and allowed himself a moment of quiet exultation. The swivel chair creaked under his hundred and twenty kilos, and those human smells of sweat and breath and habits were stronger here. He looked around the room, trying to catch the feel of a place that held the presence of a human who shared chromosomes with Amalfi Amadeus, the man who had revolutionized civilization. The room was not unlike his own office at the University, he thought, and then could not decide why. The color? No. These were ugly blue walls instead of his own restful brown. The furniture was older and tackier than his: a long couch with cushions sagging into the springs against a wall where he had his workbench and video displays; an overflowing wastebasket— Ralph had no use for anything like that, because he seldom used paper. And certainly his office had no view like Hensmacher's panorama of Lake Michigan. It had no view at all, since it didn't even have a window. But something was the same—yes. The general air of inhabited neglect. A *used* quality. You would think that a chief operating engineer of a thousand-megawatt fusion-generation plant—even a human who only played at it—would spend his time checking valves and running tests and tapping pipes with a hammer. Not this one. He seemed to spend all his time in his office.

Methodically Ralph flipped through the notebooks. It took some time. The time was not for "reading" the contents; Ralph could commit any printed pages to memory as fast as he could turn them, but this time he was not attempting to "learn" the notebooks. He simply wanted to leaf through them, to get an idea of what they contained and, most of all, what they meant in filling in the missing parts of the life story of Amalfi Amadeus. For that sort of thing Ralph's logic circuits were no faster than a human's, nor did he want them to be. For him this was pleasure. He enjoyed prolonging it.

The notebooks were spiral-bound pads. Some of the pages were tearing loose, all the edges were browned and tattered, and each sheet was filled with crabbed marks and formulae and wiring diagrams.

None of that was of much interest to Ralph. The basic science and engineering of the Amadeus fusion process was well known—was about as relevant, actually, to the plant he was sitting in as Alexander Graham Bell's first carbon-granule microphone was to the auditory sensors in his body. He wished for a moment that he had thought to insert his engineering modules before leaving the apartment. Without them, the mathematics and the diagrams made little sense; but they also didn't matter.

What struck him with a thrill of discovery was the presence, here and there, on altogether no more than a dozen pages in the notebooks, of tightly written little paragraphs that were not in any language recognizable to Ralph.

Were not in any language at all, of course. They were code.

"Hush, Cissie," he murmured absently as the malamute crawled closer to him, eyes imploring. The noise of the power plant was getting to her, but that couldn't be helped; for Ralph to leave at this point was simply impossible.

For these paragraphs, whatever they were, were *new*.

There was no doubt of that. Ralph had long since input the entire Amadeus bibliography—diaries, patents, letters, court records, incunabula of every sort down, almost, to his very laundry lists. He carried that data around with him in his store, and it did not contain anything like the paragraphs in these notebooks. He had what every researcher dreams of. He had autograph material that had never been consolidated into the main body of Amadeus materials.

It was not at all important that it was in code. Why should it be? The code had been constructed by a human being, for the use of a human being in his private records. It was impossible that Ralph's data processors should fail to decrypt it.

Ralph quickly constructed the necessary algorithms, scanned the dozen paragraphs to commit them to his data stores and then sat back. He appeared to be idle. His eyes were focused on nothing. But, inside him, his programs tried systematic substitutions all through the alphabet. First it tried displacing each letter one letter back in the alphabet, then two letters back, then three; then it tried the same thing with the alphabet reversed; then split in the middle and working both ways; then in more complex arrays. None of them worked. But then he hadn't expected them to. Since old Amadeus was going to use the code itself, it would have to be fairly easy, but it need not be that elementary. So his programs began to count letter frequencies, and to look for the most obvious groupings. Three-character groups would tend to represent words like "the," "and" or "but." Single characters, mostly "I" or "a." In view of the identity of the diarist, the program made a special search for the six-character group "fusion." . . . The whole process took less than four minutes. Ralph noted that it had indeed been a simple one-for-one character substitution, complicated only by the fact that the number of places for the substitution increased by one for each line of text and that the text was written right-to-left. Even a human being would have solved that one pretty quickly. The fact that it was not in the general data base meant that not even a human being had even looked at it since the data base was compiled.

Ralph did not exactly "look" at it, either. He didn't need to resort to anything as crude as a CRT display or print on paper. The data came direct from his internal scanners, registered on his internal stores; and it went a long way toward explaining why human beings had not included this journal in the file. It was not a document the human race could take pride in reading.

It said:

When I was an undergraduate at MIT I made my mind up to do something significant for the human race. I wanted my life to count. I wanted to end poverty, bring about world peace and liberate mankind from all its primitive fears.

The funny thing is that I succeeded. Monopole-contained fusion power made all those things possible. The only thing that went wrong was the human race itself.

This is what I hoped for:

I wanted to make every commodity and service human beings required so cheap that they might as well be free. I wanted every human man, woman and child to know that he didn't have to spend his life grubbing a living, but could use it for creative thinking, for art, for science—just for loafing, if he wanted to. I hoped for a massive explosion of creative energy in every field.

This is what I got:

A snowmobile in every driveway. A cabin cruiser in every backyard. A dune buggy plowing up every patch of sand.

When I tried to redirect the ways in which my invention was used, I was frozen out of my own corporation. So—let it be. It seems probable to me that the human race will use these new powers to destroy itself.

And, frankly, I can't wait.

At Ralph's feet Cissie raised her huge head, moaned softly and then growled. Tardily Ralph remembered to boost the gain on his audio circuits. He heard someone approaching the door.

It opened. An elderly human man stood there, peering in at Ralph and the malamute. "Who the hell are you?" he squeaked in a senile falsetto, and advanced in the room. He was cautious of the dog, not at all cautious of Ralph, the robot. "You've got no damn business messing with my things!" the old man snarled as he saw the journal open on the desk.

"I'm sorry. Are you Mr. Hensmacher?"

"I asked you first!"

"My name's Ralph. I guess you could say I'm sort of a friend of your great-uncle's."

"Now, that's a damn lie," the old man piped, "being that none of you damn robots were around when my damn great-uncle was here."

Ralph made that faint beeping sound that was the robot equivalent of a sigh: Humans were so literal-minded! "I only meant to say that I regarded him as a friend, Mr. Hensmacher." He broke off as Hensmacher, circling the malamute, snatched the journal off the desk and turned the pages with reverent haste, looking for damage. "I didn't hurt it," Ralph protested.

"You *looked* at it. You had no *right* to. You've got no

damn right to be here in the first place," he added bitterly.

Ralph stood up, snapping his fingers for Cissie. "We'll get out of your way."

"And don't come back!"

"Oh, I can promise you that, Mr. Hensmacher. There's no need to."

The old man stared at him, and then his expression changed. "Wait a minute! You mean you read it? You know what it means?"

"Certainly, Mr. Hensmacher," said Ralph. "You mean you don't?" Evidently he had overestimated human decryption capabilities, at least for this human. "Would you like me to give you the text?"

"Oh, yes! Please!" cried the old man, his anger gone away.

Ralph hesitated. It was certainly a reasonable request, and Ralph's programming was intrinsically good-natured— enough so that he wanted to grant it; but also enough so that he didn't want to be around when the old man read his collateral ancestor's last words. Ralph was not particularly fond of human beings, but he believed that all creatures were entitled to preserve their self-respect.

When he caught sight of the dictating machine on Hensmacher's desk the dilemma solved itself. He picked up the microphone and a minute's high-pitched sound, like the screaming of elves, went onto record. "If you play that back at one-tenth normal speed," he said, replacing the microphone, "you'll get the clear text. Have a nice day, Mr. Hensmacher," he added as he left; but without much confidence that it would happen.

Ralph stood in the doorway, peering out. The storm had broken. Thunder rolled around the lakefront, and rain was pounding the sidewalks so hard that each drop bounced in a coronet of spray. Cissie shivered, eyes pleading as she looked up at Ralph. He gave in and whistled for a cab.

As they got out in front of the Towers she bounded out of the taxi door and into the shelter of the building marquee, almost knocking Myron Albright over. The man was standing under the canopy with a pocket recorder, trying to keep from getting drenched while he recorded the sounds of the storm. "Ah, Ralph," he cried, "this is what I came here for! There's nothing like this in orbit!"

"You're ruining the tape with your voice," Ralph pointed out coldly, brushing past him toward the elevator. He didn't turn around. He knew that the human would be staring after him with that sad, pathetic, *organic* look, and he didn't want to be distracted.

"Take you right up, Mr. Ralph," the elevator operator said deferentially, sliding the door shut, but Ralph shook his head.

"Not up," he said. "Down. I want to go to the basement. Then I want you to get the janitor and send him down."

He paid no attention to the operator's curiosity, but led Cissie into the dark, dusty basement. It had been thoughtless of him to take Cissie along; he could hear her grunts of distress. When he engaged his olfactory systems for a moment he understood why; the garbage was getting pretty rank. "Just a little bit, honey," he said softly, patting her. "Then I'll take you upstairs—here's Jim now!"

"You wanted me, Mr. Ralph?" the janitor asked.

"Yes, I've got a job I want you to do—wait a minute. What's that?"

There was a quick movement beside the bin. "It's just the rat catcher, Mr. Ralph," said the janitor and raised his voice. "It's only us! Go into standby until we leave!" The robot beside the garbage bin was so primitive a model that Ralph had not at first recognized it. It was hardly even mobile; its one job was to squat beside the garbage until a rat came along and then, faster than any organic creature

could move, lash out with its carbon-fiber blades and slice
it in two. It was cheaper and more effective than rat poi-
son, but it was not very smart. Ralph shuddered: suppose
Cissie had blundered too close! "I always say," the janitor
said, as though he had read Ralph's mind, "you shouldn't
have organic creatures in a building. Spoils it for everybody. Probably going to have to turn off the rat catcher
here, if those human people are going to stay—"

"You won't have to do that," said Ralph. "All you
have to do is open a couple of vents."

"Vents, Mr. Ralph?"

Ralph nodded, tracing the air-conditioning ducts with
his eye. "Yes, there," he said, pointing. "I want you to
open the intake."

Jim blinked thoughtfully at the ducts, then back at
Ralph. "Air's supposed to come from the outside," he
pointed out.

"Usually, yes. I want you to change that. I want you to
make it come from right here for a while. Then later on
we'll put it back the right way. Got it?"

"I guess so," said Jim dubiously. "Air from in here?"

"That's right, Jim."

"Not from outside, right?"

"Just go ahead and do it, Jim, all right?" Ralph watched
until it was done. Then, satisfied, he took the elevator to
his apartment. He made a quick call to Sergeant Gregory,
with a report and suggestions. By the time he was finished
Cissie was moaning again. He turned on his olfactories
again and knew why: rotting garbage, dead rats and a
month's accumulation of kitty litter made a memorable
combination, and it was all billowing out of the air-
conditioning vents. The only question in his mind was
whether it was as strong on the Albrights' floor as on his
own, and the way to answer that was to go down and find
out. He didn't bother with the elevator. Without Cissie to
slow him down, he took the fire stairs.

The smell was as strong, all right. Maybe stronger. And

his call to Sergeant Gregory had produced results. From all over the building he could hear tenants' sound systems at top gain, playing Antheil and Stockhausen and rapp. Satisfied, he turned back toward the stair . . . just as the Albrights' door opened and one of them peered out. He could not at first tell which, because it was wearing a mirrored globe. Then, "Oh, Ralph," it said through the speakers at the sides of the globe, revealing itself to be Lillian, "I heard all that galumphing on the stairs. Don't tell me the elevator's broken down."

"Not as far as I know," he said, annoyed at himself for not having thought of that. Next time she asked, it would be. "I just decided to walk—for the exercise," he added; she could believe that if she wanted to.

"That's good," she said dismally. "It's hard enough for us just to walk around on the level, you know. Trying to manage those stairs would just about ruin us. And, ah"— she cleared her throat delicately—"isn't that, uh, garbage getting a little strong?"

"Always does around this time," he lied cheerfully. "Of course, they'll clear it out in a month or so."

"A *month* or so?"

"There's a new schedule," he explained, and stabbed the elevator button to end the conversation. He could not see her expression through the mirrored globe, but then he didn't have to. He could visualize it clearly enough.

When he got back to his apartment Cissie had thrown up on the rug. Cleaning it up seemed a small price to pay. Then Ralph threw the windows open. All that particulate matter would settle on the furniture, and cleaning it would be a lot of work; and Cissie hated it almost as much as she did what came through the air-conditioners. But she was an Earth-bred dog, descendant of twenty generations of malamutes that had survived to stand what had become of the Earth's air.

And it was worth it.

He was not surprised when, two days later, returning from his work, he found the elevator door open again and Charlie beaming out. The air was fresh; the radios were at normal volume; the elevator operator grinned, winked, stopped the car at the eleventh floor and leaned out to point.

The door of the Albrights' apartment was open. The furniture was gone. Painters were already getting the walls ready for the next tenant.

And somewhere, wherever the ghost of Amalfi Amadeus had settled itself at last, it rested content.